D0030577

GRACE AMONG THIEVES

"Very believable and well researched . . . [A] reliable series with an interesting setting, a capable heroine, and [an] interesting puzzle to work out." —*The Mystery Reader*

"Hyzy has done it again . . . Well crafted with the many twists and turns that readers demand in a mystery, paired with an eccentric cast of characters." —*RT Book Reviews*

"Hyzy has yet again tapped into her creative mind. There are multiple goings-on from the first page to the last, which will engage the reader's interest and involvement in the story and its mysterious aspects." —*Once Upon a Romance*

GRACE INTERRUPTED

"Hyzy has another hit on her hands." —*Lesa's Book Critiques*

"Hyzy will keep you guessing until the end and never disappoints." —*AnnArbor.com*

GRACE UNDER PRESSURE

"Well researched and believable . . . Well-drawn characters . . . are supported by lively subplots." —*Publishers Weekly* (starred review)

"A strong, intelligent, and sensitive sleuth . . . A must-read for this summer!" —*The Romance Readers Connection*

"Julie Hyzy's fans have grown to love Ollie Paras, the White House chef. They're going to be equally impressed with Grace Wheaton . . . Hyzy is skilled at creating unique series characters." —*Chicago Sun-Times*

GRACE
CRIES UNCLE

JULIE HYZY

BERKLEY PRIME CRIME, NEW YORK

**An imprint of Penguin Random House LLC
375 Hudson Street, New York, New York 10014**

GRACE CRIES UNCLE

A Berkley Prime Crime Book / published by arrangement with the author

ISBN: 978-0-425-25968-9

PUBLISHING HISTORY
Berkley Prime Crime mass-market edition / July 2015

PRINTED IN THE UNITED STATES OF AMERICA

10 9 8 7 6 5 4 3 2 1

Cover illustration by Kimberly Schamber.
Cover design by Rita Frangie.
Interior text design by Laura K. Corless.

Penguin
Random
House

For my daughters, Robyn, Sara, and Biz,
who are the sort of sisters Grace wishes she had.

Acknowledgments

Facebook is a great place to connect with readers and make friends. And Facebook friends are a wonderful resource when it comes to titling a new book. Big thanks to everyone who offered ideas for this one, but a very special shout-out to Valerie Cannata. The moment her suggestion appeared on my page, I knew this was it. Thanks, Valerie. *Grace Cries Uncle* owes its title to you!

Sincere thanks to one of the nicest people in the business, my editor, Michelle Vega, for her unwavering support, cheerful e-mails, and all-around fabulousness. Thanks, too, to production editor Stacy Edwards and copyeditor Erica Rose, who help me bring Grace and the gang to life. You are the best.

Writing these books has become more of a family affair of late. With a heart full of love I want to say thanks to Curt, who always double-checks me for inconsistencies; Sara, who catches typos and awkward wording in the manuscript before I turn it in; Biz, who brainstorms with me in the kitchen to help puzzle out solutions when I hit a story snag; and Robyn, who drags me away from the computer to do something fun. I'm the luckiest writer in the world. Love you guys!

Chapter I

I SNATCHED MY HAND FROM THE JANGLING telephone when I caught Aunt Belinda's name on the caller ID.

"Of all days," I said to Bootsie, who had perched herself on one of our kitchen chairs. "It's almost as though she knows what's up." My little tuxedo cat cocked her head and let out an expressive howl.

"My thoughts exactly," I said. Scratching under Bootsie's soft chin, I stared at the ringing phone. My mother's sister didn't call often and whenever she did it was to talk about Liza. Aunt Belinda's fascination with my estranged sister never ceased to baffle me.

I tapped my fingers against my lips. With Ronny Tooney due to pick me up in about ten minutes, I could answer now, satisfy family duty, yet legitimately keep the conversation brief. If I opted to let it go to voicemail I'd feel compelled to return the call later. And then who knows how long Aunt Belinda would natter on about Liza, urging me to reach out to her, make amends, support my sister's feckless lifestyle.

Grabbing the handset before I could change my mind, I

answered, endeavoring to sound breathless. "Aunt Belinda. How are you?"

I braced myself for the litany of health issues she'd unleash. My aunt always insisted on bringing me up to speed on her myriad visits to the doctor and regular trips to the emergency room.

"I was pretty sick for a while last month," she said. "Doctors thought it was pneumonia, but I'm finally breathing better now."

"Sorry to hear that you were ill—" I began.

She cut me off. "You haven't heard from Liza, have you?"

"No."

"Is she still in San Francisco?"

"I have no idea." Last I'd heard, Liza and Eric had tied the knot and settled in Nevada. San Francisco was news to me.

"It's been too long. I'm worried about her. She's out there in the world all by herself."

I barked a laugh. "Not quite by herself."

"Don't be spiteful, Grace, it isn't nice," she said. "What's that husband of hers like anyway? I never met him."

I rubbed my forehead. Aunt Belinda was fully aware of the fact that Eric and I had at one time been engaged. That is, until my sister had blown back into my life. The prodigal daughter had returned home in time to say good-bye to our dying mother, collect half the inheritance, and take off again, this time with Eric in tow.

"I'm hardly the best person to comment on his character."

"You're not still smarting from that romantic business, are you? Liza must have been a better match for him. Aren't you happy you found out before you got married?"

More than happy; I was thrilled. Extraordinarily so. But that was now, after I'd had time to heal and distance myself from the situation. Although I'd dodged a bullet, my relief— no matter how profound—could never dull the pain of my sister's betrayal. I doubted it ever would.

"Mom was sick for so long that all I remember from that time is that Eric was here and Liza showed up. Next thing I knew, they were both gone."

"I hear from her now and then," Aunt Belinda went on, as always glossing over details that painted Liza in a poor light. "That girl can never afford the nicer things in life, even though she works so hard."

I pressed my lips together to hold back a snippy response.

"Last time we talked, though, I got the feeling she might be having problems. Now I can't reach her."

"I wouldn't worry," I said, pooh-poohing my aunt's concerns, "Like a cat, she always lands on her feet." I mouthed the words, "Sorry, Bootsie," to my feline companion. Returning to Aunt Belinda, I said, "Liza is shrewd, tough, and has a sharp edge that keeps her safe even while those around her get sliced to ribbons."

"What's happened to you, Grace?" Aunt Belinda asked. "How did you get so calloused? You're not still working at Marshfield, are you?"

"As a matter of fact, I am." Allowing a little pride to creep into my voice, I added, "I couldn't ask for a better job."

"I don't know how you abide it there. The place always gave me the creeps."

How could I explain that, despite recent goings-on, I'd never felt more appreciated or more loved than I did working for Bennett. Ever since I'd taken the position as curator and manager of Marshfield Manor, the mansion-tourist attraction-museum that was the jewel of Emberstowne, I'd felt as though I'd come home.

I drew in a breath to explain, but thought better of sharing personal sentiments. What I said was, "This is where I was meant to be."

"Oh, I see now. It's obvious they have you snowed. You're just like your mother."

Unwilling to go down this route again, I said, "Listen, I'm a little pressed for time."

"How old is billionaire Bennett Marshfield anyway? Shouldn't he be dead by now?"

"Bennett is in excellent health, and I'm lucky to be part of his life," I said, clipping my words. How dare she say such a thing? If I had my wish, Bennett would never die. "But I really am going to have to cut this short. I have an appointment this morning."

"What kind of appointment?"

Bennett and I intended to undergo DNA testing today. His goal was to set to rest, once and for all, the question of our blood relationship. With Aunt Belinda's hateful attitude toward Marshfield and its illustrious family, I refused to bare that part of my life to her. Truth was, I harbored a secret belief that Aunt Belinda knew—or at least suspected—that her mother had carried on an affair with Bennett's father, an involvement that had resulted in my mother's birth. Tempting though it was to broach the subject, I didn't want to open that particular Pandora's box.

"I need to get some blood drawn."

"Oh." For all of Aunt Belinda's yammering about doctor visits and health scares, she was unfailingly disinterested in the well-being of others—or, at least, mine. "You'll let me know if you hear from Liza?"

"I really don't expect to. She has no use for me anymore, does she?"

"That's a real shame, you know. Liza looks up to you. You ought to reach out and offer her a hand. You have so much and she has so little."

The doorbell rang, sparing Aunt Belinda from my irate outburst. "I have to go. My ride's here."

"Oh?" Her interest piqued at last, she asked, "A new beau?"

"Not quite. Take care, Aunt Belinda. Bye."

Bootsie scampered after me as I hurried to the front door. Thank goodness I'd gotten ready early; my aunt's call could have set me behind schedule. I smoothed the sides of my navy sweater and tugged at the hem of my blue tweed skirt as I went to greet my escort for the day.

Ronny Tooney and I had taken an unlikely path toward friendship. Middle-aged, with a bit of paunch and a generally unkempt appearance, Tooney had recently attained his long-desired goal when he'd been named official private investigator to Marshfield Manor. I'd done the hiring, but only after Bennett had given his blessing. Tooney had proven to be one of Marshfield's most steadfast allies.

Cold January air spilled in when I drew open the door. In the split second it took my brain to process that the man in the gray suit wasn't Tooney, I chastised myself for not taking the time to check first. That sharp discomfort, coupled with the visitor's unwelcome step closer to the storm door, triggered my testiness.

I raised my voice to be heard through the glass. "What do you want?"

The man's high forehead scooped into his crown like an inverted *U*, giving his face a long, narrow look. He had dark, blank eyes. The barest trace of stubble along his chin. Neatly trimmed sideburns. He acknowledged my question with a slight lift of his lips. Though it had snowed overnight and temperatures were in the twenties, he wasn't wearing an overcoat.

Consulting a small notebook, he asked, "Are you Grace Wheaton?"

Bootsie joined me at the door, clambering onto a nearby table to get a better look at the fellow, her little pink-and-black nose tilting up. Even though the outer door remained secure, I lifted her into my arms.

"Who are you?" I asked.

One of his dark eyebrows twitched upward. "My name is Alvin Clark." In a smooth move, he used his free hand to draw a wallet from his breast pocket. Flipping it open, he said, "I'm with the FBI." He'd raised the endings of both statements to make them sound like questions and he accentuated the *L* consonants in his name an odd way. Not a local.

I scanned the proffered document through the glass, noting his photo, name, and the sizeable gold badge embedded in the leather, but saw nothing to indicate where he was from.

He snapped the leather portfolio shut again and returned it to his pocket. "Now, can we try this again? Are you Grace Wheaton?"

"I am," I said. "Why are you here? What do you need from me?"

With an exaggerated shiver, as though to make me aware of winter's chill, he pointed over my shoulder. "May I come in?"

My imagination didn't need more than a second to conjure up possible scenarios. Had someone outside our circle of trusted confidantes found out about today's blood test? Bennett's will stipulated that, upon his death, his stepdaughter, Hillary, would be awarded a substantial sum of money. The bulk of his estate, however—Marshfield Manor and all of its treasures—was bequeathed to the city of Emberstowne. Could the elected officials have ordered a background check on me? I had no designs on Bennett's immense fortune, but that wouldn't stop the municipality's lawyers from taking steps to protect their client's best interests.

Another thought—this one coming on the heels of Aunt Belinda's phone call: She'd intimated that Liza was in trouble. Heaven knew that Aunt Belinda had a far better finger on the pulse of Liza's life than I did. Could this Fed's sudden appearance at my house involve my sister?

"Sorry." I wanted to collect my thoughts before I answered. "I'm leaving in a couple of minutes. I have an appointment."

"Who lives here with you?" the FBI man asked.

"Why?" It was one thing to answer questions about myself. Quite another to share information about my roommates. Bruce and Scott, two men I loved like brothers, were currently hard at work at their wine shop, Amethyst Cellars. They had nothing to do with Bennett. Nothing to do with

Liza. For what other reasons could the Feds be interested in me?

"Just answer the question."

"I need to know what this is about, first."

Alvin Clark stretched his chin forward, running stub-nailed fingers down the front of his neck. "I suggest you cooperate, Ms. Wheaton. This will go much easier for you if you do."

Bootsie struggled in my arms. I let her bound to the floor and was pleased when she meandered away, having lost interest in the drama at the front door. The ever-so-slight interruption allowed me to summon my resolve.

"First of all," I began, "you haven't told me what this is about. I'd be more inclined to cooperate if I understood why you're here."

"Ms. Wheaton—" His voice was a growl.

I talked right over him. "As I already stated, I have an appointment this morning." At that moment I spotted Tooney coming up the walk, his tattered wool coat flapping open in the wind. He was clearly taken aback by the sight of the man on my porch.

He locked eyes with me from behind the FBI guy, taking the steps two at a time to position himself close to the door. "What's going on?"

Alvin Clark was momentarily rattled. He took a step backward and gave Tooney an appraising glance. "Do you live here?"

Tooney straightened his rumpled self as tall as he could and returned the scrutiny. Ignoring the Fed's question, he asked, "What do you need me to do, Grace?"

"This gentleman is from the FBI," I said. "He hasn't told me why he's here, but I made it clear that I'm running late for an appointment." I forced a smile at the agent. "If you'll excuse us?"

Clark's gaze shifted from me to Tooney, then back again. "This won't take long. Just a few important questions."

I debated handling this agent the same way I had Aunt

Belinda. Answering him now would get this over with. But Bennett was waiting, and today was an important day.

"Unless you have some sort of warrant or paperwork that requires me to answer your questions now," I said, "you'll have to come back another time."

The fact that the FBI guy didn't produce any such documentation provided a small sense of comfort.

His lips curled in hard disapproval as he shoved the notebook into his pocket. "When will you be back?"

"I can't say exactly."

"After five o'clock?"

"Probably."

"And if you are not home then?" he asked, taking a deep, irritated sniff. "What about tomorrow?"

I didn't appreciate being put on the spot, but I knew that the quicker I cooperated, the faster he'd be out of here. "I should be home all day tomorrow."

"Fine." He pivoted and strode away.

"What was that all about?" Tooney asked when he was gone.

"You got me." I shook my shoulders to release the tension in them.

"You want me to be here when he comes back tonight?"

"Maybe," I said. "Let's talk about it on the way. The FBI guy's visit put us behind schedule."

Chapter 2

I COULD HAVE DRIVEN MYSELF TO THE LAB this morning, but Bennett had insisted on an escort. Afraid that I might be light-headed from the blood draw, he asked me to indulge him by allowing Tooney to drive.

When I'd first agreed to the DNA test, I'd expected Bennett would invite his personal physician to come into the office, swab our cheeks, and then—weeks later—return with results. Bennett had other ideas. We would get our cheeks swabbed today for sure, but we'd also submit blood samples. I'd tried to reason with him, reminding him that swabs were enough, but Bennett could be obstinate. "I want more information," he'd said. "Not less. I don't plan to repeat this procedure, so let's get it done right."

Once I'd agreed, we'd settled on the first Saturday we both had free. Today.

Tooney usually drove a rattletrap sedan that boasted more dents than an aluminum shed after a hailstorm, but today he'd arrived in a shiny Buick Enclave. There wasn't a hint of snow on its shadow-gray exterior and it sported temporary license plates.

Tooney gallantly handed me into the passenger seat before closing my door and making his way around to settle behind the wheel.

"New car?" I asked.

He started the vehicle and put it into gear, his cheeks flushing pink as he shot me a quick glance. "Mr. Marshfield has been very generous with me, ever since . . . I mean . . ." Pulling away, his face now glowed scarlet. "First the house, and now a car . . ."

In an effort to better Tooney's standard of living, Bennett had snatched up the painted lady next to mine the moment it went on the market. On paper Bennett retained ownership of the property, but he had essentially handed the house to Tooney after hearing about the hovel our scruffy private investigator called home. Bennett had also arranged to have the place updated and renovated, despite the fact that it was in good shape to begin with. Hillary was in charge of that project.

"Mr. Marshfield doesn't need to do all this," Tooney went on. "He doesn't have to give me anything. I wasn't looking for a reward when . . ."

I reached across to lay a hand on his arm. "You saved my life," I said. "Bennett wants to show his appreciation."

"But you saved *his* life," he said.

"That was quite a busy evening, wasn't it?" I pulled my hand back as I recalled that memorable night from the previous summer.

"I don't deserve anything. He should be grateful to you."

"He thinks of you as my guardian angel. He believes I get into too much trouble."

Tooney's soft face twisted into a smile. "Can't argue with him there."

"I think he rests better at night knowing you're right next door."

"I sleep easier, too."

I patted his arm again. "That makes three of us."

When Bennett had arranged to have my home renovated, he'd insisted on having a burglar alarm installed. It was a reasonable suggestion and I didn't argue. At least not until Bennett's scope expanded. In light of the discovery of an underground tunnel that connected my home with what was now Tooney's, and after the catastrophic events that sent my former neighbor packing, Bennett had demanded that a second, backup, alarm be established.

The backup—on a separate circuit—would sound at Tooney's house. If he was home and the alarm went off, Tooney knew to text me immediately. If I didn't answer with the code word—*Bootsie*—he would know I was in trouble and he'd use the underground passage to get to me as quickly as possible.

I'd cajoled Bennett, bickered with him, and had argued at length that we shouldn't drag Tooney into a potentially dangerous situation without backup. It wasn't fair to ask him to come running blindly to my rescue.

Bennett had listened to my pleas and had ultimately agreed that I was right—it was unfair to require such a commitment from one of Marshfield's employees. My relief at Bennett's acquiescence had been short-lived, however, when he'd added, "We ought not to *force* Mr. Tooney to cooperate. But we can ask him if he's willing." Bennett's smile had been smug. "What do you suppose he'll say?"

Thus, both alarms were installed. I had to admit that after having lived through a number of harrowing experiences these past few years, knowing that help was right next door reassured me a great deal.

WE WERE ABOUT FIVE MINUTES LATE GETTING to Lucatorto Labs. The moment we parked I alighted from the car and hurried through the biting wind to the establishment's glass door, grabbing its handle a fraction of a second before

Tooney gallantly pulled it open for me. Two steps in, I stopped. I'd expected a generic medical testing center: mass-produced artwork on pastel walls, piles of health-centric reading material, and air thick with stinging disinfectant.

With its cushy chairs, soft lighting, and slow-tempo Bach, however, Lucatorto Labs more closely resembled an upscale spa. Walls were a warm brown accented by icy aqua and white trim. At the room's center was a trickling stone waterfall, providing both soothing sounds and the faintest whiff of chlorine.

To my left, cushy window seats overlooked a snowy courtyard. To my right and ahead, a group of business-clad individuals stood in small clusters, talking softly, sipping from ceramic mugs. All were attorneys from Hertel and Niebuhr, the firm that had handled Marshfield affairs for as long as the family had lived in Emberstowne.

A statuesque woman in natty professional attire stepped forward. I recognized her as one of the senior partners at the law firm. I'd spoken with her once, but only briefly. "Nice to see you again, Ms. Wheaton," she said, extending her hand. "As you can see, my colleagues and I are all very excited to be here for you and Mr. Marshfield today. Come on in."

"Good to see you too, Ms. Inglethorpe" I said to her, "but please, call me Grace."

"Of course. And I'm Maggie." She directed one young man to take my coat and another to escort Tooney to the window seats. "Joe will see to your comfort, Mr. Tooney." Indicating a table across the room, she added, "Lucatorto Labs has been wonderful about allowing us to commandeer the premises for the day. We have coffee, tea, and pastries set out. Help yourself. If you need anything else—some reading material, perhaps?—please don't hesitate to ask."

Cheeks pink from either the cold or the attention, Tooney handed his coat to Joe and mumbled that he was fine.

Returning her attention to me, Maggie offered a warm

smile and led me toward the gathered group. "We're very eager to get this process started."

"Where's Bennett?" I asked. There were far more people here than I'd expected. The lab was open only to us today, and even though I'd known Bennett's lawyers would be present, I hadn't anticipated such a crowd.

"He's definitely here," she said.

I caught sight of him the same moment he spotted me. Bennett, with his electric blue eyes, athletic build, and full head of brilliant white hair, put other septuagenarians to shame.

"You made it, Gracie," he said, pulling me into a hug. "Knowing how punctual you are, when you weren't here precisely at eleven I feared you'd changed your mind."

Despite the fact that I shared Bennett's confidence that he and I were, indeed, related by blood, I'd always harbored misgivings about obtaining proof. I didn't believe it necessary. Not to me, at least. I would have been perfectly content to maintain the status quo. Test or no test, Bennett would always be more to me than an employer; he was a beloved uncle. Half-uncle, if you wanted to get technical.

Bennett, however, wanted ironclad evidence and had insisted on today's gathering in order to cover every legal, moral, and ethical base he could come up with. Such formalities were important to him. From the first moment we learned of our possible connection he'd made no secret of how happy the prospect made him. I hoped he understood how much joy this relationship brought to me as well. For the first time since my mother passed away I had family. Bennett loved me and cared for me as much as I did him.

"I wouldn't miss this for the world," I said.

The group of lawyers, witnesses, and what have you opened their circle to allow me in. One of the senior partners, Ted Hertel, grasped my hand in both of his. "Wonderful to see you again, Grace. Today is a big day. We're thrilled to be part of it."

"Thank you," I said, feeling a little overwhelmed. The fact that conversation had ceased the moment I'd joined them set me on edge. "Sorry I'm late. I had an unexpected visitor at my front door right as I was leaving."

"Visitor?" Bennett asked, picking up on the disquiet in my tone. "Who was it?"

With the exception of the assistants who kept to the sidelines, the people gathered here today were all middle-aged or older. Every one of them dignified, polished. There were men and women in different shapes, sizes, and colors, but they all bore intelligent, curious expressions as they waited for me to answer. Even though I wore a perfectly presentable sweater and skirt ensemble I felt young, underdressed, and out of place.

I tucked my hair behind one ear. "A gentleman from the FBI, believe it or not," I said with a little cough-laugh.

If I'd suddenly pulled out flaming sticks and begun juggling them, the lawyers couldn't have expressed more surprise. The group—almost as one—reacted with arched-brow, openmouthed expressions of concern.

"What did he want?" Ted asked.

"I don't know, exactly. I told him I had an appointment and didn't have time to answer his questions."

Bennett's brow had tightened, so I hastened to add, "I'm sure it's nothing important. He let me go." Another little laugh. "It's not like he had a warrant for my arrest or anything."

Whoops. Mustn't joke with lawyers, I thought, as the attorneys exchanged uneasy glances and began discussing this among themselves. One of them turned sideways and spoke softly to Ted, though loudly enough for me to hear. "Could this be related at all to today's tests? Should we delay until we have answers?"

"We aren't delaying another moment," Bennett said over the din. Turning to me, he asked, "Gracie, what did he say?"

My discomfort level was high, but I didn't hesitate. "He

knew my name, but wanted to know who lived in the house with me. I didn't tell him anything."

"Did he show you identification?" Maggie asked.

"Yes, right away."

The lawyers were apparently aware of Bruce's and Scott's presence in my life, because this new piece of information got them chatting again, this time musing about my room-mates and their business interests.

Wishing I'd never opened my mouth, I said, "I'm sure it's nothing. Otherwise, why would he be willing to come back later?"

Bennett still wore an anxious expression. "When will that be?"

"He asked if I'd be home after five."

Maggie spoke up. "If you like, Bennett, I'll be there with Grace when the agent returns." She sent a pointed look around the rest of the assembled group. "Let's not get worked up about this. For all we know one of Grace's neigh-bors may be under suspicion for illegal activity." To me, she asked, "Would you mind my involvement?"

"Not at all," I said. "That's very generous of you."

"My pleasure. Five o'clock then?" She pulled out her phone and began tapping notes into it.

"I'm not even certain he'll return tonight. He asked about tomorrow, too."

She nodded, as though this was of no consequence. I appreciated her direct, businesslike attitude. "Here," she said, handing me her business card. She'd written her cell phone number on the back. "Call me when he shows. I'm not that far from you; I can be there in ten minutes. Don't answer a single question until I get there."

"Thank you," I said.

She nodded. "Shall we get started, then?"

Chapter 3

TWO TECHNICIANS LED US THROUGH mahogany-paneled doors into the functional area of the building, where glaring fluorescent fixtures illuminated shiny white and blue walls. Our shoes snapped against the navy tile floor and the smell of Pine-Sol was so intense I would have bet that the maintenance folks had finished swabbing only moments earlier.

Bennett and I followed directly behind the two techs, and I wasn't surprised when the rest of the entourage crowded in after us. We trooped past tiny examination rooms on either side of the quiet hallway, taking several maze-like turns until we arrived in what appeared to be the heart of the place.

The white-and-blue theme carried into what had to be the main lab. Stainless steel fixtures lined the perimeter and two islands sat at the expansive room's center. Chilly and clean yet cluttered, the space was chock-full of microscopes, refrigeration units, computers, what looked like incubators, and machines I couldn't begin to identify. An emergency shower and drain took up one corner.

Two men and one woman in lab coats stepped forward to greet us.

The older of the two men took point position. He wore heavy-framed glasses and a magnifier/lamp contraption perched atop his bald head. "I'm Dr. Lucatorto," he said before introducing his colleagues. Indicating the smiling, dark-skinned man behind him, he said, "My partner, Dr. Rabbat." He shifted to point toward the woman. "And, per your request to have a second laboratory process your specimens, this is Dr. Lyon, from Sarear Labs."

Bennett and I shook hands with all three of them. Dr. Lucatorto sent an appraising glance over the others. "These measures are a bit excessive," he began, "but as I've assured your counsel, Mr. Marshfield, Lucatorto Labs is AABB accredited. As is Sarear Laboratory." Waving a benediction over the passel of lawyers gathered behind us, he added, "While we appreciate your generous compensation for our time, I can promise that there is no need for this level of involvement."

Bennett's expression was mild. "Perhaps not," he said. "But I make it a habit to over prepare rather than be caught short."

Dr. Lucatorto used a knuckle to tap his glasses higher up his nose, as though to convey that it made no difference. "Well then," he said, "shall we begin?"

The two techs who had led us in, Wanda and Valerie, turned out to be phlebotomists, one from each of the two labs. After Bennett and I were seated in identical swing-out armchairs across from each other, Valerie began to prep my arm as Wanda ministered to Bennett.

"Do you know your blood type?" Valerie asked me.

"B-positive," I said.

Bennett smiled. "Same as mine."

"We will, of course, confirm that information," Dr. Lucatorto said.

They did. We matched.

Bennett said, "We're off to a good start."

Maggie pulled out a small camera and snapped several pictures. "Documentation."

There was no music in this part of the building and the entire audience of attorneys remained breathlessly quiet. Except for the humming of equipment, and the occasional directive from our phlebotomists, the place was awkwardly silent. I wished for privacy. Getting my blood drawn didn't bother me; the scrutiny of our wide-eyed onlookers did.

I watched as the deep red liquid from my veins streamed into the first vacuum tube.

"You aren't squeamish?" Bennett asked.

My nerves were so taut that the absurdity of his question hit me hard. I began to giggle. "After all we've been through these past few years?"

His mouth twitched. "Good point, Gracie." He raced his gaze along his extended left arm and the needle protruding from it. "This really is nothing, isn't it?"

Nervousness, being in the spotlight, and the awkwardness of it all, built a bundle of hilarity in my chest that jounced around my insides, desperate to escape. I giggled again.

The vials filled quickly. Bennett and I were required to sign identification labels for the samples before the two techs switched positions to repeat the process. The attorneys murmured among themselves and Maggie continued to take pictures.

Wanda and Valerie had us sign the second set of samples before Valerie said, "That's it. We're done taking blood."

Dr. Lucatorto explained the next procedure for obtaining DNA, which involved collecting samples from the insides of our cheeks. He also reminded us that this step was redundant. His detailed description took longer than the swabbing itself. Like the techs had, Drs. Rabbat and Lyon administered the test to us one at a time, then switched positions to test the other.

"All done," Dr. Lyon said when she and Rabbat completed

their sampling. "Sarear Labs should have results to you within about a week or so."

"That long?" Bennett asked.

Dr. Lucatorto gave him an indulgent smile and knuckled his glasses again. "If you recall, Mr. Marshfield, you opted for the more comprehensive analysis, involving a greater number of genetic markers. Such excessive measures require more time."

Bennett knew this. I knew this. Bennett's impatience was getting the better of him.

Dr. Lucatorto addressed the entire group. "I admonish you all to remember that the tests we have administered today may either prove the likelihood of kinship between Mr. Marshfield and Ms. Wheaton with a high degree of statistical probability, or they will ascertain that they share no family ties whatsoever."

It wasn't until after I'd finally agreed to Bennett's request to be tested that I'd realized how much I was anticipating a positive result. How much I wanted it to be true. I'd considered going through my mother's belongings—most of which remained packed away in the attic and garage—to find something of hers that could have been used to lift her DNA. We had plenty of paperwork, photos, and circumstantial evidence to presume the truth. I had no doubt that my mother and Bennett were half-siblings. Yet I'd chosen to forgo searching for my mom's DNA. Once I'd made the decision to move forward, I knew I wanted the test results in my name, wanted confirmation that Bennett and I were, truly, uncle and niece.

We'd been in the utilitarian section of the lab for less than twenty minutes—and if we hadn't had to sign so many documents, it could have been fewer than five—but the room's chill began to make me shiver. I got to my feet and inspected the bandages on the insides of both my elbows before pulling my sleeves back down to my wrists.

Their responsibilities complete, the doctors released us. The lawyers crowded close, conferring among themselves and taking turns to shake our hands and express hope for positive results.

In the midst of this, Bennett turned to me, taking my hands. His were warm and steady. His eyes were, too.

"Whatever the outcome, Grace," he began, effectively silencing the cheerful chatter, "whatever these tests confirm or dispute, you are my family and you always will be."

It was as though we were the only two people in the room. He continued to stare down at me and I got the impression he was trying to convey more than he had words for.

"I know," I said softly. Heat gathered behind my eyes and in the back of my throat.

"No matter what," Bennett said very quietly.

I nodded. "No matter what."

Lifting his gaze to encompass those surrounding us, he let go of my hands and said, "Did you all hear that?"

Maggie answered. "We did."

"Bennett," I said, keeping my voice low, "you know I didn't agree to the test for any reason other than to keep you happy."

He continued to speak loud enough for everyone to hear. "And what will make me happiest of all is to make you my heir."

"No, Bennett, no," I said, tugging at his arm. "You know that's not what this is about."

"I know that, Gracie. This is about family."

One of the men in back wagged a finger. "It will be so much more straightforward, so much easier for us to rewrite your will if DNA tests prove kinship. Who knows what sort of challenges we may encounter if you bequeath your estate to a young woman who is not related by blood."

Bennett offered the man a cool smile. "I certainly hope for proof," he said. "But I don't pay you for easy."

Chapter 4

BENNETT'S DRIVER HAD DROPPED HIM OFF AT the lab, leaving Tooney responsible to return us both to our respective homes. "You see how little blood they took?" I asked, when we were all bundled up and tucked into the Enclave. "I would have been perfectly fine driving myself."

Tooney had started the car, but was waiting for the frosty windshield to clear. "I didn't mind," he said.

Bennett leaned forward from the backseat. "Then how could I have possibly convinced you both to join me for lunch afterward?"

Tooney half turned to face him. "Both? You mean me, too?"

"Yes, Mr. Tooney, I feel like celebrating. What do you say, Gracie?" He winked at me. "I promise to have you back before your FBI friend returns at five. You promise to call Maggie when he shows up, won't you?"

"I will," I said.

Bennett tapped the back of Tooney's seat. "Let's have lunch at Octave. You know how to get there?"

Tooney's face went slack. "I'm wearing blue jeans," he said. "They're not even new ones."

Settling against the backseat, Bennett waved him off. "You'll be fine."

BENNETT WAS RIGHT. OCTAVE'S MAÎTRE D' welcomed us warmly, making no comment about Tooney's faded jeans, nor his high-top black gym shoes. In fact, if it hadn't been for the host's ever-so-brief glance at our private eye friend, I might have believed he hadn't noticed Tooney's casual attire at all.

About half the restaurant's tables were occupied and the maître d' chose a winding path through the sea of white linen, crystal, and subdued conversation. An older man glanced up as we passed, did a double take, then shot to his feet. He tossed his napkin aside and made his way toward us. "Bennett Marshfield." He spoke with a Southern drawl. Texas, I thought. "How you been keeping yourself, old man?"

Bennett blinked, then glanced to me before smiling and greeting the interloper. Though he projected warmth, I sensed wariness on Bennett's part. "I'm doing very well, thank you, Neal. How are you?"

Neal's "Couldn't be better" reply came across as perfunctory, almost absentminded. With a quick glance, he appraised Tooney and me. His curiosity was unmistakable as he waited for Bennett to make introductions.

"Are you in town for the convention?" Bennett asked.

"Of course. What else?" Neal studied Bennett. "Heard some rumors. Thought I'd get here early to see what's what."

"I hope you enjoy your stay in Emberstowne." Bennett started to move away. "Good to see you again."

The dismissal clearly stung. Neal's bushy brows came together. "Thought I'd stop by your estate one of these days. You wouldn't have a problem with an old friend coming to call?"

Bennett seemed uncomfortable for a moment but regained his composure as politeness won the day. "I would be delighted to have you visit Marshfield. I'll instruct the staff to roll out the red carpet."

Neal tipped an imaginary hat brim. "I'm hoping to steal a little bit of your time, Bennett." He winked. "Satisfy my curiosity about a few things."

Bennett worked his mouth as though searching for the right words. "You are always welcome at Marshfield."

When we moved off again, trailing the maître d', who had waited patiently to seat us, I whispered to Bennett, "Who was that?"

He waved away my question as though it was of no importance. "Neal Coddington. If you wouldn't mind, please let the front desk know not to charge him an entrance fee. I'd never hear the end of it."

"Do you want them to alert you when Mr. Coddington arrives so you can greet him personally?"

Bennett slid a glance sideways as he leaned down to whisper, "Absolutely not."

Within moments we were seated at a quiet table overlooking snow-covered Emberstowne. "This is beautiful, Bennett," I said.

Octave took up the eighth floor of one of the city's office buildings and was known for its outstanding French cuisine as well as its impeccable service. Paneled walls, cozy antiques, fresh baguettes, and Edith Piaf's softly warbling voice surrounded us with tranquil bliss.

"You've dined here before?" he asked.

"First time."

Tooney opened the large leather-bound menu and made eye contact with us both over its edge. "Same here," he said. Leaning my way, he asked, "How do I know what I'm ordering?"

"Gracie can help you there," Bennett said. "She was masterful at translating when we were in Europe last year."

"Hardly masterful," I gently corrected him. "But I think I can decode the menu. What do you like?"

Bennett ordered Champagne and when the waiter asked if we were celebrating anything special, said, "Yes, we are, indeed. Life is good and it's made even better when surrounded by family and friends."

"The best reason of all to celebrate," the waiter said.

He returned with a vintage that probably cost more than my salary for a week, offering the label to Bennett for approval before popping the bottle open and pouring.

Tooney placed a meaty hand over the top of his flute. "None for me, thanks. I'm driving."

"Commendable, Mr. Tooney. But won't you take enough in your glass for a toast?"

He agreed, and the moment the waiter was gone, Bennett lifted his glass. "I owe you both for my well-being and my happiness. Until the two of you entered my life, I was a lonely old man who had nothing better to do than manage my wealth and plan for my demise. Thanks to the two of you, I am invigorated, I am stronger, and I am happy." He touched his glass to mine. "You are my family." He touched his glass to Tooney's. "You are my friend. May good fortune keep company with us all."

AFTER DINING, AS WE ENJOYED CAFÉ AU LAIT and macarons, our conversation eventually turned to the upcoming Fine Art and Antiquity Collectors' convention.

"That starts a week from today, doesn't it?" Tooney asked. Before I could confirm that it did, he went on. "I'm surprised the organizers didn't want to host it at Marshfield."

The Fine Art and Antiquity Collectors' convention, or FAAC, drew an upscale crowd of collectors and antique dealers from around the globe. The convention's location changed from year to year, keeping its wealthy clientele traveling from Amsterdam to Zephyrhills in their pursuit of rare treasures.

The FAAC produced documentaries that were broadcast on travel channels and advertised on public broadcasting stations. The format was similar to that of the popular *Antiques Roadshow*, except that most attendees were experts themselves, and items reviewed on camera were generally valued in the millions rather than the thousands.

"They approached us," I said, "but they have very specific space requirements because of the lighting equipment, cameras, and security. While Marshfield Manor has plenty of room, we would have had to close the house to tourists for the duration of their stay."

"That's why they're taking over the two biggest hotels in town?" Tooney asked.

"Three, from last I heard."

Bennett had been silent through all of this, steepling his fingers in front of his mouth.

Tooney gave a half smile. "January isn't exactly the most tourist-friendly time of year for Emberstowne. Guess we got lucky that the FAAC decided to host it here this time."

"We did," I said. "The Marshfield Hotel is booked up, too, and that rarely happens in the winter." Turning to Bennett, I said, "You're very quiet. I would have expected you to have plenty to say. What days do you plan to be there?"

His eyes held an alertness I didn't understand. As though he wanted to join in our conversation but was holding himself back. I couldn't imagine why.

"I . . ." He drew the word out. "I will not be attending this year."

Tooney seemed as surprised as I was. "You always make time for the FAAC convention," I reminded Bennett, "and the last two were out of the country. This one is, literally, in your backyard. Why *wouldn't* you go?"

Shaking his head, Bennett pulled his napkin up to pat

his lips. "No desire this time. Too many people, and you know how much I dislike crowds."

In the world of fine art events, the word *crowd* was less like the press of humanity attempting to exit after a Disney extravaganza, and more like a fancy cocktail party where everyone smelled good, wore thousand-dollar ensembles, and chitchatted about one-of-a-kind finds.

"You love that sort of thing." I took a sip of coffee. "I can't believe you'd want to miss it."

His napkin on the table before him now, he worried it with the fingers of both hands. "I'll not be missing it entirely." He cleared his throat. "I'm hosting a small reception on the last night of the FAAC."

I lowered my china cup into its saucer so quickly it clattered. "Reception?" I repeated. "I don't know anything about that. Where are you hosting it?"

Bennett's cheeks grew a faint shade of pink. "Marshfield. A week from Tuesday."

"At Marshfield?" I asked, continuing to repeat Bennett's words as though doing so would help them sink in better. None of this was making sense. "Who organized this? Why don't I know about it?"

Bennett patted my arm. "No need for you to worry. It's a small affair, probably no more than a hundred people or so."

"That's not small." Thinking quickly, I asked, "Did Frances help you put this together?" My assistant was usually the first to know everything that was going on. I'd be furious if she'd kept this from me, but relieved to know that Bennett's plans were in good hands.

"We're keeping it quiet," Bennett said. "So, no. She does not."

I jumped on the word. "*We?* Who's we?"

That seemed to unnerve him. "Allow me to rephrase." Sitting up straighter, he met my eyes. "I didn't tell you about this because it has nothing to do with regular Marshfield business. This is simply a whim. I'm hosting a few of the . . .

shall we say . . . higher-rollers at Marshfield for an intimate get-together at the conclusion of the FAAC event. When I use the term *we*, I mean that I've been in contact with the organizers."

As curator and manager of the estate, I was in charge of all events, big or small, that took place in the house. "I can't imagine why you wouldn't have brought me in on this, Bennett. You had to have had a reason."

He pulled his lips in, stopping himself from answering.

I was hurt to have been excluded. "You obviously don't want me there," I said. "I guess I'd like to know why."

Leaning forward, he placed a hand on my forearm. "No, no, Gracie. I've made a mess of this. I simply didn't want to bother you with organizing another big event."

Now it was a big event. A moment ago it was an intimate get-together. "What aren't you telling me, Bennett?"

Tooney piped in. "Is there a particular antique you were hoping to pick up from one of these people?" he asked. "Is that why you're inviting some of them to your home? So you can negotiate with them privately?"

The sudden shift in Bennett's expression told me that Tooney had hit a nerve.

Flustered, he waved his hands. "It's nothing." He again picked up his napkin and ran it between his fingers. "Like I told you. A whim."

"Bennett," I said, keeping my voice low, "you know that you can tell me anything. I'll keep your confidence. We both will. Why all the secrecy?"

He regained his composure and said, "Today is our day for celebrating." Taking a final sip of his Champagne, he signaled for the check. "Let's drop the FAAC topic for now. All will be explained, though probably not for a while. You'll have to trust me on this one, Gracie."

Chapter 5

IN WHAT HAD OF LATE BECOME A SUNDAY morning ritual, my roommates and I sat around the kitchen table, drinking coffee and reading the newspaper.

Scott always reached for the business section first while Bruce snagged the front page and I grabbed travel. After devouring those, we moved to other sections as we shuffled through the entire edition, exchanging, sharing, and occasionally commenting on interesting tidbits as we came across them.

Bootsie settled onto the back windowsill, staring out, blinking with drowsy contentment.

Scott folded down the front of the paper. "You think Bennett will make a formal announcement once the DNA results are in? I mean, do you think he intends to make your relationship public?"

"I hope not." I tamped down a tickle of unease. "He's agreed to keep it to our circle of confidantes for now."

"A circle that keeps growing," Bruce reminded me. "Seriously, Grace, who *doesn't* know about the DNA testing?"

I shifted in my seat. "You think I'm fooling myself believing that we can keep this quiet, don't you?"

Scott and Bruce exchanged a glance before Scott went on. "Your assistant, Frances, has been in on this from the beginning and you know what a gossip she is."

"She promised," I said.

"What about Hillary?" Bruce asked.

"Hillary has to be kept in the loop," I said. "And as Bennett's stepdaughter it's in her own best interests to keep this quiet. If it turns out that I am related to Bennett—"

"As we all know you are," Bruce said.

"*If* I am," I continued, "that knocks Hillary down a peg, at least in the public's eye. No, she won't say anything."

They exchanged another glance.

"What?" I asked. "Why do I get the feeling that the two of you are hiding something from me?"

Scott gave his partner the "Why not?" look, and Bruce laid down his newspaper to look me straight in the eye. "We overheard a conversation between a couple of patrons during a tasting last night."

I sat up straighter. "Who was it? What did they say?"

"We don't know them," he said. "Not by name, at least. They've been in a few times. It seems the trip you and Bennett took to the lab, as well as your celebratory luncheon afterward, didn't go unnoticed. Tongues are wagging and there's speculation about what's really going on."

"We're pretty sure they wanted us to overhear their conversation," Scott said, "because they know we all live together."

"What do they think is going on?"

The corner of Scott's mouth twisted upward. "There are a couple of theories out there, but the front-runner is that you and Bennett are planning to get married and all these tests are to rule out social disease."

Laughter burst out of me so quickly that I was glad I hadn't just swigged a mouthful of coffee. "Are you kidding me?"

Bruce sobered instantly. "The thing is, Grace, the temptation to correct them is real. Scott and I won't to say a word because we have your best interests at heart. But what happens when Hillary, or Frances, or Tooney is confronted? Will they be able to hold back?"

Bootsie howled, interrupting us. Alert and on her feet now, though still perched on the sill, she stared out the back window. Her black-and-white face moved side to side, as though tracking a large animal.

Bruce's question lingered in the air as I got up to see what held the little cat's attention. The moment I rose, however, Bootsie bounced off the ledge to stare at the back door.

"Maybe that FBI guy showed up after all," Scott said.

Our back bell rang. One second later came an extended and forceful knock.

Before answering I parted the curtains to check to see who it was.

"Flynn?" My voice went high with surprise as I grasped the knob and pulled the door open.

The young detective seemed as shocked by my quick answer as I was to see him in my backyard. He wore a simple black jacket with its collar turned up against the cold and a navy blue knit hat over his bald head. Clouds of breath poured out of him. I got the impression he'd jogged his way over.

"What are you doing here?" I asked.

Wiry and perpetually impatient, Flynn took time to scowl before answering. "This isn't a social call, I can tell you that much."

Bootsie jumped onto the countertop nearest the door to get a better look. I took her in my arms, unlatched the outer door, and pushed it toward him. "Come on in. Would you like coffee?"

Flynn eyed my seated roommates, offered a perfunctory greeting, and sniffed the air. "If it's made."

Scott took Bootsie, freeing me to pour Flynn a steaming

mug. As I handed it to him I noticed his hands were bare and red-chapped with cold. "What's going on?" I asked.

"Have a seat," Bruce said.

Flynn took a sip and shook his head. "Prefer to stay on my feet."

The unexpected arrival of a homicide detective in my kitchen probably should have thrown me into a panic, but I'd gotten to know Flynn—and his partner, Rodriguez—fairly well over the past couple of years and I knew that their chief often called one of them in to assist on less-deadly matters when the department was shorthanded. While I didn't count the two as friends, we were cordial acquaintances.

"I hear Rodriguez is back from medical leave," I said. "How's he doing?"

"You'll see for yourself in a minute. He's on his way."

"Rodriguez is here, too?" I asked. All of a sudden Flynn's presence took on a far more ominous significance. "What's going on?"

"Let's see. Two homicide detectives and a crew of evidence technicians? Not to mention the coroner. What do you think is going on?"

Scott's face drained of color and he pulled Bootsie closer to his chest. "Has someone been killed?"

Flynn held the mug in both hands as he took a sip. "Good coffee. The call came in about an hour ago." He pointed toward the house next to mine, the opposite side from Tooney's.

"Who was it?"

"Relax," Flynn said. "Nobody we know. Well, at least nobody from around here. We're canvassing the neighborhood. The 911 caller thought he was a drunk sleeping it off but worried he might die of exposure."

"Is that what happened?" Bruce asked.

Flynn smirked over the rim of the mug. "Only if you count exposure to gunshots. Two." Nodding appreciatively at our pained reactions, he took another drink of his coffee.

Rodriguez arrived, wrapping me in a bear hug the moment

I opened the door. "So good to see you, Miz Wheaton," he said close to my ear. Stepping back to hold me at arm's length, he grinned. "How've you been?" He raised a hand to my roommates. "Looks like we disturbed a comfortable morning here. My apologies. I hope you are all doing well?"

Taken aback by his effusive greeting, I stammered, "We're great, thanks." A second later, I recovered conversational footing. "But you," I said, "you look wonderful. How much weight have you lost?"

"More than I'm willing to admit." He patted his middle. "Still a long way to go, but I'm finally on the right track."

Rodriguez had suffered a massive heart attack some months ago and had subsequently undergone surgery to repair a ruptured aortic valve. He'd been a large man for as long as I'd known him, but had ballooned in weight in the months before his attack.

"I'm happy to hear it," I said, patting him on the shoulder. "Very proud of you."

"My doctors and my wife have been battling me about my weight for years." He pointed to his chest. "It wasn't until my ticker got in on the action that I decided to listen up."

"We're all very glad you did."

Next to him, Flynn fidgeted. "Are we done with the warm and fuzzies yet? Can we get back to our homicide?"

"Of course, amigo." Rodriguez flicked a judgmental glance at the coffee mug in Flynn's hands. "Forgive me for interrupting your expert interrogation. Pray continue." Though his words were sharp, the amusement in Rodriguez's eyes never dimmed.

Flynn took a final slug of the coffee then placed the mug on the countertop next to the sink. He flipped open his notebook and pulled out a pencil. "Were any of you home yesterday between noon and three?"

Bruce pointed to himself and then to Scott. "We were both at the wine shop."

I raised a hand. "I was at Lucatorto Labs, then out for lunch. Ronny Tooney was with me. We left here a little bit after eleven."

"That's right," Rodriguez said. "When will you and Mr. Marshfield get the results back to find out if you're related?"

"You know about the test?"

The older detective shrugged. "Everything having to do with the Marshfield family is big news. I can't say that the town is buzzing about it yet, but word is getting around."

"We were hoping to keep it quiet."

Rodriguez held a finger to his lips. "No one will hear it from me."

"Getting back to the investigation," Flynn said with an annoyed glance at his partner, "we were planning to talk to Tooney, along with your neighbors on the other side. Once we ID our victim, we'll also want to know if anyone noticed suspicious activity yesterday."

"You don't know who the victim is?" Scott asked.

"No wallet, no ID. Evidence technicians are going over the scene right now," Rodriguez said. "Who robs someone in a residential backyard? In this neighborhood? What was the guy doing there anyway? I don't think he was planning to be outside for very long; he wasn't even wearing a coat. Don't like it. Doesn't compute."

"Hang on a minute," I said. "What did he look like?"

Flynn and Rodriguez lasered their attention on me. "Holding out on us?" Flynn asked.

"There was an FBI agent here yesterday asking questions. I didn't have time to talk with him because of my appointment with Bennett. He said he would come back later, but never showed up. He wasn't wearing an overcoat, either."

Rodriguez lowered his chin and stared at me. "FBI?"

"What did he want with you?" Flynn asked.

"I never found out."

The younger detective pinched the bridge of his nose. "Why am I not surprised?"

"You don't think that's who your victim is, do you?"

The two men exchanged a glance. Rodriguez tugged the collar of his jacket tight around his neck. "You want to grab a coat, Miz Wheaton? Maybe you should come take a look."

Chapter 6

RODRIGUEZ MADE HIS LABORIOUS WAY UP THE slight incline that ran along the back of my property. Flynn and I stayed with him even though we both could have made the trek in about half the time.

"Snowed again yesterday." Rodriguez swung an arm out, pointing at the footprints ahead of us. "These, leading to your house and back, are from me and my partner." His words came out in billows of white, chopped and heavy with effort. "No footprints around the body, except for the kids' who found him. So we know he was there for some time."

"The uniforms first on the scene said the victim had snow on him, too. That's probably why no one noticed him until this morning."

"Kids found him?" I asked.

"Yeah. Your neighbor's son and daughter went out to play. Wanted to make snow angels. Found the guy 'sleeping' in their yard. Turned out to be dead instead."

"Grace, hello? Grace?" I turned toward the high-pitched

greeting to find my neighbors from across the street, an older brother-sister team, making their way toward me.

I let out a little groan.

"What's wrong?" Flynn asked.

"Nosy people," I said under my breath. "What's worse is that I can never remember if their names are Carl and Chris, or Chris and Carla."

The siblings, both in their sixties and wearing identical blue parkas and forest-green rain boots, slogged uphill on short legs. He was slim, she was not. By the time they reached us, their breath was puffing out from their slack lips, shooting into the cold air like smoke from a steam train.

The brother asked, "What's going on?"

"I don't know yet," I said.

The sister pointed. "That's the coroner's van, isn't it? Is somebody dead? What have you gotten into this time, Grace?"

When she started walking uphill again, Flynn stopped her. "This is a crime scene," he said. "I can't let you go any farther."

"You're letting *her* go up there." The brother pointed at me, looking petulant.

"Miz Wheaton may be able to identify the victim," Rodriguez said. "Now, if you'll excuse us."

"Identify the victim?" the brother repeated as his sister yelped. "Is it someone we know?"

Rodriguez held up a hand to quiet their rising hysteria. "We'll update you as soon as we can." He pantomimed scanning the street. "Which house is yours?"

They pointed at the same time, their extended arms forming a giant *V* behind them. "That one," they said in unison.

"I will be sure to stop by to talk with you when we're done here." Rodriguez may have noticed Flynn's impatience as the younger detective bounced on the balls of his feet, but missed Flynn rolling his eyes. "Why don't you wait for me there?"

The siblings seemed disappointed to have gotten all dressed

up in their heavy outerwear only to be turned away, but when Rodriguez added, "And I'll tell you as much as I can, all right?" they acquiesced.

"Don't forget us," the sister said.

Flynn raised his voice to their departing backs. "Not a chance of that."

The far end of my property backed up to three other yards: Tooney's place to the west, a neighbor I didn't know to the north, and a family with two kids to the east. As we headed uphill, I caught sight of a handful of uniformed officers rubbing their hands together and breathing into their fists as they stomped the ground to stay warm.

"We talked with the kids' parents, who are about as eager to get out of this town as your buddy Pedota was," Flynn said, with a scathing look at me. I thought about Todd Pedota and his involvement in the last murder investigation. Flynn was right. The moment my former neighbor had been exonerated, he'd put his house up for sale and disappeared. "They're horrified to have their kids stumble across a dead man, as you might imagine. And because of all the murders that have taken place at Marshfield, they're convinced you're somehow involved."

"I'm not," I said.

Flynn smirked. "Those two people in the parkas seemed ready to blame you, too."

The coroner's van was parked between two homes, back end doors open in anticipation of its grisly cargo. Rodriguez raised a hand in greeting to the two men standing next to the dark vehicle. "That's the new coroner," he said. "You meet him yet?"

A heartbeat later it registered that he was talking to me. "Uh, no. No reason to."

"Good guy." Rodriguez's words were still breathy and brief. I found myself wishing he'd stop talking and conserve energy.

Two of the uniformed officers around the body stepped

aside to give us a better view. The victim was lying faceup, arms spread on either side of his body, as though entreating the skies for help. As heavily stained as it was with blood, I recognized the suit. And even though his expression—eyes closed and openmouthed—was unfamiliar, I recognized the man immediately.

"That's him," I said. "That's the FBI agent who came to my door."

I shivered as the evidence technicians finished taking photos, collecting samples, making notes, and conferring with Rodriguez and Flynn. Yesterday's chill was nothing compared to the icy cold we were experiencing today and I wasn't properly outfitted. Expecting this to have been a quick trip out to my yard and back, I'd pulled rubber rain boots over my fuzzy socks and grabbed the nearest jacket I could find—my trench coat. No hat, no mittens. The coat was lined, but against the sharp breeze it was like wearing a bedsheet. My hair twisted up and around my head; my eyes watered.

"We need to ask you a few more questions, Miz Wheaton," Rodriguez said when he noticed me rubbing my nose with the back of my bare hand. "But there's no reason for you stand out here in the cold."

"It's not that bad." As uncomfortable as it was out there, I didn't want to leave until I knew what had happened.

He waved aside my lie and called to one of the two men standing by the idling coroner's vehicle. "Hey, Dr. Bradley, would it be okay if Miz Wheaton warms up in your van? She's our best witness so far."

The taller of the two men stepped forward. Brown curls twisted out from around his knit cap and although he looked to be only in his late thirties, he walked with a cane. His shiny black jacket sported the county emblem rendered in gold with his title, "Coroner" embroidered beneath. With his alert eyes and serious demeanor, he definitely looked the part.

"I'm fine," I said.

"So this is the legendary Grace Wheaton," the man said.

Letting go of his cane long enough to remove one glove, he extended his right hand to me. "I understand you kept my predecessor busy. I'm Joe," he said as we shook. "Happy to meet you."

"Same here," I said instinctively, although I would have been content not to have dealings with our county coroner. Now or ever.

"Your hands are freezing," he said. "Come on, the cab section ought to be toasty."

"I'm fine, really."

He'd tugged his glove back on and grabbed hold of his cane again. Lifting it slightly off the ground, he tapped it against his leg. "Injury," he said, even though I hadn't asked. "I pretend I'm Willy Wonka. Come on."

I didn't want to be a bother, but I was beginning to lose feeling in my fingers. "Thanks."

We trudged around the vehicle together. "I know that spending time in the coroner's van is probably not on anyone's bucket list"—though his words were deadpan, amusement sparked his eyes—"but it will keep you out of the wind."

When he opened the passenger door, a wave of blissful heat engulfed me so completely that I was suddenly okay with the idea of hanging out in the death-mobile. "It's wonderful in here," I said. "Thank you."

"There's not something I hear every day."

I pointed to the driver's side. "Are you joining me?"

Sliding a glance outside to where the body lay, he seemed to consider it. "I've done a preliminary examination, but they may need more input before they move him. As delightful a prospect it would be to enjoy the warmth, it's probably best if I make my way back."

Across from me, the driver's-side door opened, bringing a rush of icy air. Flynn climbed in, settling himself behind the wheel before pulling the door closed again. He blew air into his fists then leaned forward to talk across me, addressing the coroner, who remained outside holding my door.

"Thanks, Doc. This shouldn't take long. We'll be out of your hair before you load up."

Dr. Bradley gave Flynn a nod of acknowledgment. To me, he said, "Again, it was very nice meeting you. Too bad it was under these circumstances." The man didn't smile, but I swore I detected humor in his eyes. "Be well, Ms. Wheaton. I would say I hope to see you again soon, but most people don't take that the right way."

When I laughed, a tiny corner of his mouth tipped upward. He nodded and shut the door.

Flynn pulled out a tissue, blew his red nose, and got right down to business. "Are you one hundred percent certain that's the guy who came to your door yesterday morning?"

"That's him. No doubt about it."

"What did he want?"

I recounted the brief conversation to the best of my ability, reminding Flynn that I'd cut the exchange short and that the FBI guy said he'd be back later.

"Do you remember his name?" Flynn asked.

"Alvin Clark."

He seemed impressed that I was able to come up with that. "Which office was he out of?"

"No idea," I said. "Except for the badge, his photo, and his name, there wasn't much real information there."

"And you have no idea what he wanted to ask you about?"

"None whatsoever. He wanted to know who else lived with me, but I wouldn't tell him."

"Why didn't you call us?"

"Why would I?" I asked. "Having an FBI agent show up at one's front door isn't usually a reason to alert homicide detectives."

"What if the killer is really looking for you, but shot this FBI guy because he got in the way?"

"Why would anyone be after me? That doesn't make any sense."

"Yeah, but the situations you get involved in don't always follow logic. You ought to be more careful, you know."

I couldn't see how answering the door for an FBI agent constituted reckless behavior but I didn't feel like arguing. Flynn asked me a few more questions, but I had little more to add.

"Want me to walk you back to your house?" he asked.

"I think I know the way."

"That's it, Grace. Be a smart aleck. Things happen around here, and they always seem to involve you. You ought to think about taking precautions."

"I have," I said. "We installed a very sophisticated alarm system. If anyone tries to break in, the service and the police department will be alerted."

"Uh-huh. But what happens when you open the door for the killer and let him in? No alarm will go off then, will it?"

I didn't know why he was trying to scare me, and I wasn't in the mood to take any more. "We're done here, right?"

He gave a quick nod.

I hesitated, but plunged ahead. "If you find out, would you mind letting me know why this Alvin Clark was here and what he wanted?"

"Yeah, sure."

"Thanks," I said.

I was about to open the passenger door when Flynn said, "One more thing, Grace."

I turned.

"A burglar alarm provides only limited protection. In the time it takes to transmit notice of a break-in and then for help to arrive, a murderer could kill you and be out of your house, leaving you bleeding on the kitchen floor. Maybe we catch him, maybe we don't. But at that point it's too late for you, isn't it?"

"Wow, thanks, Flynn," I said.

Chapter 7

MONDAY MORNING, MY ASSISTANT STOOD IN front of her desk, arms folded. Her tethered rhinestone glasses were perched at the end of her nose and she stared at me over their tops, her tadpole eyebrows arched. "Well?" she asked before I could even say hello. "When will the lab have results?"

"Good morning, Frances." I pulled off my winter coat and hung it on the nearby rack. "How was your weekend? Did you do anything fun?"

"Stop stalling. I had my doubts you'd go through with it but I hear that you did. The lab must have given you an estimate." Tapping her foot now, she continued to glare. "And while you're at it, bring me up to date on the dead guy in your backyard."

"Not my backyard. My neighbor's."

"Same difference. Who was he?"

"Don't tell me your gossipy minions missed the part about him being an FBI agent?"

Frances's brows jumped even higher.

I gestured. "Have a seat. I'll tell you all about it."

Frances settled herself behind her desk and I took one of the two chairs opposite. My assistant loved nothing better than to gossip; she'd be eager to share my up-close-and-personal details with members of her clandestine grapevine.

Before I started, I held up a finger. "I want to remind you not to share anything about the DNA test with anyone."

"Tongues are wagging around town," she said, "even though I haven't breathed a word. My friends have been trying to get me to confirm." She shook her head, making her chins waggle. "They're getting nothing from me. But the fact that I'm not talking is almost admission in itself."

I sighed. "I really wanted to keep this quiet."

"Best you can hope for at this point is keeping the results quiet. You never answered. When will you know?"

"About a week or so. Two labs are running separate tests. They'll wait until both sets of results are in."

She gave a brief nod. "Now, back to your FBI guy." Pushing up her purple sweater's sleeves, she leaned forward on thick elbows to listen.

Frances interrupted only twice during my summary: once to comment derisively on Bennett's generosity toward Tooney, and the other to ask what I thought the FBI agent wanted from me.

"Maggie Inglethorpe suggested that one of my neighbors may be under investigation," I said.

"But you don't think so."

"I don't know what to think," I said. "The fact that the agent was found shot to death so close to my house has me on edge."

Frances's mouth twisted. "At least the murder wasn't on Marshfield property this time."

At the sound of Frances's door opening, I turned. Bennett strode in, his brow tight, his mouth set in a line.

"Gracie," he said, his voice a growl. "What happened yesterday? Why didn't you call me?"

I got up to greet him. "There was no reason to alarm you.

In fact, I was just telling Frances about how Rodriguez and Flynn are on top of things. The fact that the FBI agent wanted to talk with me is simply a curious coincidence. I don't believe there's anything for me to worry about."

"Anything having to do with your safety concerns me," Bennett said. His gaze was still heated and direct. "I worry about you."

I led him toward Frances's desk, where we both took seats. "I'm sure we'll find out more soon enough. I asked Flynn to keep me updated."

Frances harrumphed. "And you think he will?"

"He'd better," Bennett said. "I'm very concerned about this FBI agent's inquiry. The minute you hear more, I want to know about it. And if we discover the detectives are holding back on us, I'll have a talk with the chief of police myself."

"Let's not get ahead of ourselves." I held my hands out to both of them. "Flynn has been better lately. And Rodriguez seems particularly elated to be back on the job."

Frances harrumphed again. I ignored her.

"What about that reception you talked about, Bennett?" I asked, in an effort to shift subjects. "I hadn't yet gotten to that topic with Frances. I really believe that she and I ought to be involved in the arrangements."

Frances sat up straighter. "What reception?"

"It's nothing, really," Bennett said. "I'm hosting a small get-together here at the conclusion of the Fine Art and Antiquity Collectors' convention."

Frances looked from me to Bennett and back again. "The convention starts Saturday," she said. "When were you planning on telling us?"

Looking as uncomfortable as he had when he'd first broached the topic, Bennett tried to dismiss its importance. "I've had my personal staff arrange everything. It's too much work for both of you and it has nothing to do with Marshfield Manor. This is purely a personal whim and I didn't want to trouble either of you."

Frances, eyes narrowed, appeared to be having the exact same reaction I had. "Who's coming?"

Bennett waved a hand in the air. "It's a short list, really. A few experts, a few key collectors in the world of antiquities."

"And you didn't think Grace and I should be in on the planning?" she asked.

Bennett shot Frances a stern look. "I am allowed to comport my business dealings without your involvement, am I not?"

Frances tilted her head, not buying any of this. Nor was I.

"Not to put you on the spot, Bennett, but when you first mentioned this, you told me that you were working with the organizers of the FAAC. Now you say you put your personal staff in charge. You also just referred to it as a small get-together, but aren't more than a hundred people expected to attend?"

"A hundred guests?" Frances echoed.

Bennett shifted in his chair. "Did I say that?"

"You did," I said. I didn't enjoy making Bennett feel uncomfortable but this situation felt wrong. "You are, of course, entitled to keep secrets from us. I understand if you don't want to trust us with certain—"

"This is not a matter of trust." His brows came together again. "Certainly not."

"It's okay, Bennett," I said. "Whatever your reasons for keeping us away from this reception"—I made eye contact with Frances—"we may not understand, but we'll accept your decision. If you prefer we stay away, we will stay away. All we ask is that you keep us updated so that we're not blindsided when things like this come up."

Bennett looked away, staring at the ceiling. He flexed his jaw, then said, "The reception is Tuesday night. The list of attendees hasn't been finalized yet and likely won't be until the last minute. There may be more than a hundred guests. Perhaps double that number. Much will depend on what items change hands during the course of the convention.

The organizers have been working with my personal staff and even I don't know all the plans for the evening."

I studied Bennett as he continued.

"Because I was approached to host this event, I thought it best to allow those in charge to manage the details, thus sparing you both the additional responsibility." He held out his hands, fingers spread. "You see why I didn't feel the need to mention anything?"

Despite his explanation and assertions, I sensed he was still hiding a key point from us, though for the life of me, I couldn't imagine what it was.

"Before we move on, two questions," I said.

He sighed theatrically and folded his hands across his middle. "Proceed."

"Why aren't you attending the actual FAAC convention like you usually do?"

"You're not attending FAAC this year?" Frances asked.

"He claims he doesn't care for the crowds," I said. "And that he has no desire to go this year."

Bennett's eyes sparkled and he pursed his mouth before answering. "Had I known I was to face the Spanish Inquisition I may have reconsidered visiting this morning." Inhaling deeply, he said, "Allow me this one secret. I am, indeed, staying away from FAAC this year, and am instead hosting a separate event after its conclusion. My reasons are my own and you will both simply have to trust that I know what I'm doing."

I knew we'd taken the issue as far as we could. "Which leads me to the second matter," I said. "Tooney asked you if there was a specific item you're hoping to acquire and if this reception is the means to accomplish that. Is that what's going on?"

He looked away again, scratching the side of his temple, buying time. After what was probably no more than fifteen seconds, but felt much longer, he made eye contact with us both. "Mr. Tooney's talents are grossly underrated. I'm glad we have him on retainer as Marshfield's ally."

Frances snorted.

"What is it you're looking for?" I asked, eager to join in on the journey. "Is there anything we can do to help?"

For reasons I didn't understand, my words seemed to cause Bennett pain. "I'm sorry, Grace. Not this time. I've already told you more than I should have. There is an item I hope to acquire, and I have it on good authority that its owner plans to attend the FAAC event. I prefer to conduct business here in my home, where I have the advantage. At this juncture I prefer not to divulge further information about the item and I will thank you both to put an end to this particular line of questioning."

He stood. "If I'm lucky, I will receive news of this item as early as today, and perhaps all will be settled before the FAAC event begins. If that happens, I will be free to attend the convention after all." Pointing to each of us in turn, he added, "That's enough for today. Grace, please keep me updated with regard to the murder investigation. And, more important, stay safe."

When he left, Frances stared after him, tapping her fingers on her blotter as she chewed the inside of her cheek. "That's not like him at all."

"I know," I said. "It has me worried."

She shifted to chew the other side. "Maybe you should let the matter drop."

"This? Coming from you?"

She blinked a couple of times. "Know what I think?"

"Tell me."

"He's buying you a present. For when the DNA results come back. You both already know what they're going to say, but once it's official he will want to commemorate the moment by giving you a gift."

"I hadn't thought of that."

"You think I'm wrong?" she asked.

"I don't know," I said slowly. "That makes perfect sense." And though it did, something still didn't feel right.

Chapter 8

IN MY OWN OFFICE LATER THAT AFTERNOON, I decided to call Rodriguez and Flynn to find out if they'd had any luck discovering who'd killed Alvin Clark. Neither detective was at the station. I considered trying their cell phones, ultimately deciding not to disturb them. I left a voice-mail instead.

Seconds after I dropped the receiver back into its cradle, my phone rang. From the display I knew that the call originated from our main welcome desk on the first floor.

"Want me to answer that?" Frances shouted from her office.

"I got it," I said, and picked up. "Grace Wheaton."

"Miss Wheaton, this is Evelyn down at the front desk," she said.

I would have recognized her warbling voice without clarification. "What can I do for you?"

"There's a Mr. Krol here to see Mr. Marshfield."

Bennett hadn't mentioned anyone by the name of Krol to me. But then again, Bennett had been keeping secrets lately. "Does he have an appointment?"

"He says he was supposed to be here earlier but his flight was delayed. I tried upstairs but Mr. Marshfield isn't picking up his phone. His butler, Theo, doesn't know where he is, either. I thought you might."

"Unfortunately, I don't know have any idea where he is at the moment. Did Mr. Krol tell you what this is in regard to?"

Evelyn placed her hand over the mouthpiece, though I couldn't imagine why she wanted to shield her conversation. When she returned, she said, "Mr. Krol says that he has a business arrangement with Mr. Marshfield." She lowered her voice to a whisper. "He won't give me any details."

"That's fine, Evelyn. I'll come down to meet him while Frances locates Bennett. Sound good?"

"Yes, thanks, Miss Wheaton."

Having overheard, Frances had already taken up the quest. "Who do you suppose this visitor is?" she asked as I crossed her office. "The Mister usually keeps you updated on his appointments."

"Not this time, apparently."

"I'm telling you," she shouted to my back as I headed out, "he's planning a surprise. Mark my words."

I took a staff stairway down to the main level and let myself through a segment of the velvet-rope barricade that delineated tourist boundaries. Hurrying across a corridor where a family of six walked abreast, taking up the entire width, I excused myself and pushed through.

I caught sight of Bennett's guest from about thirty feet away. Tall, with the kind of blond hair that managed to look tousled and professional at the same time, he cut a dashing figure in his charcoal suit. Seventy-five-year-old Evelyn stared up at him with undisguised adoration, and although he was about half her age, he appeared to be enjoying Evelyn's company.

"I'm Grace Wheaton," I said when she regretfully directed his attention to me. "I'm sorry Bennett Marshfield isn't available at the moment. How may I help you?"

He shifted the camel overcoat he carried in order to shake my hand. "Very pleased to meet you," he said in a warm Australian accent. "Evelyn informs me that you're the palace manager for the estate."

I doubted Evelyn had used those exact words. *Palace manager* wasn't a term I encountered often, but it always made me smile. "I suppose you could say that."

"I'm Malcolm Krol." He handed me a business card.

These days, when anyone can achieve quasi-professional results using a desktop printer, business cards are generally unimpressive. Not so that of Malcolm Krol. I recognized the high-quality linen stock and noted the raised printing. Deep maroon lettering against a creamy background provided the man's name and phone number, nothing more.

"What business are you in, Mr. Krol?" I asked.

Our visitor either perpetually maintained an amused expression, or he recognized me as a gatekeeper and decided to play along. His eyes were unreadable but he appeared to be tamping down a tolerant smile.

Evelyn piped in, clearly eager to rejoin the conversation. "He had an appointment with Mr. Marshfield this morning at eleven," she said, adding absolutely no useful information whatsoever. "His plane was delayed."

Krol reached across the desk to touch Evelyn's arm. "That's right. And if the airline had gotten me here on time, I would have had my meeting with Mr. Marshfield and been out of your hair."

I waited for him to answer my question. Instead, he lowered his voice. "Have you any idea when my colleague will be available?"

Colleague? That label suggested he and Bennett had worked together in the past or had plans to work together in the future.

"Malcolm?"

I turned to see Bennett jogging across the main hall. He

waved a greeting and closed the distance between us in seconds.

As the two shook hands, Bennett gestured toward me. "I see you've met the estate's manager." To me, he said, "Thank you for greeting my guest. Frances let me know you were down here." Bennett's smile was strained.

"My pleasure," I said. "I was just asking Mr. Krol about his business." Holding the man's card aloft, I casually flipped it back and forth. My message was clear—I wanted to know more.

"Of course," Bennett said, lifting it from my fingers. "I will be sure to talk with you later. For now, Mr. Krol and I have much to discuss. And I believe Frances requires your assistance upstairs."

There was no question about it; I was being dismissed. I didn't like it one little bit.

"I'll talk with you later, then," I said.

"Very nice to make your acquaintance, Ms. Wheaton," Krol said. "I hope we meet again."

FRANCES DIDN'T REQUIRE MY ASSISTANCE, BUT I wasn't surprised to discover Bennett's fib.

"He probably doesn't want you to know what he's planning for you," Frances said when I explained his odd behavior.

"I think there's something else going on. I can't put my finger on why, but Bennett seemed extremely bothered by the fact that this Krol and I were talking."

"You have a knack for figuring things out. Of course the Mister would be upset. A little bit of digging on your part and you'll spoil his fun."

"If that's true, then Krol would have known who I was. He didn't seem to have ever heard of me before."

"Oh, ho," Frances said, pushing herself back in her chair and affecting a haughty air. "Aren't we a little full of ourselves?"

"You know what I mean. Whether I like it or not, Bennett tells everyone about my role here. Which is why the DNA isn't much of a secret anymore. Bennett has a very tough time keeping things to himself."

"You are right about that. And you say this guy's card didn't have much information?"

"A phone number. And I don't even have that information to trace because Bennett plucked the card out of my hands."

"Do you remember the area code at least?"

I closed my eyes and did my best to envision it. "I think it was either four-one-five, or four-one-nine. But I can't be certain."

Frances had taken a while to warm up to the idea of using computers but now surpassed me with her speed at Internet searching. She tapped her keyboard. "Marin County, California, or"—more tapping—"Toledo, Ohio." Glancing over at me, she got a gleam in her eyes. "You could always ask your friend Ronny Tooney to find out more about this guy for you. How many Australian Malcolm Krols could there be?"

"Tempting though it is, I can't. If Bennett wants to keep secrets, I need to respect his privacy. Using Tooney to investigate—when Bennett pays his salary—seems very wrong."

"Have it your way." The glint in her eyes dimmed.

As I crossed into my office, I heard her mutter, "Goody Two-shoes."

Chapter 9

BRUCE AND SCOTT WERE WATCHING TELEVI-
sion in the living room. I was in parlor, about to shut my book
and call it quits for the night, when the doorbell rang.

I glanced at the clock on the mantel; it was a few minutes
before ten. Bootsie had been asleep on my lap prior to the
interruption. Now we were both on our way to find out who
was visiting at this late hour.

Bruce reached the front door a couple of steps ahead of
me. "Are you expecting anyone?"

"I left a message with Rodriguez and Flynn this afternoon," I said. "Maybe they decided to stop by?"

The look on his face let me know that he didn't believe
that scenario to be likely, either.

"Check first," I warned.

Bruce flipped on the porch light and peered out. "It's a
woman," he whispered.

Scott came around to join us. "Maybe it's another Fed?"

Bruce swung open the door. "Can we help you?"

She was slim, wearing distressed blue jeans and a dark

navy pea coat. Her fluffy red scarf was decorative, rather than sturdy, and her cowboy boots were covered in snow.

"Hi," she said, focusing her attention on me, "are you Grace?"

"Do I know you?"

She had golden hair that fell to her shoulders and heavy, straight bangs. With hollow cheeks, big eyes, and a heart-shaped face that ended at a rather narrow chin, she was more gaunt than pretty.

"No, not yet." She laughed. "My name is Nina Buchman." She peered into the house, as though looking for something. "Can I come in?"

Just like the FBI agent had the other day, Nina affected a shiver. She carried a brown leather tote that appeared filled to bursting, and she shifted from foot to foot, tapping her boots against each other to dislodge accumulated slush. The tote appeared weather-beaten and well-worn. The boots looked new.

"Maybe if you tell me what it is you want?" I said, with a lilt to phrase it as a question.

"Sure, sure. Of course." She laughed again. Her teeth were big for her small mouth, and with her über-narrow face and shiny hair she reminded me of a thoroughbred. Attractive, strong, willful.

Bruce backed up, allowing me to take point. I felt him touch the back of my arm—a silent gesture of warning. But I'd felt it, too.

She brightened her smile. "I'm new in town and interviewing for a job. I need somewhere to stay until I find a more permanent place."

I turned to Bruce and Scott. They looked as perplexed as I felt. "Why are you *here*, though?" I asked. "At our house?"

Her eyes went wide. "Don't you have a room here to rent out?"

"No," I said. We did have a spare bed and bath upstairs and, at one point, had considered taking on another roommate to help with expenses. We'd scuttled those plans, however, once Bennett had insisted on paying for renovations.

"You don't?" The tone in her voice went far beyond disappointed. More like disbelief. As though she knew about that vacant spot upstairs. How could she? A second later, her tone shifted completely. "Is someone else living here?"

I started to close the door. "Good luck with your search."

"Wait." Again, she tried to see deeper into the house. "Could I come in for a little bit? Maybe you can give me ideas of where to look?"

"Are you telling us that you moved to a new city with no place to stay?"

"I have a hotel," she said. "But I don't care for the place. I really prefer a more homelike environment."

"There are a couple of nice bed-and-breakfasts right off Main Street." Scott indicated the general direction. "Three blocks that way and one block up. You can't miss them."

She sucked in her top lip and gave another shiver. "What about for a few nights?" she asked. "You don't have room for *one* person for a couple of nights? I could sleep on the couch."

"I thought you had a hotel."

"I do," she amended quickly. "But the, um, convention is messing me up. I'm really in a bind, here. Can't you help a girl out?" Tears formed in the corners of her eyes. She held a gloved hand to her mouth. "Please?"

Bruce made a sound low in his throat. I couldn't tell whether that meant he was caving in to her pleas or reminding me to stand strong.

Too many odd things had happened in Emberstowne in the years I'd been here. Too many suspicious occurrences. Flynn's warnings about the limitations of my burglar alarm popped like mini-fireworks in my brain. This woman looked helpless, but a nagging feeling of something being amiss—that tingle of fear that so many of us ignore—decided it for me.

"I'm sorry," I said. "We can't help you. Good luck."

"But—"

"Sorry," I said again. And as difficult as it was, I shut the door.

"Grace," Scott said. "Are you sure we can't do anything for her?"

"What if she killed the FBI guy?" I asked.

Scott blanched. "Do you really think so?"

"I don't know. We can't know. But don't you think it's weird that she knew my name? She knew we had a room here?" I pointed upstairs.

"That was a little odd," Bruce said.

Scott and I made our way into the parlor. I picked Bootsie up and cuddled the little cat close as I made my way to my favorite wing chair and sat down.

"The FBI guy, Alvin Clark, knew my name, too. And he wanted to know who else was living here," I said as I stroked Bootsie's fur. "This is too much of a coincidence. I don't like turning my back on people in need . . ." I let the thought hang.

"Her story about the hotel seemed suspect," Scott agreed. "At one point she made it sound as though she had nothing for tonight, but then when we pressed, she backpedaled."

"Exactly. This doesn't add up to anything good. And are we to believe she's going door to door looking for a room to rent?"

Bruce finally rejoined us. "I turned off the light inside the hallway," he said. "So I could watch her without being seen. She stood on the porch for a minute, assessing the house."

"Why would she do that?" I asked.

He shrugged. "She finally turned around and headed back to the street, but not toward the bed-and-breakfasts. She headed west."

"There's nothing that way but more single-family houses," I said.

Bruce shrugged again.

"Two strangers at our door in the past three days," I said. "And one of them was murdered. I'm not feeling bad about turning her away."

Scott nodded. "When you put it that way, neither am I."

I pulled out my phone. "I think this is worth mentioning to Rodriguez."

FRANCES STOMPED INTO MY OFFICE THE NEXT morning, hands tight at her hips. She wore eggplant-colored wool pants, sensible shoes, and over her white knit shirt, a thick beige cardigan embroidered with violets. She'd been about to say something, but stopped herself with a frown of displeasure. "It's cold in this room. Something wrong with your heater?"

I tugged my own sweater close as I gestured with my chin. "The price of my beautiful view."

She stared out the tall mullioned windows that took up much of my southern wall. "I don't remember a winter this cold. Not for a long time."

I offered a one-shouldered shrug. "When my family lived in Chicago, we got used to subzero temperatures." I followed her gaze. The sun, behind heavy cloud cover, brought to mind the image of a shiny quarter submerged in slush. The gray glow did nothing to animate the flat blanket of white covering the rolling grounds below. "We haven't dropped below the teens since I've lived here. And today we're predicted to hit the low thirties. Practically a heat wave."

She wrinkled her nose, then gave me a once-over. "Cold-blooded animals adapt to temperature changes better than warm-blooded ones do."

Ever since Frances and I started getting along better, it had become more difficult for her to get under my skin. She didn't stop trying, of course. Sometimes I ignored her, sometimes I played along.

"And what am I to deduce from that pronouncement?"

"Stating a scientific fact." Her halfhearted attempt to provoke me hadn't hit its mark. She shrugged off the disappointment. "I came in here to tell you that I couldn't find anything on that Malcolm Krol in either Ohio or California. There are links to uncover home addresses—for a fee, of course—but nothing at all about who he is or what he does for a living."

"I thought we agreed to let Bennett have his secrets."

She pointed. "You agreed. Not me. What kind of amateur sleuth are you to leave this matter hanging? Which brings me to another matter—the dead guy in your yard? What are you doing about that?"

"Not my yard, and nothing." I sliced my hands sideways across the top of my desk in emphasis. "This time it's up to Flynn and Rodriguez. Let the professionals handle it."

"Hmph." She was about to say more when the sound of her door opening silenced us.

"Yoo-hoo. Anybody here? Grace? It's Hillary. I have a big surprise for you." Frances folded her arms across her ample chest and shot me a "What now?" look.

I got to my feet. "In here," I said.

While Hillary and I would probably never be close friends, we'd reached a point in our relationship where we respected one another and were now wary allies.

Frances spoke under her breath. "What kind of surprise do you think she has this time?"

I had no idea. I probably wouldn't like it very much.

Hillary walked into my office looking, as always, like a model who'd stepped fresh off the cover of a woman's magazine. Blonde, pert, tiny, and perfectly dressed and coiffed, she came in smiling until she caught sight of Frances.

"Oh, you're here, too? I suppose that's fine."

"Don't keep us in suspense, please," Frances said, arms folded.

Hillary wagged a finger at my assistant. "The surprise isn't for you." She pointed. "It's for her."

I'd remained standing behind my desk and worked to inject cheer into my tone. "What's up?"

Hillary waggled her head and grinned broadly, more

pleased with herself than I'd seen her in some time. "I came in to see Papa Bennett today and when I arrived I met someone downstairs at the welcome desk asking for you." Her eyes were wide and full of merriment. "I thought it would be a fun surprise to bring that someone up here."

"Who is it, Hillary?"

"See for yourself," she said, then waved to whomever waited in the next room.

When Liza walked in, I nearly lost the ability to stand.

"Hey, Grace," she said with an impish smile. "Long time no see."

Chapter 10

THERE ARE MOMENTS IN LIFE WHEN QUICK recovery isn't possible. This was one of them. My knees were unable to keep me steady. I swayed forward, balancing my weight on the tips of my fingers. Splayed across the top of my desk blotter, their pads were white, growing numb from the pressure of keeping me vertical.

I was neither afraid of my sister nor threatened by her. Not physically, anyway. The shock of her sudden appearance in my office hit so unexpectedly and so hard, however, that my mind and body seized up in stupefied paralysis.

Little observations prickled at my brain: Liza's skin had lost its youthful glow; she had tiny wrinkles near her eyes and grooves around her lips. Had she started smoking again? Her blue jeans were too long, faded and frayed at the hem. Her over-filled purse looked like a cross-body saddlebag with leather straps straining against the weight of its contents. She carried a bright orange trench coat—no match for current temperatures.

Through it all I was vaguely aware that Hillary had antici-pated a far different reaction. "This is your sister, isn't it?"

Six inches shorter, with darker coloring and a curvier build than mine, Liza and I were too dissimilar to share clothes or makeup when we were young. She gravitated toward tight, revealing outfits, where I'd always leaned toward tailored and classic. I kept my straight blond hair shoulder-length; hers, which was brunette, had always been worn wild and wavy down her back.

Liza's chestnut mane was gone now. She'd pulled what was left into a nub of a ponytail, errant strands popping out all over. She'd cut bangs in again, too, wearing them straight and full across her forehead.

I didn't say a word. I couldn't. I had no idea what might come out.

Liza broke the strained silence. "Aren't you happy to see me?"

A hundred questions exploded in my brain at once, firing up and dissolving too quickly for me to catch even one long enough to put into words. I'm sure she was convinced the bangs made her look younger. Of course, the last time she'd worn them that way she'd been eighteen and thought they made her look smarter.

Frances took a predatory step toward my sister. "You're Liza?"

"Oh, you *do* talk about me," Liza said, inching away from Frances and nearer to me. I hoped she didn't expect me to come around my desk and welcome her with a giant hug. "That makes me so happy. I was afraid that after our last disagreement you might hold a grudge."

Frances snorted loudly. "Is that what you're calling it? A disagreement?"

My assistant had recovered from my sister's surprise appearance. That was more than could be said for me.

Frances knew the whole sordid tale—I'd told her about how Liza had eventually married my former fiancé and had squandered her inheritance on a get-rich-quick scheme that had left the two nearly penniless. I'd warned Frances about

my sister for this very reason: I couldn't predict when Liza
might show up, and I didn't want my assistant duped into
helping her. Too bad I hadn't thought to mention this to Hillary.
Anyone who ever helped Liza was eventually sorry they had.

Liza grabbed Hillary's hand and tugged her close. "This
wonderful woman rescued me downstairs. I didn't know
where to begin asking for you." Directing what could only
be described as a loving gaze toward Bennett's stepdaughter,
she went on. "I don't know how to thank you, Hillary."

"Um . . . it was my pleasure," Hillary said. Her eyes
asked a million questions.

"What are you here for, Liza?" I asked.

Thrusting out her bottom lip, my sister strove to affect
puppy dog eyes. "Is that really the first thing you're going
to say to me after we've been apart so long?"

"Seems to me you probably have more to say to Grace
than she has to say to you," Frances said, in a fierce and
welcome show of solidarity.

Hillary seemed to finally grasp that she hadn't engi-
neered the happy family reunion she'd expected. "You know,
I always wished I'd had a sister, but unfortunately I'm an
only child." In an obvious attempt to lessen the tension, she
did what Hillary always did best: She talked about herself,
picking up speed as she went on. "I grew up here. I was a
teenager when my mom married Papa Bennett. But it was
really lonely here all by myself."

"That had to be difficult," Liza said, offering Hillary a
placating tone while maintaining eye contact with me. "I
was lucky to have Grace as a big sister to look up to."

Taking time to choose the right words, I breathed deeply
and ordered my weak limbs back into action. They complied. Now all I needed to do was quiet my tempestuous
heartbeat. I worried every person in the room could see the
veins throbbing in my neck.

Hillary didn't handle awkward silence well. "Grace will
have to tell you about how I renovated her house. It turned

out beautifully, I must say. All new windows, new siding. A complete re-do inside and out." She glanced my way long enough to notice that I still wasn't engaged in the conversation. "I'm doing the home next door now, too. They're mirror images. Sister houses, I like to call them."

One beat later she seemed to realize what she'd said. "I mean," Hillary went on, "it's not like they're really identical. Close. Like I said, mirror images. Brothers built them, did you know?"

Liza held a hand up, silencing her. What in any other situation would be construed as a rude gesture, seemed to provide Hillary relief.

"You renovated Mom's house?" Liza asked.

"*My* house."

Liza pulled her cheeks in, an expression, which she'd never outgrown, of frustration. "Things must be going pretty well for you if you can afford that kind of investment."

Hillary's brows jumped. The temptation to spill the truth that Bennett had paid for the project was bright in her eyes.

"Emberstowne has been very good to me," I said.

"You're the manager of this place?"

"I am."

There was no comfort in this room. No warmth. The four of us stood like enemy combatants who'd stumbled upon one another in the middle of a war. Liza had positioned herself directly across the desk from me. Next to her, Hillary gazed longingly at the door. Frances, feet planted shoulder-width apart, kept her arms folded and her gaze fierce.

"So, does that mean you work with the Marshfield family?" Liza asked.

"Papa Bennett is my stepfather," Hillary said. "I'm part of the Marshfield family."

"Papa Bennett?" Liza repeated, as though finally understanding. "Bennett Marshfield?"

Hillary's incredulous expression seemed to ask what rock Liza had crawled out from under. "Yes, of course."

"I would really love to meet your stepfather." Liza's blatant appeal oozed friendship, but—for me, at least—there was no missing the calculation in her eyes. "Do you think I could?"

"I don't see why n—"

"Bennett is very busy," I said. "Sorry. Not happening."

"But if he's *your* stepfather," Liza persisted, addressing Hillary. "Shouldn't it be your decision?"

"Grace sets the Mister's schedule," Frances said.

Liza pulled her cheeks in again, struggling to neutralize her frustration. "I don't understand."

"I'm afraid Frances is right," Hillary said. "You'll have to work through Grace."

I could have reached over and kissed Hillary for that. Instead, I simply said, "Thank you."

Liza drew a sharp breath. Tossing her head back—a significantly less impressive move than it used to be with that stubby ponytail—she asked, "Who else, then?" Before we could ask what she meant, she added, "Marshfields, that is. Who else lives here?"

"No one else," I said, eager to put an end to this. "You never answered my question, Liza. What are you doing here?"

Her eyes sparkled in a way that made my stomach lurch. "Are you telling me that Bennett is it? There are no other Marshfields?"

Frances and Hillary immediately glanced at me. I couldn't blame their instinctive reaction. I wondered how soon it would dawn on them that if the DNA tests came back positive, that meant Liza was related to Bennett, too.

I swallowed before answering. "I have a very busy day planned. Your visit, while I'm certain it will be brief"—I offered a frosty smile—"is unexpected. Why don't you tell me why you're here and we can both get back to our lives?"

She gave a halfhearted shrug. "I need a place to stay," she said. "Not for long."

"Why here? Why now?"

"I've hit a bit of a snag," she said.

She shifted her weight and with that trifling gesture the energy in the room shifted, too. From the moment she'd breezed in, taking me by surprise, she'd held control. Marching in here demanding answers about my life, demanding to meet Bennett, she'd been all bluster and bravado. It had been a performance that had worked until the moment she admitted needing my help. I was sure it rankled her mightily, but now the power was mine.

"What kind of snag?"

Her gaze didn't waver as she struggled to regain dominance. "Life."

A snarky reply shot to my lips but I wrestled it back. "Is your husband with you?"

She winced at the question, but lifted her chin. "Eric and I are no longer together."

I wasn't happy to hear it. I wasn't distressed. I felt no level of satisfaction or the temptation to gloat. I felt . . . nothing at all.

Silence stretched between us and I could sense Liza's discomfort grow. She threw impatient glances at Frances and Hillary, making it clear she'd prefer to air our family grievances without an audience.

They remained in the room, unmoved by her transparent hints. My allies, such as they were. Two years ago I could never have predicted this moment. Right now, I wanted to hug them both.

"Fine." Liza huffed impatience. "I'm here because I have nowhere else to stay. I have no money, either. There. I said it. Happy now?"

"How much do you need?"

"I'm not asking for money. That is, I'd rather stay at the house." Liza's smile was as fleeting as it was weak. "I thought I'd stay with you. In the spare room. It is our house, you know."

"It's my house now, Liza. We divvied everything evenly. I got the house. You got the cash."

"But the house is worth so much more now. It's not fair."

Anger had built up in me over the years and the outrage

flaming in my chest right now terrified me. I blinked hard to regain control. "Of course my house has gone up in value. If you'd bought a home instead of squandering your money . . ." I stopped myself from saying anything further.

Our mother had done her best to split her estate fifty-fifty and it was true that we'd both walked away with equal shares. It was also true that my property had appreciated in value, the way real estate usually does. But the harder truth, the one that had stopped me mid-sentence, was knowing that my home's worth in the market was exponentially higher than it would have been without its recent renovation.

Hillary and Frances both watched me, neither saying a word. Part of me knew that I owed Liza nothing. She'd spent every penny our mother had left her, and I refused to be the enabler who prevented her from growing up and accepting responsibility for her choices.

Part of me grappled with the knowledge that, if not for Bennett's intervention, I could be facing serious financial issues now, too. I'd benefited from Bennett's assistance because he believed us to be blood relatives. Liza was my sister. Even though I never wanted her to know the nature of my relationship with Bennett, couldn't I afford to be a little charitable?

Hillary and Frances continued to stare and I wondered if they could read my mind. Or if I was reading theirs.

I thought briefly about the young woman who'd come to our door last night. If I'd rented the spare room to her, I would have been able to truthfully tell Liza that we were full up.

I didn't know what was fair—what the right answer was. Not yet, at least. Until I did, until I could make peace with myself on the matter, I decided to punt. "How long do you plan to stay?" I asked.

The sparkle in Liza's eyes was back. She knew she had me. She didn't know the reason for my change of heart, but it clearly didn't matter. "A week? Ish?"

Chapter II

WE DECIDED THAT LIZA WOULD MEET ME BACK at home that evening. Most of the locks had been changed or recalibrated during the renovation and—even if Liza had kept her set of house keys—she couldn't have gotten in.

Frances offered to escort my sister out of the mansion with such cloying consideration that she couldn't have been more obvious if she'd chased her out with a stick. With one brow arched dramatically—another move Liza couldn't possibly have missed—Frances smiled, showing teeth. "This way, dearie. I know a shortcut."

When they were gone, I turned to Hillary. "Whatever you do, don't trust her," I said.

Hillary crossed her arms and leaned one hip against my desk. "So I gathered. What happened between you?"

Emotion tumbled over me, sucking me under like a rip current after a killer wave. Liza's sudden appearance had reignited old pain, heaving buried resentment from tight, protected places in my heart. The effort it had taken to keep my temper in check was now exacting its toll. I sat.

"It's a long story," I said slowly. "One that probably started when we were little. I always wanted to love and trust my sister, but I don't. I suppose I've finally come to terms with the fact that I never will."

"That's sad," she said, without compassion. "Do you really think it's fair that you got your family's house and she didn't?"

I looked up at Bennett's stepdaughter and wondered if she was regarding me the same way Liza did. Bennett had made little secret of the fact that despite my many and vocal objections, he intended to name me heir to his estate—a status Hillary had been jockeying for, for years. My familial position, if DNA confirmed it, would usurp Hillary's. I wanted nothing but to keep Bennett in my life forever. I wished talk of heirs and estates and bequeathing property would just go away.

Too tired to do anything but answer honestly, I said, "I think my mother knew us both well enough to make the decisions she did. If Liza had gotten the house she would have sold it on the spot, probably for even less than her cash settlement. She would have frittered away her windfall, leaving her in exactly the same mess she is in now. The only difference is that the house would have been lost to the family. Our mom knew me. Knew I'd keep it."

Hillary straightened from her perch. "Good thing she left it to you then," she said. "Otherwise I may have never had the chance to renovate."

I felt a smile work its way to my lips. That was the Hillary I knew.

"One more thing," I said as she started to leave.

She turned back. "Yes?"

"Don't tell Liza about the DNA test, okay?"

Hillary wrinkled her nose. "What happens if you and Bennett *are* related?" she asked after a thoughtful moment. "Will you tell her then?"

"I don't want to. Liza will do everything in her power to weasel favors from Bennett. She's relentless."

"But if she is family, Bennett will know."

"At this point, there's no proof so we have to keep it quiet." Frustrated, I ran my fingers up my head, grabbing handfuls of hair. Squeezing, I fought the fear twisting my stomach. "I should never have agreed to the test." I clenched my eyes. "I should have told him no. Now how can I protect him?"

Hillary said nothing. I sat there, eyes shut, for an extended moment.

I opened them to see Hillary regarding me with a curious expression. "You really do love Bennett for himself and not for his money, don't you?"

I nodded.

She reached forward to pat me on my forearm. "You will have to tell him that your sister showed up. And when the results come in, you'll have to tell her the truth, too."

"Do you have any idea what she'll do with that information?"

Hillary looked as serene as I'd ever seen her. "He tamed me, Grace. You watched it happen. My stepfather is a shrewd man, not easily bulldozed."

"He's also desperate for family," I said, not wanting to point out how long it had taken him to effect her taming. "I don't want him to get hurt."

She made a so-so motion with her head, acknowledging the point. "I won't say a word to your sister about the DNA test, and I'll let you worry about how to keep her out of trouble. But as for Papa Bennett?" She knocked her knuckles against my desk. "Don't underestimate him. He hasn't gotten where he is by being a fool, you know."

"You're right," I said. "But until I figure out how to deal with the consequences, I'm going to do my very best to keep Liza and Bennett apart."

"It's interesting."

"What is?" I asked.

"You," she said. "You're always the one in charge. The one who's so sure of herself."

I nearly blurted, "Me?" but stopped myself from interrupting.

"It's interesting to see you vulnerable." She waved neat, manicured fingers in the air. "Don't get me wrong, it's not like I'm enjoying it. Well, maybe a teensy bit. I'm seeing a different side of you." She wrinkled her nose again. "Makes you a little more likeable. A little less perfect."

"Perfect?" I did laugh then. "Hardly."

"To Bennett you are. I can't begin to compete."

"It's not a competition."

Hillary brought her face closer to mine. "You're a class act," she whispered, "and Bennett recognizes that. I wasn't ever his favorite person in the world, but when you showed up, I no longer stood a chance."

I wanted to reassure her otherwise, but she sensed the interruption and stopped me.

"You may be a decade younger than I am, but you've become a role model." Straightening, she shimmied her hands down her hips to smooth her skirt, then fixed me with a pointed glare. "Tell anyone I said that and I will make your life miserable."

The honesty in Hillary's eyes as she'd spoken, however, made it clear she'd been sharing from the heart.

I was blown away by her candor. Enough to offer some of my own. "When I came back to Emberstowne, my life fell apart." I managed a weak smile. "It's been a long journey, but I'm better. Working at Marshfield helped, but it was Bennett and his belief in me that allowed me to recognize my own strength. I'm hardly perfect, but I am happy here. With him. With all of you."

Hillary got a faraway look in her eyes. "Bennett has been good to me, even though I haven't always been kind to him. Bringing me back here and cutting off my funds may have been one of the best things he's ever done for me." Making eye contact with me again, she added, "He takes care of family, doesn't he?"

Doing my best to ignore the knot in my stomach, I nodded.

Moments after Hillary left, I heard Frances return to her office. There was enough noise to alert me she wasn't alone.

"Guess who I found downstairs looking for you?" she asked. "You are Miss Popularity today, aren't you?" Flynn and Rodriguez followed Frances in.

"Detectives, so good to see you." Their unexpected appearance flooded me with pleasure, taking me by surprise. "How are you?" What did it say about me that, after a clash with my sister, homicide detectives were a welcome sight?

Confused by my warm greeting, Flynn didn't answer. He ran a hand along his shaved head. Rodriguez, however, broke into a giant smile. "Miz Wheaton," he responded in kind. "Gorgeous day, isn't it?"

I turned to face the windows, noting the overcast sky, graying snow, and general dreariness of Marshfield's expansive grounds. A dismal scene. To a man who'd recently faced his own mortality, however, every day on earth was a magnificent gift.

"Absolutely," I said.

Frances interrupted. "Sure, beautiful. All that snow, the cold, the slush, the lack of sunshine. Yeah, I see it." When she rolled her eyes, I got the impression that Flynn was tempted to high-five her.

"What can I do for you gentlemen?" I asked as we settled ourselves.

Frances waved a hand in the air. "Coffee all around, I assume," she said, and was out the door before any of us could respond. From the other room she shouted, "Don't discuss anything interesting. I'll be back in a second."

Flynn sat on the edge of his chair, hands clasped. "Sorry to disappoint your sidekick," he said, "but we do have news and we plan to get right into it."

"About the man who was killed in the neighbor's yard?"

"The same," he said.

"First though," Rodriguez said, interrupting his partner, "we couldn't find anything on that woman who visited your house. Ran her name. Nothing popped."

"No record, then?"

"Or it's an alias. Most likely she simply had bad information. If she shows up again, let me know."

"Will do."

Frances bustled back in carrying a silver tray laden with four cups of coffee and an assortment of cookies and treats. Her breath rasped with effort and the ceramic mugs jiggled against each other as she hurried to lay the tray on my desk before us.

"No way, Frances," I said. "No way you poured coffee and arranged snacks that quickly. It's not humanly possible."

Flynn had already brought a steaming mug to his lips, but grinned before he took a sip. "Who says she's human?"

Frances narrowed her eyes at him. "Next time maybe I'll find something special to add to yours." She turned to me with a self-satisfied expression. "When I found these two downstairs, I called to the kitchen to send this up." Again to Flynn, she said, "Of course I don't know why I bother when my efforts go unappreciated."

"I appreciate you, Frances," I said. When she turned back, clearly smug, I thought about the unwavering support she'd shown less than an hour earlier. "I really do."

She took up a perch on the nearby sofa, her favorite spot for listening in when the local detectives came to call. She wiggled backward into the cushions, lifted her chin, and blinked expectantly. "You can go ahead now."

Chapter 12

FLYNN TWISTED IN HIS CHAIR TO GLOWER AT Frances. "How kind of you to grant us permission to do our jobs."

Rodriguez leaned forward to tap two fingers on my desk, thereby reclaiming everyone's attention. "Our victim," he began, "the man who came to your door—"

"The FBI agent," I prompted.

Flynn shook his head. "Not."

"The dead man in my neighbor's yard wasn't the guy who came to my door?" I asked. "But I saw him. It was the same man. I'm sure of it."

"Yeah, well—"

Rodriguez stopped Flynn with a look. "Slow down, amigo. One step at a time." The older detective's eyes were dark and heavy-lidded. Although his mood had dampened a bit since they first walked in, he still maintained a cheerful demeanor. "I believe that the victim is the same man who came to your door. What we are here to tell you is that he was not part of the FBI."

Frances gasped.

"And his name wasn't Alvin Clark, either," Flynn interjected. "It's Emilio Ochoa."

"I . . ." Wracking my brain, I tried to conjure up a memory. "That name means nothing to me. What was he doing at my house? What did he want?"

"That, Miz Wheaton, is what we're here to find out." Rodriguez had already pulled out his notebook. "Let's go over your conversation with him one more time, okay?"

I repeated what I'd already told them, trying my best to remember any details that I may have forgotten to mention the first time. I came up empty.

"It was a really short conversation, mostly consisting of me trying to get him to leave so I wouldn't be late for the blood test." I held my hands up and shrugged. "Did you talk with my neighbors? Maybe they have more to add."

Rodriguez shook his head. "You seem to be the only person he visited."

"Why my house?" I asked. "Why me?"

"Isn't that the big question?" Flynn said. "Have you ever lived in Los Angeles?"

"No."

"But you've visited there?"

"Sure," I said. "A couple of times. What does that have to do with anything?"

Reading from his notes, Rodriguez said, "Emilio Ochoa, age forty-two, multiple arrests for fraud, embezzlement, and international trafficking." He gave me a sympathetic glance before continuing, "You had no reason to doubt him. Seems like he's an old hand at these games. Served a couple of stints in his late twenties but then disappeared."

"Until now," Flynn said.

"Meaning he went straight for a while?" Frances asked from the sidelines.

"Meaning he probably got smarter and flew under the radar," Flynn said with a little snap in his voice. "No sign of him in LA, nor anywhere in the state. His last parole officer recorded that Ochoa planned to relocate to Idaho to be closer to family."

"What we need to find out," Rodriguez said, "is what brought him out in the open and why."

Their mention of Los Angeles set me on edge. "My sister was living in San Francisco for a while," I said, repeating what Aunt Belinda had told me. "She showed up here, today, at Marshfield. Do you think that may be connected?"

In my peripheral vision I noticed Frances sit up straighter, but Rodriguez had already begun to shake his head. "I don't understand. What would your sister have to do with our victim?"

"I don't know," I said. "That's what I'm asking you."

Flynn's mouth had curled up at one corner. "San Francisco is not exactly next door to Los Angeles. It's a big state."

"I know that, but I also know that my sister gets into trouble."

"Runs in the family then," Flynn said.

I ignored him, directing my words to Rodriguez. "I know it sounds wacky, but she showed up here today, out of the blue. I haven't talked with her in years but she turned up two days after a stranger—another person from California— was killed in a nearby backyard."

"It's a little thin," Rodriguez said. "But I'm not willing to dismiss your hunches, either. We know better than that, don't we, amigo?" He elbowed Flynn. "Is your sister staying with you?"

I gave a terse nod. Frances snorted.

"Ask her about this guy," he said. "Give her both names. See if she recognizes either one. If she does, let us know. We'll come talk with her."

"You seem awfully eager to throw your sister under the bus," Flynn said.

Not willing to go there, I continued to address Rodriguez. "What else can you tell me about the victim?"

"He never married. Parents still alive, in Idaho. They swear he turned his life around and went straight. But they lost touch with him again about ten years ago."

"This news has to be devastating for them," I said.

Flynn piped up, "They also said that Ochoa was a fortune chaser. Took shortcuts. Thought that easy street was right around the corner, and wealth waited for him with the next big deal."

This was sounding more like Liza every minute. "I'll check with my sister," I said.

When they left, Frances sat across from me. "You don't really believe this murder is connected to your sister, do you?"

"I'm not ruling it out."

Frances's fleshy face froze in horror. "You don't think *she* shot the guy? In cold blood?"

"No, no. She's not a nice person, but she's not a murderer," I said. "Liza will do almost anything to further her own interests, but she's never physically harmed me, or anyone I can think of."

Frances worked her mouth to one side, as though literally chewing on that information. "The Marshfield Hotel is booked up, isn't it?" she asked. "You're stuck with her at your house."

"I suppose I could make a few phone calls around town to see if there are any open rooms this week," I said. "The FAAC convention has eaten up all the good places."

Frances adopted a singsong voice. "And you're too much of a soft touch to force your sister to stay in one of the seedy hotels."

"It's not that, not this time at least," I said. "Did you ever hear the famous saying? I think it comes from Sun Tzu, in *The Art of War*. He says, 'Keep your friends close and your enemies closer.'"

Frances smirked. "Words I live by every day of my life."

I didn't quite know how to take that.

Chapter 13

BEFORE LEAVING WORK, I CALLED SCOTT AND Bruce to alert them to the Liza situation. They had both met her, briefly, before my mom died, and were as happy to hear of her return as I'd been. "Hang in there, Grace," Bruce said before we hung up, adding, "Thanks for the forewarning."

Liza wasn't at the house when I arrived. I wasn't surprised; she'd never been particularly prompt, especially when she had it in her power to make another person wait. The difference was this time it didn't bother me. If she'd changed her mind and taken off again for parts unknown—whether she bothered to notify me or not—I could live with it.

I parked on the driveway and let myself in the back door, cheered by the sound of Bootsie scampering down the stairs. Her paws slid on the floor as she spun around the corner to greet me. "How are you, baby?" I deactivated my alarm system then scooped her up and nuzzled her neck. Though she'd grown a great deal since she'd first arrived, she still held tight to kitten behaviors and now batted soft paws against my face, wanting to play.

When she bounded to the ground, I washed my hands. Though I'd dunked them under running water less than thirty seconds after I'd freed the little furball, it still hadn't been quick enough. My eyes began to water and I sneezed four times in a row. "Totally worth it," I said aloud.

On my drive home I'd had time to think about Liza's stay here, time to come up with a few ground rules. I jotted them down on a notepad and dug out an extra key to the front door. If she needed to come and go, as I suspected she would, she'd require the means to get in. One key. Just one. That way as soon as she was gone for good I could call my buddy Larry the Locksmith to re-key one set of doors.

Moments later, as I was pulling out ingredients for rata-touille, Liza showed up. Keeping vigilant and watching for Bootsie, I opened the door.

"I'm back," Liza said, extending her hands up, on either side of her head. "Party time."

"I thought you might change your mind."

"Not a chance, sister."

"Come in." I closed the door behind her.

She stomped her feet on the small braided rug we kept just inside the house, shaking the snow off her cotton flats. "Cold out there."

She wore the orange trench and carried the filled-to-bursting saddle purse. "Your coat is too flimsy for this weather. Your shoes, too. Where's your luggage?" I asked.

"This is it." She patted the bag's curled leather straps. "I left in a hurry."

One second later, her eyes went wide as she focused on the floor behind me. "What is that?"

I turned. "I took in another roommate," I said, scooping her up. "This is Bootsie."

Liza recoiled. "You have a *cat*?" She reacted as though she'd spotted raw sewage running through my kitchen. "Mom hated cats."

"Mom did not hate cats. She was allergic." I sniffled. "Seems I inherited that."

Putting her hands out as though to say, "Keep it away from me," she continued to stare at Bootsie as though she'd never encountered a feline before. "Does it have the run of the house?"

"I'll keep her out of your room," I said, "but remember, you're the guest here. She's not."

"I'm probably allergic, too," she said.

"Probably. I suggest keeping your distance."

"Don't worry. I will."

Bootsie, for her part, seemed content to study our visitor from the safety of my arms. She was usually eager to flirt with a new person. Not this time.

"One more thing—when you come in and out of the house, you need to make sure Bootsie doesn't get out. She's an indoor cat and wouldn't stand a chance against the feral ones, not to mention the coyotes and other hungry critters we have out here."

"Fine," she said as she pulled her coat off. "Any other surprises I ought to know about?"

I pulled up the list I'd compiled. "Basic stuff. Housekeeping. I reserve the right to add new rules as I see fit."

"What's happened to you, Grace?" she asked. "I haven't been back here in years and you don't seem to be the least bit concerned about what I've been through."

I bit my tongue before rising to the bait, before jumping down her throat over her "all about me," question.

Instead, I turned away, letting Bootsie go. As she ran into the dining room, I washed my hands again. "I'm about to make dinner. It'll take a while."

She dropped her coat and bag on one chair and lowered herself into another. "I knew you were finally home because your car was on the driveway. How come you don't use the garage? Is it still chock-full of garbage?"

"Mom's papers and a lot of her belongings are still out there, yes," I said. "I'd hardly call it garbage."

"You knew what I meant."

I began slicing zucchini and peeling eggplant, watching Liza out of the corner of my eye. She kept her head bent, quietly reading my list of rules. Every so often, over the sound of my knife hitting the cutting board, I heard her grunt. With amusement or disapproval, I didn't know.

Eventually, she raised her head. "Seems fair," she said.

I'd expected pushback on a few of the items. "Good. Now that we have that settled, I need a few answers."

"What if you don't like what you hear?"

I turned to face her, unable to prevent myself from sighing. "I don't care, Liza. I don't care what you did, what you didn't do. I don't care who you are, or where you plan to go next. All I do care about is the truth. On a couple of very simple matters."

"What do you want to know?"

My big chef's knife in my hand, I gestured. "First, and most important, who is Alvin Clark?"

That was clearly not the first question she'd been expecting. "Who?" The look on her face told me that she wasn't faking bewilderment. That much I knew I'd be able to tell. Over the years I'd grown adept at recognizing when she was lying. The name didn't register with her.

"All right," I said, still watching her. "What about Emilio Ochoa?"

She shook her head slowly. Again, I could detect no prevarication. "Where are you coming up with these names? Who are these people?"

"Is there any reason that a man from Los Angeles might be looking for you?"

She blinked. Surprised again? Yes, but this time there was something more behind her eyes. Fear? "No, I can't imagine . . . Why are you asking? What's going on?"

I fixed my gaze on her. "Let's try this again. Can you think of any reason why someone would track you here? Are you in trouble again?"

"So high and mighty, aren't you?" She twisted her mouth to one side.

Remaining silent, I waited.

Liza stared up at me. "I left Eric."

"So you said."

"Maybe he sent someone here to find me." She shrugged. "That's the best guess I can come up with."

"Trouble in paradise?" It wasn't kind, but I needed to cut through Liza's stalling to find out what had really brought her back to my doorstep.

"I got tired of him." She began making fingertip circles on the kitchen table.

That was an out-and-out lie. "Tired of him?" I repeated. "How so?"

"He's boring; you know that." She made eye contact again with that truthful statement. Eric *had* been boring. I'd just been too busy with dealing with my sick and then dying mother to notice.

"Let's leave the 'why' alone for now," I said. "Why would he send a scout here to look for you? Why not simply call?"

"These men . . . they came here? Looking for me? What did you tell them?"

"One man. Two names," I said. "And he never mentioned you. He didn't have the chance."

"An alias?" Liza seemed genuinely confused. "Why would you think this has anything to do with me?"

I was about to answer when the house phone rang. Wiping my hands, I reached for it. "It's Aunt Belinda."

Liza jerked in her chair. "Don't let her know I'm here."

My hand hovered over the receiver. "Why not? She's forever calling me, worried about you. Asking for news."

"Just . . . don't. Please? Not yet."

The fleeting fear I'd glimpsed in Liza's eyes a moment ago had returned with intensity, whitening her lips as she

sat ramrod straight. She gripped the handles of the saddlebag purse on her lap, her knuckles pale as her face.

"Hello, Aunt Belinda," I said when I picked up the phone.
"So nice to talk with you again."

She skipped right over niceties. "Have you heard from
Liza?"

Aunt Belinda's voice was loud enough for my sister to
hear halfway across the room. Liza shook her head, begging
me with her eyes.

"Are you okay?" I asked my aunt. "You sound upset."

"I've been trying her cell phone, over and over again. Usually when I call her it goes to her answering machine." *Voice-
mail*, I mouthed silently. "There's nothing at all anymore. I
get that loud noise and then a message that the number isn't
in service."

"Glitches happen," I said. "I'm sure there's an explanation."

"No, something is really wrong this time. Eric called
here not five minutes ago, asking if I'd heard anything.
When I asked him why Liza wasn't with him, he said that
they'd had an argument a couple of days ago. She stormed
off. Hasn't been seen since."

Holding the receiver slightly away from my ear to allow
Liza to listen in, I raised my eyebrows, asking the silent
question, "What haven't you told me?"

"I'm sure she's fine," I said into the phone. "Probably just
working off some steam. You know how hotheaded Liza
can be." I delivered that last line with a smile. She stuck her
tongue out at me.

"I don't know," Aunt Belinda said. "He sounded really
worried."

"Let's not overreact," I said, working to inject calm into
my tone. "Did Eric give you any other information?"

"No."

"Maybe Liza is coming to see you," I said. "Maybe she's
on her way right now."

"You think so?" Aunt Belinda asked. The hope in her voice was unmistakable. "I don't have much to share, but if she came, I could offer her a place to stay at least."

Watching my sister, who seemed to be growing more agitated by the moment, I said, "I'm sure she'd be happy to know that."

But Aunt Belinda wasn't finished trying to convince me of the magnitude of this situation. "He was desperate, I tell you. I've never heard anyone so tormented in my life. You can't fake that kind of panic. You know what I mean?"

"I do," I said. I was witnessing exactly that: the kind of panic that can't be faked. Liza had curled in on herself, fists covering her eyes, looking smaller than she had seconds earlier. She breathed hard enough for me to hear. In that instant I realized that my sister was in genuine anguish. And with that awareness, a small part of my resentment dissolved.

"Maybe there's more to the story than we realize," I said into the phone.

Liza's head jerked up. She stared up at me with grateful eyes.

"Maybe," Aunt Belinda said, "but there's no good reason for her to be out on her own. She ought to know she can reach out to family if she's in trouble."

Liza continued to watch me, waiting.

"Let's hope she isn't in trouble," I said, "and this is simply a lovers' spat."

"I don't know . . ." I could tell Aunt Belinda wanted to turn this conversation into an endless loop of conjecture and speculation.

"I really ought to go," I said before she could get rolling. "I'm in the middle of making dinner."

"You'll let me know if you hear from Liza?" she asked.

I hesitated. "I've told you before, Aunt Belinda, the likelihood of Liza contacting me is slim. Less than slim." I shrugged at Liza. She offered a weak smile.

"I'm just so worried about that poor girl. You could be a

better sister to her, you know," Aunt Belinda said. "You could try to connect with her yourself. You don't have to wait for her to come begging at your door before you lend her a hand."

"And with that, it's time for me to hang up," I said before my temper flared again. "Have a good night. Talk soon."

The second the receiver hit home, my sister erupted with thanks. "I didn't know if you'd cover for me, Grace. I can't thank you enough."

She would have gone on longer, but I didn't want this gush of gratitude.

"Here's what's important," I said. "The man who came here—Alvin Clark/Emilio Ochoa, whatever his name is— told me he was an FBI agent."

Liza's jaw dropped. "And you thought this had something to do with me?" Moments ago she'd seemed buried under the weight of her secrets. Not so anymore. Indignant Liza had resurfaced. "The FBI? How could you even think such a thing? I may have had my share of problems but never anything that—"

"I said he *told* me he was an FBI agent." I raised my voice to be heard over hers. "Remember the alias?"

She stopped talking, but maintained a piqued expression.

"He lied. Not a Fed. Okay?" Before she could say another word, I added, "And he's dead, by the way. Murdered." I pointed. "Back there, in one of the neighbors' yards."

Liza was rarely rendered speechless. If it hadn't been a murder that rendered her mute, I may have enjoyed the moment.

"The man was killed Saturday, found on Sunday. Detectives came today to tell me that he wasn't a federal agent after all. That he was originally from Los Angeles, with a police record."

Finding her voice, Liza asked, "And because he was from California, and has a record, you associate him with me?"

"He showed up here," I said, repeating information, hoping that this time it would sink in, "at this house. He wanted to know who lived here. It was only because I was on my way out that I didn't answer him, or find out what he was looking for." I pointed right and left. "He didn't visit any of my neighbors. Didn't talk to anyone else in town. He came here." I pointed at her. "And two days later, you show up."

Liza may not be the most reliable person on the planet, but she wasn't stupid. I could see comprehension dawn. "Coincidence," she said, but I could tell she was rattled.

"You said you thought Eric may have hired a guy to track you down," I reminded her.

She looked away again. "God, I hope not."

Chapter 14

ONCE LIZA WAS SETTLED IN THE SPARE ROOM, I returned to the main level to clean up after dinner. As I loaded our dishwasher and rinsed the baking pan in hot, sudsy water, I reflected on my sister's behavior this evening. Like a pinball, she'd careened from one emotional bumper to the next: terrified, irate, grateful. I could barely keep up.

Crusted ratatouille had baked itself into one corner of the pan and wasn't giving up without a fight. I pulled my watermelon-slice scrubby from its dish and set to work on the corner, exorcising my frustration as I dug at the resistant chunk.

Bootsie appeared at my side, staring up at me with an expression that seemed to ask "Why?"

"I don't have an answer for you," I said.

"Answer to what?" Liza asked.

I jumped a little bit, twisting to face her.

"Sorry, didn't mean to frighten you."

"I'm not used to anyone else being here," I said with a glance at the wall clock. "At least not at this time of day."

"What time do your buddies come back?" she asked, crossing to stand next to me at the sink. She leaned back against the countertop, too close.

With my hands still submerged, I winged my elbows. "A little room, please."

She scuttled sideways, not bothering to offer help.

"They come home after the wine shop closes. Depends on business that day. Most of the time they're home by ten."

She made a face at the clock. "Do they know I'm here?"

"They do." With a victorious flourish, I wedged the final hunk of ratatouille out of the dish. Rinsing the pan thoroughly, I added it to the bottom dishwasher rack.

"And?" Liza asked after protracted silence.

I turned to face her. "And what?"

"What did they say about me?"

"Why do you want to know?" I asked as I wiped up the countertop and grabbed a drying towel for the items I'd hand-washed. Liza scooted farther down the counter to allow me access. "They're my friends and they're supporting me. That's really all that matters."

She huffed, then sat at the table. "Ever since I got here, I've had to answer all the questions you've thrown at me."

"With varying degrees of honesty, I'd imagine."

No response to the jab. "Now you. You have to answer questions for me."

"Have to? Really, Liza?" I turned to face her.

"That is," she amended quickly, "I'd like to ask you some questions. Get to know you again—maybe better."

I wondered what her game was, and at the same time felt sad and sorry to have that be my first response. Yet, such was the nature of our relationship. I needed to remain vigilant. Otherwise I risked her hurting me, and those I loved, again.

"I'll share the highlight reel." I held a finger up. "As you know, I work at Marshfield." Raising another, I added, "I love my job there." Continuing to tick off points, I counted on my hand. "Bruce, Scott, Bootsie, and I have settled into a very comfortable life here together, and I am not currently involved in a romantic relationship. That about sums it up."

"Pretty cut-and-dried," she said.

I shrugged. "It's all you need to know."

"You used to get excited about history and old antiques. Do you get to work with stuff like that now?"

"All the time."

"I'll bet you're pretty good at it. You always were a super achiever."

"As I said, I love my job."

She offered a timid smile, manufactured just for me. "What's it like, working around all that wealth? Is it amazing? Do you know how much everything in the house is worth?"

My sister, always hyper-attentive where money was concerned. "Sorry." I shook my head. "No more Marshfield talk."

"Fine, then. What do you do for fun?"

I thought about Adam and how he and I had almost forged a bond together last year. He'd been great company and a good friend. I'd had a lot of fun when I was with him. He was a lovely, kind man. But I'd never felt for him the way he felt for me. He deserved a woman who did.

"Fun," I repeated, feeling a wry smile crawl up the corners of my mouth. Who had time with all the excitement that went on around here? That's how I'd met Adam, in fact. Smack in the middle of a murder. Two, to be precise. And these were two of, how many now? Sadly, I was losing count.

"Hard to say, really," I began. "I've been tied up." *Umm . . . literally.* "More than a few tough moments."

She folded her arms. "If you expect me to apologize for taking Eric away, I won't," she said, putting on a pout. "I did you a favor. He turned out to be a loser. Leech with a capital *L.* As soon as all Mom's money was gone, he turned on me." She looked away. "You think *you* had it tough."

It took me a beat to understand what she was talking about and why she'd suddenly brought Eric's name into the conversation. When I did, I could barely keep my voice down. "You think my 'tough moments' refer to you skipping out with Eric?" My laugh came out hoarse and crazed. Her audacity astounded me.

When I managed to settle myself again, I regarded her with a sadness I hadn't felt for her before. "It's always about you, isn't it, Liza?"

She tilted her head. "You're different now."

"People change."

"Exactly." She pulled a leg up onto the chair so that she could wrap her arms around it and rest her chin on her knee. "Which is why I want to know more about you. I want you back in my life. I'm different, too. Really."

I didn't believe that for a minute, but was too tired of fighting to challenge her.

Chapter 15

I DECIDED TO STOP BY AMETHYST CELLARS ON the way home the following day. There was so much I wanted to talk with Scott and Bruce about—things I dared not voice with Liza in the house. Parking around the corner from their shop, I picked my way along the icy sidewalk to make my way in.

January in Emberstowne was traditionally quiet, providing downtime for shop owners. The smattering of visitor traffic in winter allowed proprietors to catch up on indoor maintenance and concentrate on plans for the coming tourist season.

This January, however, with the Fine Art and Antiquity Collectors' convention in town, local businesses were enjoying a brisk bump in sales.

Thus, when I stepped out of the biting wind into the cozy warmth of Amethyst Cellars, I wasn't surprised to find it buzzing with happy patrons, sipping, sniffing, and chattering about wine.

The high-ceilinged shop, furnished with cherrywood

cabinetry and granite countertops, had become a destination spot in Emberstowne. Bruce and Scott had taken this bare storefront and turned it into a gathering space, with two bar areas set up for group tastings, a refrigerated glass case to showcase gourmet chocolates and other delectable treats, and kiosks strategically placed around the room in a way that encouraged people to mingle, while enhancing traffic flow.

Gift baskets took up a fair share of one outside wall. Their cellophane wrappings shimmered under soft spotlights. Two couples perused the display while sipping from amethyst-stemmed glasses. This shop was the picture of gentle cheer and I adored visiting. Every time I did, I marveled at how wonderfully my roommates had brought their vision to life.

One of the female employees, talking to four rapt listeners, described the flavor notes to look for in this month's featured cabernet. Two other employees led small groups, taking them through the order of wines they might choose and explaining the tasting process.

Bruce was in the middle of ringing up what appeared to be a robust sale for an elderly Asian couple. Next to him, Scott chatted them up, and when he noticed me at the door, waved me over.

"Grace, we were just talking about you," he said.

The couple turned to face me, their eyes bright with pleasure. I guessed them to be in their early sixties. The man was close to my five-foot-eight height, the woman considerably shorter. Both had smile-line wrinkles around their eyes and ebony-black hair. His was scrub-brush short, but full. Hers was a luxurious bob, with silvery strands that sparkled when they caught the light.

"About me?" I asked.

The gentleman bowed his head slightly. "We are enraptured by Marshfield Manor and intrigued by Mr. Bennett Marshfield and his wondrous collection."

"I was telling them that you run the estate," Scott said.

"Mr. and Mrs. Tuen were delighted to hear of our connection to you."

The man placed a hand on his chest. "I am Jim Tuen." Using that same hand to gesture, he added, "And this is my beautiful wife of thirty-six years, Daisy."

Daisy nodded, smiling. "We are very pleased to meet you."

"I'm very happy to meet you both," I said. "I hope Bruce and Scott haven't been telling too many stories out of school."

Scott gave me a mischievous grin. "Only the good parts."

"We arrived in Emberstowne this morning," Daisy said. "Once we were settled in our hotel it was too late to begin our tour of the mansion, but my husband and I plan to spend time there over the next several days, at least until the convention begins."

"I take it you mean the Fine Art and Antiquity Collectors' convention?"

She gave an eager nod. "It is the highlight of our year."

While she and I talked, Jim finished his transaction with Bruce, who handed over a weighty shopping bag. Addressing me once again, Jim said, "Part of the joy in traveling to the show is experiencing new cities. We are finding your Emberstowne to be highly charming."

"It is a beautiful town," I said. "Even more enjoyable when the weather cooperates. You should consider returning in the fall."

"We may have to include such a visit in our plans," Jim said. "Bennett Marshfield speaks often about how proud he is of his home."

"You know Bennett then?" I asked.

Daisy shook her head. "We have heard him speak at the convention many times, but have never had the opportunity to meet with him face-to-face."

Jim added, "We are hoping to do so this year. With the convention in his hometown, I suspect Mr. Marshfield will spend a great deal of time mingling with other collectors."

Although I knew Bennett had no plans to attend the FAAC this year, I didn't want to dash their hopes with too brusque a reply. "As I'm certain he'd be honored to meet you."

Scott joined in as we continued with small talk, while Bruce rang up the next customer. From what I gathered, the Tuens were extraordinarily wealthy—not in the same league as Bennett, but well-off enough to have amassed what sounded like an impressive collection of antiques. They admitted to being partial to ancient Chinese art, but found they had a soft spot for abstract expressionists like Helen Frankenthaler and Willem de Kooning.

After we'd talked for a while, Jim touched his wife's arm. "We must leave these good people to their business," he said. "We are taking too much of their time."

"I hope you'll remember to ask for me when you visit Marshfield," I said.

"You are very kind," Daisy said. "But we would not wish to impose."

"They seem very nice," I said when they left.

"They are. Gina helped them with their tasting and they not only tipped her very well, they bought four bottles and arranged to have a case shipped home."

"That's wonderful."

"Excuse me." A woman who had been paying close attention to our conversation stepped forward the moment Jim and Daisy Tuen exited the shop. Mid-forties, taller than me by a couple of inches, wearing thick cinnamon lipstick that matched her wavy, shoulder-length hair, she regarded me with interest. "I couldn't help but overhear; you work with Bennett Marshfield?"

The question had been asked with doe-eyed innocence, but because I'd spotted her attentiveness earlier, my guard immediately shot up.

"I do."

Cat-green eyes shifted from entreating to calculating in

the space of a blink. "Oh, how wonderful," she exclaimed, her tone rapturous. "I am absolutely delighted to make your acquaintance."

She held a giant coat draped over one arm. I hoped the fur was faux. Wearing shiny black boots that came up to her knees and an emerald-green clingy dress that skimmed her legs mid-thigh, she was both thin enough and tall enough to be a model. She certainly carried herself with a model's bearing and confidence. Her skin was the color of hand cream, with such pale brows and lashes that I knew her hair color was natural. Or at least had been, once upon a time. She wore almost no makeup except for the lipstick. The bright stain in her otherwise colorless face made her mouth look bigger, wider, and more hostile than it probably should have.

Still beaming, she pumped my hand. "My name is Phyllis Forgue. I've known Bennett for years. Years." Bringing her face closer to mine, she asked, "And who might you be?"

"My name is Grace Wheaton," I said, extricating my hand from her exuberant grasp. "Very nice to meet you."

"I understand—again from a tiny bit of eavesdropping I hope you can forgive—that you run Bennett's estate? How extraordinary. How long have you worked with that devious man?"

Devious? "I'm sorry," I said, "how is it you know Bennett?"

With a look that communicated pity rather than disappointment, she said, "Oh dear, it seems Bennett hasn't mentioned me to you." A fat designer purse hung at her elbow alongside the furry coat, but she lifted that hand to cover her lips, affecting a mischievous grin. "How embarrassing to have to explain."

Scott, who had been called across the room, veered behind Phyllis Forgue to face me, waggling his brows and rolling his eyes. Next to me, Bruce gave a throaty chuckle.

"Is there anything I can get for you?" he asked Phyllis in an effort to derail what was shaping up to be a disagreeable conversation.

"Not now." In answering Bruce, she raised her hand high, making a chattering motion with her fingers. "The girl over there has been helping me. I'll get back to her shortly."

Thus dismissed, Bruce shrugged, mouthing "Sorry" as he left.

"Bennett will attend the FAAC opening ceremonies, I presume," Phyllis said, far more loudly than was necessary. "I do so enjoy spending time with Bennett. He's a natural. So intelligent. With an eye for quality, if you know what I mean?"

"You were about to tell me how you know him," I reminded her.

Running her long, eggplant-painted fingernails along the side of her neck, she huffed. "Well, of course we know one another from our years attending FAAC." She shook her head as though I was a clod. "He and I always vie for the same objets d'art," she said, adopting a French accent. "It's as though we are one brain. One person. Uncanny how it happens. We always find ourselves competing to own one particular piece. Every single time."

"Uncanny," I repeated.

"Yes!" She poked one of those eggplant nails against my shoulder and pushed. It hurt. More than a little. "You have that exactly right."

I desperately wanted to tell this woman that Bennett had no intention of attending the FAAC this year if only for the pleasure of watching her react. *Be nice*, I told myself.

I thought about the item Bennett had hoped to procure. Could this Phyllis Forgue be after it, too?

"And what is it this time?" I asked.

She blinked, confused.

"What item are you and Bennett vying for this time?"

"Oh." The question took her by surprise, though I couldn't imagine how. Recovering, she placed an index finger across her lips. "I'm not saying. It's a secret."

"Not even a hint?" I asked. "Come on." I pretended to look around the room for spies. "I won't tell anyone."

Blinking those giant green eyes, she shook her head, very slowly. "*You* tell *me* what Bennett is looking for this time; I'll let you know if you're right." She lifted her chin, grinning. "I'll bet you have a clue."

If I did, I wouldn't be trying to pry it out of you. I smiled, keeping it light. "I'm afraid we are at an impasse," I said, winking. "Confidential, you understand."

Undaunted, she shuffled closer. "I would dearly love to connect with my old friend before he's swept into the maelstrom of fake camaraderie that lies at the heart of FAAC." She tossed her long red waves back, then ran her fingers up along her hairline. "Can you arrange that for me? I'd be most grateful. He and I have much to discuss. I'm open tomorrow. Say around two?"

"I can't answer that without clearing it with him first. Do you have a business card?"

The cinnamon lips twisted inward as she attempted to hide her disappointment. "Of course," she said. Digging one out of her purse, she proffered it, all smiles again. "An hour. Not even," she said, tapping her phone number. "Call me."

"Nice to meet you," I said again, promising nothing.

She hefted her coat and purse, pushed up another smile, then returned to the tasting bar, where she'd already identified six bottles for purchase. From the looks of things, she intended to add more.

Scott made his way back over to me, a lock of his blond hair falling forward as he leaned in to whisper, "I'd love for Emberstowne to host the FAAC every January."

"I'll bet you would. But hey, the reason I stopped by was to ask if you and Bruce have had a chance to talk with Liza?"

"Not at all. She was closed in her room when we got home last night and apparently still asleep this morning when we left. What's going on? Why is she back?"

"I wish I knew," I said. "She says she left Eric."

"She did?"

"Our aunt Belinda called last night, frantic because Eric

called her, looking for Liza," I said, keeping the update as succinct as I could. "When Aunt Belinda asked if I'd heard from Liza, I didn't tell her Liza was sitting in front of me."

Scott affected an exaggerated gasp. "You lied?"

"I deflected," I said. "But the fact remains that I'm uncomfortable with my sister in the house, and having to dance around the truth isn't helping my state of mind."

Bruce accompanied another patron to the cash register and began ringing him up next to us.

"One more thing," I said to Scott. "I've talked with Tooney and asked him to help me keep an eye on Liza."

"Is that necessary?" Scott asked.

"I've had too many run-ins with Liza to expect anything but trouble when she shows up."

"More to the point, will she cooperate?"

I shrugged. "Who knows? It's the best idea I can come up with."

"There's not much more you can do," he agreed. "But if you need anything, just ask."

Bruce leaned sideways. "Or even hint broadly. We've got your back, Grace. You know that."

"I do. And I appreciate it."

Chapter 16

WHEN I GOT HOME, I HUNG UP MY COAT AND said hello to Bootsie, who seemed unusually eager to snuggle. Walking from the kitchen into the dining room, I called out, "Liza? You here?"

"Yeah," she replied from the front of the house.

From her raspy reply, I got the feeling my shout had woken her. Still holding Bootsie, I continued through the parlor and crossed the front foyer to find my sister in the living room. She was sprawled across the long sofa in front of the television, whose volume was so low I had to step in front of it to see what she was watching.

"Six o'clock news," I said. "Anything of interest happening in the world?"

She boosted herself into a sitting position and ran her fingers through her disheveled hair.

"Six o'clock?" she repeated. Stretching her arms as she clenched her eyes, she yawned then blinked and regarded the window quizzically. "At night or in the morning?"

She was wearing the same yoga pants and T-shirt I'd given her last night before bed. "Have you been sleeping all day?"

Rubbing her ear, she stared up at me. "That thing." She pointed at Bootsie. "That thing kept waking me up."

"I told you to close your bedroom door."

"I don't mean last night. I meant during the day, here." She patted the sofa cushions on either side with her palms. "That cat wouldn't leave me alone. It tried to sit on my chest. I've got hair all over me." To emphasize her point, Liza spread her fingers and wiped at the front of her shirt.

"I don't see any hair. Are you sneezing? Sniffling?"

That stopped her, mid-wipe. "Huh," she said. "No."

I shrugged. "One thing I forgot to do yesterday was show you how to work the burglar alarm."

She blinked again, as though willing herself awake. "You have an alarm system?"

"When you're more alert, I'll show you how it works." I made a mental note to remember to change the security code the moment she moved out. "If you ever leave the house, I'd like you to set it."

She grumbled something about how I was able to afford such a thing.

When I started back for the kitchen, she padded behind me in stockinged feet. "You don't have much to eat here."

I half-turned. "There's plenty. We have leftovers from last night. Not to mention vegetables in the bin and basics in the pantry." Bootsie had been nuzzling against my fingers, hinting for a head rub. I accommodated her and pointed with my chin. "Did you even look?"

"Of course I did." Her tone was defensive. "I was looking for, you know, easy things like frozen dinners I could heat up in the microwave. I had to eat cold cereal."

"Poor baby," I said. "Why didn't you have the leftover ratatouille? I'm sure the boys didn't finish it up."

She looked away. "Meh. I hope you have something better planned for tonight."

As much as I wanted to suggest that she was perfectly capable of making dinner for herself—if not for us all—I held my tongue. Once she began contributing to the household she moved from guest to roommate. I didn't want her to get that comfortable.

"I hope pork tenderloin meets with your approval," I said, "but before I get started, two more things."

By this time, we'd returned to the kitchen and I'd let Bootsie scamper away. She knew her dinner was coming soon and that I'd need both hands to get it for her.

"What's that?" Liza asked.

"Aunt Belinda mentioned your phone was out of order. What's up with that?"

My sister looked away. "Got behind on the bills. They canceled my service."

"Do you still have the phone?"

She shook her head. "I had to sell it for money to get here."

The situation was worse than I'd feared. At this rate, Liza might be staying with us for months rather than days.

"What's the second thing?" she asked.

"I have a friend I'd like you to meet. His name is Ronny Tooney."

"Boyfriend?" she asked with a spark of interest. "I thought you said you weren't involved with anyone."

"A friend," I repeated, scribbling Tooney's number on a piece of paper and handing it to her. "I'll arrange for you to meet in person in the next day or so. If you need help while I'm out, though, that's who to call."

She gave the paper a cursory glance, then studied me. "Seems weird. Why would I need anyone's help while you're gone?"

"Who knows, Liza? If there's one thing I've learned to expect from you, it's the unexpected. I intend to be prepared for anything."

* * *

THE NEXT MORNING I CALLED BENNETT FROM my office. After he answered and we covered a few basics, I said, "I ran into Phyllis Forgue last night at Amethyst Cellars."

He repeated the name. "Why does that name sound familiar? Do I know her?"

"She seems to know you. In fact, she seemed to want everyone within hearing distance to know what close friends you two are."

"Phyllis Forgue," he said again as though trying to conjure up an image from the feel of the words on his tongue. "Oh, wait. Is she a tall, striking woman, lots of red hair, convinced that every eye in the place is on her?"

"That's the one."

"She does command attention. She would be so much more attractive if she didn't flaunt how fascinating she finds herself."

I giggled even though I shouldn't. "Perfect summation."

"You didn't tell her that I won't be attending the FAAC this year?"

"Of course not. But I get the impression she'll be crushed when you don't show."

He made a noise of impatience. "Unfortunately, she's one of those expected to attend Tuesday night's reception here."

"And she didn't mention it?" I asked. "She strikes me as the type to wave an invitation in the air for everyone to admire."

"We've sent notice to key players in an effort to generate buzz, but have made it clear that the party is open to all FAAC attendees." He seemed eager to change the subject. "Phyllis Forgue is one of the many reasons why I've chosen to skip the event this year."

"She wants to meet with you privately. Today, in fact. I promised I'd call her to let her know. I assume you're busy?"

He didn't answer immediately. "Let me handle that one," he finally said. "What's her number?"

I gave it to him. "Are you sure? I'd be happy to take care of this for you."

Again he hesitated. "No need, Gracie. I'm perfectly capable. Thank you."

When we hung up, I stared at the phone for a long moment. It wasn't like Bennett to hedge. What was going on?

RODRIGUEZ AND FLYNN SHOWED UP LATE IN the afternoon. Their unanticipated appearance seemed to throw Frances for a loop. "They want to see you," she said without ceremony. "How many times do these two need to stop by?"

Flynn rolled his eyes as he loped across the room and sat down across from me.

Still at the door, Rodriguez addressed my assistant. "My apologies," he said to her, though I caught the hint of amusement in his eyes. "This is a matter of some urgency."

"It better be," Frances said.

"As much as we enjoy the delicious coffee and cookies you always provide for us, I'm afraid we don't have time to spare today."

That perked her up. Following Rodriguez in, she took her usual spot on the couch.

"It's about the victim," Flynn began. "We uncovered a little more information. We found out why he was in Emberstowne. He was looking for someone."

"My sister?" The words leapt from my mouth before I could think twice.

Rodriguez must have read the alarm on my face. He leaned forward and narrowed his eyes. "She worries you that much?"

"I'm jumpy, I admit. Let's start again. The fake Fed was looking for someone, got it." I pulled in a deep breath. "Do you know who?"

Flynn consulted his notebook. "We have the guy's name

but it doesn't mean anything to us. He's not a resident of Emberstowne. He lives in California, but started out in New York."

"California again," I said.

"Yeah," Flynn said. "We can't figure out what this guy's tie to Emberstowne is, and since the victim visited your house, we decided to check with you. Does the name Eric Soames mean anything?"

"Eric? He was looking for Eric?"

Frances knew precisely who Eric Soames was. Her posture rigid, her expression gloriously shocked, she stared at me, openmouthed.

"You know him?" An accusation rather than a question. Typical Flynn.

I pinched the bridge of my nose. "He's my sister's husband."

Rodriguez gave an extended grunt of surprise. "There's a twist I didn't see coming."

I wanted to remind him that I'd suggested Liza's appearance in Emberstowne might have been connected with the victim's visit to my house.

"Did you ask your sister about this man?" Rodriguez asked. "Give her both names we came up with?"

"I did," I said. "She didn't recognize either one."

"Eh," Rodriguez said without skepticism. "He might have other aliases we haven't uncovered."

"What did this fake Fed, the victim, want with Eric?" I asked.

"We don't know yet," Rodriguez answered. "That's part of what we're trying to find out. We had no idea why he came to Emberstowne, but the tie to your sister explains a lot."

Flynn had been studying me closely. "Have *you* seen him?"

"Eric?" I asked. "No. My sister thinks he may come after her, though. She left him last week."

Flynn started to ask another question but Rodriguez cut

him off. "Miz Wheaton, we don't understand what's going on here yet, and we're relying on you to help us put these pieces together."

I gave a brief nod.

"How well do you know Eric Soames?" Flynn asked.

Out of the corner of my eye, I noticed Frances press her hands down on the tops of her knees as though fighting to stop herself from leaping into the conversation. It was clearly taking every ounce of restraint for her to keep from spilling the juicy story.

"I . . ." Putting it into words myself, however, was difficult. I faltered. Flynn's left leg bounced an exasperated rhythm. Rodriguez waited patiently. My two-heartbeat hesitation bothered me more than sharing the truth.

"Eric and I were engaged at one point." There. Done. It was out. Lifting my hands in a motion that I hoped suggested c'est la vie, but probably conveyed helplessness, I said, "Though seeing as he took off with my sister while I was busy settling my mom's estate, I think I can honestly say that I didn't know him very well at all."

Frances had leaned sideways to watch the detectives react. Flynn's mouth dropped open. He closed it quickly.

"They're married now, from what I understand," I added.

Rodriguez rubbed a hand over his chin so roughly I was afraid the stubble would abrade his palm. "This Eric," he began oh-so-carefully, "would you say he's capable of murder?"

A knee-jerk response bubbled up. I was about to say, "No, of course not," but the truth was I had no idea. My helpless hands came up again. "I don't think so."

"At least now we know why you're so willing to throw your sister under the bus," Flynn said.

I shook my head. "She did me a favor," I said, practically parroting Liza's words. "I dodged a bullet with that guy."

Flynn smirked. "Our victim didn't."

"If Eric turns up, I'll let you know immediately," I said.

"More important than that"—Rodriguez leaned forward—"you were right. Your sister is probably involved."

I resisted the urge to gloat that I'd told them so. "You believe Eric killed that FBI agent, don't you?"

"He's a person of interest, no doubt about it," Rodriguez said. "I prefer not to assign guilt until I have all the facts in front of me."

Flynn was giving me the evil eye. "Maybe your sister did it," he said. "You believe she's capable of murder, don't you?"

I'd answered an almost identical question from Frances. "I do not," I said.

"Couple days ago you thought this dead guy might be connected to your sister," Flynn said, inching forward. "Now that he is, you're telling me she's innocent."

"My sister is far from innocent," I said. "And while I can't account for her whereabouts the day the fake FBI guy was killed, I can tell you that murder is not in her nature."

Rodriguez raised his droopy lids, revealing a steely gaze. "What about self-defense?"

I thought about my own actions when I'd faced those who would do me harm. "I suppose it's possible."

"If Eric Soames didn't kill Emilio Ochoa, then whoever did is probably looking for him." Rodriguez's dark gaze met mine. "The killer is in Emberstowne. As is your sister. Whoever is looking for Soames may be looking for her, too. It's a coincidence we can't ignore." He wagged a finger at his partner. "Let's go talk with the other Miz Wheaton." To me, he asked, "Do you know where she is right now?"

"My house," I said. "I don't believe she had any plans to leave during the day. I'll give her a call and let her you're coming."

"She might be able to help our investigation," Rodriguez said. "She might also be in grave danger. Tell her not to leave the house. We'll head right over."

"You got it," I said, then sat up when an idea hit me. "I'll have Tooney sit with her until you get there."

The minute they were gone I called Liza, getting the impression I'd woken her again. When I told her what was up, however, her lethargic cadence fell away.

"You're kidding," she said. "The murdered guy was looking for Eric? Are you sure? Why did he come to our house?"

My house, I mouthed silently. "Detectives Rodriguez and Flynn are on their way over to talk with you." I described the two men so she'd feel safe answering the door. "They want to ask you some questions. As do I."

"I don't like the sound of that," she said.

"Whatever you're hiding, Liza, it needs to come out. Do you understand? You and I need to talk. Soon. But right now, when the detectives show up, please tell them the truth. Tell them everything you know. Don't play games with them, okay? They're here to help."

"You have such a low opinion of me."

"I'm going to ask a friend to come by and hang with you until they get there," I said. "You know that phone number I gave you? Ronny Tooney? As soon as you and I get off the phone, I'm going to call him." I took a moment to describe the amiable private investigator.

"Seriously?"

"Humor me," I said. "The detectives are about twenty minutes away. Tooney can be there in less than five."

"Oh joy," she said. "A babysitter."

"We could have avoided this if you'd been upfront with me from the start. You and I need to have that serious discussion—I want to know what's really going on."

"You got it, Sis."

The moment I clicked the phone to hang up, it rang again.

I picked up immediately. "Tooney," I said. "I was about to call you."

"Hey, I wanted to tell you, when you told me about your sister, I did a quick background check on her. Eric Soames, too. Thought it might help. You told me they were married, right?"

"That's what Liza told me," I said. "Couple of years ago."

"Couldn't find proof of that, but no matter. The important thing is that there are no convictions for Liza Wheaton or Liza Soames. Nothing anywhere under that name, which is why I asked if they were legally married. People call themselves married when they're not sometimes."

"That's true." I wanted to hurry him along, but didn't want to skip any pertinent info. "Anything else stand out?"

"Your sister has poor credit history. Nah . . . worse than poor. Her credit is about as bad as it gets. Sorry, Grace."

"That's okay, I need to know these things."

"Soames's credit history is almost as bad," he went on, "but worse, he's got a rap sheet. Couple of arrests and one conviction for fraud and theft."

"Oh boy," I said.

"He got a light sentence, reduced even further because he wasn't considered dangerous and because the prisons were overcrowded. Served about three months, then paroled for six. He's a free man now."

Sounded a lot like Emilio Ochoa's record to me. "Was all this in Los Angeles?" I asked.

Tooney grunted a negative. "Arrests in Nevada and Utah, conviction in Nevada."

"Thanks a lot," I said. "This gives me something to work with when I talk with Liza again. In the meantime, here's the reason I was about to call you."

I told him everything Rodriguez and Flynn had shared with me and let him know that the two detectives were on their way to my house. "Can you sit with Liza until they get there?" I asked. "And when they're done, would you mind taking her over to your house for a little while? If the killer is looking for her, it might be better if she wasn't alone."

"No problem," he said. "I'll head over there right now."

I was about to hang up when he said, "Uh . . . Grace?"

His whispered tone caught my attention. "What's up?"

"You do know that Hillary is here, right?" I could tell he was cupping his hand over the receiver.

"Do you think Liza will be in her way?"

He hedged. "Hillary is a force to be reckoned with when she's on the job," he said, still whispering, "but that's not my biggest concern. That guy she works with—Frederick— he's here right now, too. He shows up most days, you know."

I'd forgotten about Frederick. "Our circle of confidantes keeps widening," I said. "Remind Hillary and ask Frederick to keep the DNA testing to themselves, please. And let them know that Liza might be in danger and to keep her where- abouts to themselves, too."

He promised he would and hung up.

I placed both hands on the receiver and heaved a great sigh. Frances stood in the doorway, watching.

"It isn't easy to keep my sister contained," I said, "but this time I think I'm good."

Chapter 17

FRANCES DIDN'T HAVE A CHANCE TO REPLY.
The door to her office opened and a few seconds later Bennett strode into my office.

"I understand our local detectives were here," he said. "I take it there is news about the murder that took place near your home? What did they have to say?"

The fact that Bennett wanted to keep on top of this didn't faze me; his timing did.

"Wow," I said as we settled into our seats. Frances, no longer relegated to the sidelines, occupied the chair next to Bennett's. "That was fast. They left here no more than ten minutes ago."

He gave a lighthearted shrug. "Have they figured out who killed the man yet?"

Frances snorted. "Those two? When do they ever solve a murder without our help?"

Bennett's brows came together. "You aren't getting involved in this, are you, Gracie? You really should let the police handle it."

Frances's lips, poofy and pursed with agitation, coupled

with an "If you don't tell him, I will" look in her eyes, gave me no choice.

"I may already be involved," I said.

Bennett sat forward. "What do you mean?"

"The victim, the man who told me he was an FBI agent," I began, "was looking for my sister's husband." Although Bennett was fully aware of my difficulties with my estranged sister, I took the opportunity to provide recent updates.

The three vertical lines between Bennett's brows deepened. His eyes sparked with anger. "The dead man was looking for Eric?" he asked. "The dead man knew to come to your house? That Liza had lived there at one time?" As he spoke, his agitation grew. "What's this all about, Gracie?"

"Rodriguez and Flynn are on their way to talk with Liza right now," I said. "She may have information that can help. Before you know it, the police will have this wrapped up."

Frances snorted again.

Bennett jerked a thumb toward my assistant. "I'm inclined to agree with Frances," he said. "When have our homicide detectives ever brought the guilty to justice without your assistance?"

"Bennett," I said, doing my best to calm him, "I have Tooney looking out for her. We're going to keep a close watch on Liza for as long as she's here. Tooney will keep her safe."

"Who will keep *you* safe?" he asked.

"They're not after me. We don't even know that the killer is after Liza. All we know is that Eric is involved. I plan to help Rodriguez and Flynn as much as I can, and I plan to pressure my sister into helping them, too. Before you know it, the streets of Emberstowne will be safe again."

He didn't seem convinced.

Before he could press further, I changed the subject. "That fellow who came to see you the other day," I began, "Malcolm Krol. What was that all about?"

The question took Bennett by surprise. He sputtered a moment before asking, "What brought that up?"

"Curious," I said. "On Monday when we asked you about that mysterious item you were hoping to acquire, you mentioned that you might be hearing an update. That's the same day Malcolm Krol came to visit. I thought the two circumstances might be related."

Bennett forced a quick chuckle. "You do see conspiracies everywhere."

He hadn't answered my question. "Did you find out any more about that item? What is it, by the way? I know you were reluctant to—"

My desk phone rang. The display indicated it was a staffer from the front desk calling me the same way Evelyn had when Malcolm Krol had arrived. What were the odds of him showing up while he was being discussed?

I picked up the receiver as Frances wagged a finger at Bennett. "Saved by the bell."

It was Evelyn again, but this time she had a different message to convey. "There are two people here at the front desk, Ms. Wheaton," she said. "They told me you said they should ask for you."

I made that offer to a lot of people. "Who is it?"

"It's a Mr. and Mrs. Tuen." In my mind's eye I saw the couple I'd met the day before at Amethyst Cellars. "They said that they don't want to bother you, but if there was any chance of meeting Mr. Marshfield . . ." She let the thought hang for a moment before adding, "I thought it best to check with you, first."

"That was a good idea, Evelyn," I said.

Still seated across from me, Bennett stared out the window, clearly preoccupied with matters from our discussion.

"Hold a moment, please," I said, and clicked so she couldn't hear. "Bennett, there is a couple down at the front desk. Jim and Daisy Tuen."

The names sparked recognition in his eyes. "FAAC attendees?"

"Right before I ran into Phyllis Forgue at the wine shop,

I met the Tuens. I told them to ask for me if they visited Marshfield."

He seemed perplexed as to why I was sharing all this. "I know you and the Tuens travel in the same circles. I didn't promise that you'd meet with them, but if you wanted to, I know they'd be thrilled."

"I can't. No. Sorry."

Frances piped up. "That's not like you."

"What about Phyllis Forgue?" I asked. "Did you call her back?"

"That woman," Bennett said. "She follows me around and bids on the same things I do. She's wealthy enough to make trouble. I've learned to bid on smaller items I have no interest in simply to keep her busy while I work quietly to procure the pieces I prefer."

"From her perspective it's as though you and she are of one mind," I said. "Uncanny."

"The only thing uncanny is her ability to get on my nerves."

He hadn't answered my original question. "Were you able to get in touch with her?"

He made a so-so motion with his head. "She's been invited to the reception. That's enough to appease her."

Why was Bennett being so mysterious?

"Seeing as how you aren't attending the FAAC this time, I would have thought you'd jump at the chance to connect with a few of the other collectors," Frances said.

He set his jaw. "The Tuens are probably attending the reception, too. I'll talk with them there."

Probably? My first thought was to ask why, this close to the reception, he didn't know who was on his guest list, but I let that go.

Part of me wanted to meet the Tuens downstairs and give them a personal tour, but I hadn't had the chance to spend a lot of time with Bennett the past couple of days and I wanted to push for a little bit more information about this elusive item he was reluctant to discuss.

"Please express my regrets," I said to Evelyn when I reconnected. "Today is a very busy day. I'm certain Mr. and Mrs. Tuen will understand, but be sure to offer them free refreshments in the Birdcage Room as an apology."

When I hung up, I crossed my arms. "You came in to find out what's going on, Bennett, but I'm turning things around. You're being oddly circumspect about this object, artifact, antique . . . whatever it is."

Lacing his fingers in his lap he said, "If you must know, it's an artifact. A very valuable one, but at this point I would rather not tell you more about it because—"

The door to Frances's office opened, but before any of us could get up to see who it was, Liza burst into my office. "I'm here," she said with an absurd level of glee.

I jumped to my feet. "What are you doing here?"

In an instant, Liza gave the room shrewd scrutiny. I watched cagey delight suffuse her features as she made a beeline for Bennett's chair. Thrusting her hand out to him as he stood, she wore an expression of fawning appreciation and injected the same into her voice. "You must be Mr. Marshfield. I am honored to meet you. Grace has told me so much about you and your wonderful family."

"No, I haven't."

Bennett accepted her proffered hand and shook. "And you must be Grace's sister, Liza." Considerably taller than my sister, he regarded her with bright eyes alight with curiosity. "I'm pleased to make your acquaintance."

I hadn't seen Liza this giddy since we were children. Once they'd completed their handshake she gave a perfunctory glance around the room, nodding a dismissive greeting to a frowning Frances, before returning full attention to Bennett. She reached, grabbing both of his forearms, tilting her face up. "I hope I'm not interrupting anything important." She offered him a timid smile. "I can be so oblivious sometimes. Am I bothering you?" Adding a little flirtatious blinking, she took a step closer. "Should I leave?"

Bennett gently extricated himself from her hold. "Your sister is in a better position to determine that than I am."

"What are you doing here?" I asked again.

The soft warmth in her eyes didn't completely die when she turned to me, but I caught a shadow of snappy anger behind them. "You said we had to talk. You said it was important. I came here straight away."

It was taking all my self-control to maintain my equilibrium. "I said that the detectives were on their way to talk with you. I told you to stay home and wait for them."

She gave a careless shrug. "Oops."

My cell phone registered an incoming text. I ignored it. "Liza, I—"

But she'd already turned back to Bennett. "I would *adore* it if you and I could get to know each other better," she said, reaching for him again. Touching his hand, she smiled ever so blithely. "You must have fascinating stories to share about this wonderful home and your vibrant family history. And the amazing treasures you have here . . ." She clasped both hands against her chest as though in rapture. "I can only imagine the tales you have to tell. Would you consider giving me a quick tour? You'd enjoy a chance to show me around, wouldn't you?"

Bennett's mouth twitched ever so slightly. Liza must have noticed it as well, because her animation grew. As if she hadn't piled it on thick enough, she added, "What a treat that would be."

My cell phone rang. I noted the caller, Tooney, then silenced the device.

Poor Frances. The only person still seated in the room, she was doing her very best to express annoyance with grunts, scowls, and sniffs of displeasure. No one paid her any mind.

"As enchanted as I am by your proposal," Bennett said, "I am dependent on your sister's judgment." He locked eyes with me even as he answered her. "If Grace believes it is in my best interests for you and me to spend time together, I am confident she will arrange for it." He winked at me.

"What about right now?" she asked, her refusal to be deterred giving rise to desperation. "It seems quiet around here today. Just a quick tour?" Bennett opened his mouth to reply, but she cut him off, again clasping her hands to her chest. "Getting to know you better, and getting to know this magnificent estate better would be a dream come true for me."

The faint sparkle of amusement in Bennett's eyes faded, replaced by his steely blue gaze. He pressed his palms together prayerfully at his lips, taking his time before answering. "One must not be fooled by appearances," he said at last. Giving that a beat to sink in, he added, "While we appear to be idle, the reality is that I have obligations I must attend to."

He reached for her hand to shake.

She hesitated, then complied. "It's that I really—"

"I'm pleased to have made your acquaintance, Liza." Dropping his hand, he turned to me. "You'll keep me updated on the matters we discussed, Grace?"

Grace. Not Gracie. Bennett was choosing to protect our relationship from Liza's scrutiny, too.

"Of course," I said.

He nodded to all of us. "Then I shall take my leave. Good day."

Liza maintained a tight smile until he was gone.

My desk phone rang. Toorcy. I picked it up and said, "My sister is here. I'll get back to you later."

"Got it, Grace."

When I hung up, Liza said, "I underestimated you, Sis. You managed to wrap one of the wealthiest men in the world around your little finger." With a cocked eyebrow and sassy head waggle, she went on. "My, my, my. I misunderstood. You really *have* changed, haven't you?"

Frances shot to her feet, full-tilt. "How dare you suggest

such a thing." Bringing a pudgy index finger to within a hair of Liza's nose, she fairly growled, "If you knew how things really are around here, you'd be purple with jealousy."

Liza pounced. "Jealous of Grace? This I have to hear. Enlighten me about how things 'really are.'"

Dread seared a stinging path from my gut into my throat. Knowing all too well how much my assistant loved to gossip and—even more—put people in their place, I panicked that she'd spill everything about me and Bennett, right here and now.

My assistant didn't break eye contact with Liza. "Your sister is a whole lot more important to Mr. Marshfield than you could ever imagine."

"Frances," I said, "let's drop it. We don't owe her, or anyone, an explanation."

Her cheeks still flushed with emotion, my assistant blinked. Twice. She opened her mouth to continue, closed it, then began again. "Your sister," she said, "is very dear to Mr. Marshfield."

Liza might not have been able to detect the subtle falter in Frances's attack, but I did.

"Your sister," Frances continued after a swift glance at me, "is more than simply an employee here. She . . . she . . ."

Liza smirked. I willed myself to keep breathing.

"She's the Mister's most trusted assistant." On a roll now, Frances tucked her fists into her hips and stepped closer to Liza, offering her own version of a head waggle. "She's the best thing to happen to Marshfield in a long time and I'll thank you to keep your snide comments to yourself. Or you'll answer to me."

Liza managed a quick laugh but I could tell she'd been thrown. "Well, now I'm really worried."

Warmed beyond words by Frances's rant, I fought to contain my emotion as I caught her eye. "Thank you."

She twisted her mouth to one side, making a show of looking at her watch. "Getting late," she said. "Before I leave,

I'll have a talk with our security staff. They need to be reminded that protocols require visitors to wait at the front desk for *permission* to come up here." She sent a pointed scowl toward Liza, who had sucked in her cheeks. "No exceptions."

"An excellent idea," I said. "Thanks. I'll leave the matter in your capable hands."

Chapter 18

LIZA FUMED IN SILENCE. WHEN WE FINALLY made it home, I said hello to Bootsie and turned to shut off the burglar alarm. Liza threw herself into one of my kitchen chairs, pouting like a four-year-old.

I pointed to the wall-mounted keypad. "This was never set."

She gave an exaggerated look around the room. "Does it look like anyone broke in?"

"That's not the point. You should have set the alarm before you took off."

Elbows on the tabletop, chin cupped in her palms, she rolled her eyes. "I can't do anything right, can I? No matter how hard I try, I always fall short."

"Stop right there, Liza. You're not turning this one around. You knew the detectives were coming to talk with you. You were supposed to wait with Tooney until they got here. You didn't. And even if I could overlook those things, I asked you to set the alarm whenever you leave the house. How, exactly, do you see that as trying hard?"

"Nothing is ever good enough for you, is it?" Liza said, adopting her favorite poor-me argument. "I can't wait until I'm away from here."

"That makes two of us."

We were both silent while I sorted through the refrigerator. I stared at the cold leftovers and condiments. I wasn't hungry. When I shut the door again, I asked, "What's keeping you here? You don't like me. I don't like you. Why stay?"

"I don't have anywhere else to go."

"Why didn't you want to talk with the detectives?" I asked. "What are you afraid of? What kind of trouble are you in?"

"I'm not in any trouble at all," she said. "Why do you always assume that?"

"Avoiding the police kind of makes me suspicious."

"I told you, I came to see you today because you said it was important that we talk. I'm not avoiding the police."

"Then you won't have a problem if I call them right now and let them know we're home."

I had started for the house phone when the front doorbell rang. Exasperation got the better of me. "Who is it now?"

As I hurried to answer, I wondered if it might be Rodriguez and Flynn trying again to connect with Liza. "Do not leave this house," I shouted over my shoulder.

I grasped the knob and pulled open the door to find a tall, sturdy man on my doorstep. Military-short dark hair, hooded eyes. He wore a heavy charcoal coat open over a gray suit, white shirt, and gray tie. I didn't open the storm door.

"Good evening," he said through the glass. He gave a perfunctory smile, allowing the briefest glimpse of deep dimples and bright white, even teeth. His eyes, however, were shark-dead, reflecting neither life or light. "Are you Grace Wheaton?"

"Why? Who are you?"

He held out a leather wallet. "Sam McClowery, FBI. I have questions to ask you about Eric Soames."

"No, no, no," I said, grabbing the edge of my heavy door. "Fool me once, maybe. Fool me twice? Not happening."

He continued to regard me with that blasted, blank expression. "Ms. Wheaton, if you have information about Eric Soames or his whereabouts and you refuse to share it with me—"

"Take your fake ID and get off my property," I said. "Tell your cohorts that I know nothing about Eric. Nothing at all. If I had information on where he is, the first thing I'd do is pick up the phone and call the police. You got that? The police."

As my voice rose, it dawned on me that I might be shouting into the face of the very person who'd killed the first fake Fed. The storm door glass between us wouldn't offer much protection if this guy decided to take me down. In that instantaneous way the brain has of reasoning out a problem when facing danger, I knew that my best defense was to convince this guy that I had nothing to offer.

"I'm not kidding, either," I said in an effort to make a good show. "You want to find Eric? Get in line. I was engaged to that loser a few years ago but he threw me over for someone else." I chose not to mention that the someone else happened to be in my house right now. "You got that? Engaged. You think if I had any knowledge of where he was I wouldn't gleefully hand it over to you or one of your thug brethren?"

"Ms. Wheaton, I assure you—"

"No, I assure *you* that I'm finished fielding questions about that lowlife scum. The last guy who came asking about Eric wound up dead in the neighbor's backyard. I suggest you watch your back."

With that, I slammed the door. Unfortunately, because it had recently been replaced with a solid-core, steel-encased, draft-proof model, and because the storm door was equally airtight, the slam came out more like an indignant *whoosh*.

Liza had been watching from the parlor. "Wow," she said.

I left her staring and made my way to the kitchen. Picking up the house phone, I dialed from memory Rodriguez's cell phone number. When he answered, I told him about the new fake FBI agent on my doorstep and provided a description.

"Miz Wheaton," he said with a sigh, "trouble certainly seems to find you, doesn't it? My partner and I will be out there shortly."

"One more thing: I know you missed my sister this afternoon."

"That we did. We planned to follow up in the morning."

"She's back now. I'm sure she'll be delighted to answer your questions. It's like getting two for one."

His soft chuckle made me believe he knew exactly how pleased Liza would be to see them. "We'll be there in less than twenty. Don't go anywhere."

"I won't," I said.

"What happened to you?" Liza asked when I hung up. She'd followed me into the kitchen, but probably hadn't caught much of my conversation with Rodriguez. "You turned into a crazy woman with that guy at the door. I've never seen you like that."

"Get into enough battles, you learn how to stand up for yourself," I said, opening the refrigerator again. This time I *was* hungry. Grabbing a plate of leftover meatloaf, I sliced a helping, placed it on a smaller dish, and popped it into the microwave before returning the original plate to the fridge.

Liza watched me as though I were a species she hadn't encountered before.

"This isn't the most balanced meal, but"—I shrugged, licking a wayward drop of coagulated gravy off my finger—"a girl's gotta eat."

"Yeah." She reclaimed her seat at the table.

"Help yourself, by the way," I said. "I'm not making dinner tonight."

"Okay, sure."

Ravenous by the time the microwave dinged, I polished

off the meatloaf in five bites, grabbed a few raw carrots for crunch, then ended my hasty meal by peeling a navel orange. Liza puttered about the kitchen, keeping silent.

When she sat down across from me with her own cobbled-together dinner, she said, "So, Ms. Superhero, that Frances was awfully quick to come to your defense this afternoon."

Frances's words had meant the world to me, but I shrugged as though it was no big deal.

"She's pretty convinced that there's nothing going on between you and Bennett Marshfield, but that's not what I think."

Flush from my success at getting the stranger off my front porch, I wasn't about to let my mood be ruined by Liza's speculations. "Good thing I don't really care what you think."

"You keep telling me you're not in a romantic relationship," she continued. "Maybe you're in one, but don't want the world to know."

I popped an orange segment into my mouth and talked around it. "Give it a rest, Liza. You're wrong."

She wiggled her shoulders and cocked her head. "Then why so protective? Why not let me spend time with him? Are you afraid I'll steal him away like I did Eric?"

Thank goodness I'd swallowed, otherwise I would have gagged. "Yeah, Liza. That's it. You found me out. I'm worried that Bennett will fall in love with you and cast me away forever." I gave a snort, one Frances would be proud of.

"It has to be true," she said. "That's the only thing that makes sense."

The doorbell rang again. Rodriguez and Flynn to the rescue, for once. "Yep," I said as I got up to answer the door. "You got it. Give the girl a gold star."

She shouted after me, "Don't try reverse psychology stuff. You're hiding the truth from me. I can tell."

I was very glad she couldn't see my face at that point, because it probably would have broadcasted the fact that yes, I was hiding the truth from her. It was, however, a truth she couldn't begin to guess. As long as she maintained the preposterous belief that I'd lured Bennett into a decidedly not-platonic attachment, the reality remained safe.

"Thanks for coming," I said as I ushered Rodriguez and Flynn into the house. They were both wearing more casual clothes than they usually did during the day. Blue jeans and hockey jerseys from two different teams. Flynn carried a folder. "Big game today?" I asked as I took their coats.

Rodriguez pointed to the colorful Blackhawks logo across his chest. "Love these guys," he said. "One of the original six." He indicated Flynn. "Playing his team today."

I didn't recognize the logo. "Which one is it?"

"The Buffalo Sabres," Flynn said. "You got a problem with that?"

Weren't we starting out well? "Come on in," I said, leading them into the kitchen.

"I can't believe that guy came back," Liza said as I walked in. Her mouth dropped open when she spotted the two visitors behind me. It wouldn't have taken a rocket scientist to figure out who they were, especially as I'd described both men in detail earlier in the day. I could read alarm and disappointment on Liza's face.

"Guess what? My friends Detectives Rodriguez and Flynn were able to make time for us tonight."

"When you said you were calling the police, I thought . . ." She didn't finish whatever she'd planned to say. "Hello." She got to her feet and turned on the charm. "I'm Grace's sister, Liza. Really sorry about missing you today. I can't imagine how I misunderstood." She giggled, bobbing her head from side-to-side. "Oops."

I invited the men to sit at the kitchen table. "Can I get you coffee? Water?"

They waved me off with thanks, turning their attention to Liza. "This new visitor who showed up tonight," Rodriguez began, "did you get a look at him? Recognize him?"

Liza glanced at me before she shook her head.

"He was asking about your husband, Eric Soames, is that correct?"

Again, Liza turned to me before answering. I held up my hands.

"Miz Wheaton," he prompted, then frowned. "As we have two Miz Wheatons here, do you mind if I use your first names?"

"Go ahead," I said. Liza shrugged.

"Liza, then," Rodriguez continued, "where is your husband now?"

She was slouched across from me. The detectives sat at either end of the table. "I have no idea. I left him and didn't look back."

"Could he have followed you here?"

"Maybe," she said, "but I made it clear it was over between us."

"What kind of business is your husband in?"

She shrugged again and looked away. "He finds work when he needs to."

Flynn made an unpleasant noise. "What kind of work? Specifically?"

Liza loosened her arms, sat forward and stared straight at Flynn. "He didn't talk about his business with me. Can't help you there."

Flynn pulled a sheet out from the folder on his lap. He didn't shift his attention from Liza as he slid it toward her and turned it faceup. It was a photo of the first fake Fed who'd come to my door. Even viewing it upside-down, I recognized the man. Not a mug shot from decades earlier. This was a recent likeness, full face, close up.

"Do you know this man?" Flynn asked Liza.

She wrapped her arms around herself again, leaning back. "No." Affecting a bored-with-this-nonsense tone, she asked, "Who is he?"

Flynn glanced at me and I got the impression he was

asking whether I believed Liza or not. I couldn't tell, so I shrugged.

"This is a copy of the man's passport photo—a passport he had using an alias. That ring any bells with you?" Rodriguez stood and brought his chair around to Liza's side. He sat next to her, his bulk encroaching on my sister's personal space. Using a fleshy finger to slide the photo closer, he said, "Think hard. Maybe you didn't know this man. Maybe you saw him before, though? With your husband?"

"Maybe. I don't know for sure. He looks like a lot of people."

Flynn brought his chair around to Liza's other side. He sat. It was clear he was aiming for casual, but his steady hawk-like glower gave him away. "Does the name Tomas Pineda mean anything to you?"

With all the attention in the room on her, Liza's subtle, startled blink was impossible to miss. "Wow," she said. "You guys are full of oddball questions, aren't you? Who is this guy, anyway? Why is he so important?"

Rodriguez hadn't moved his finger from the photo's edge. He slid it closer still. "You recognize the name." Not a question.

Tight between the two detectives, Liza made herself small. Her bravado eroding by the second, she kept her teeth firmly clamped on her lower lip and sent me a look, pleading for help. Nothing I could do here. Nor would I. The man in that picture was dead. If my two detective friends believed Liza could help find the murderer, I wasn't about to stop them.

"Who is this guy?" she asked again. "Why are you interested in him?"

"One more time, Liza," Rodriguez said softly, bringing his face very close to hers. I'd never found the portly detective to be particularly intimidating, until now. The man possessed a power I'd never seen before. "We're unsure whether you recognize the face, but you most definitely know the name.

Why don't you make things easy for yourself? Who is Tomas Pineda? How is he connected with your husband?"

Liza covered the sides of her head with both hands. "I don't know. I don't know. I don't know. Leave me alone."

"Cut the dramatics, Liza," I said.

The hateful look she directed across the table was one I would remember for a long time. I could have sworn she hissed, too. "I have never seen this man before in my life," she said, anger chopping her words. "The name. Yes. I heard the name. I don't remember much. Eric said that name once or twice. I don't think Eric liked him. But I can't be sure."

"Is Eric capable of murder?" Rodriguez asked in that scary-soft voice of his.

"No!" Fully alarmed now, Liza leaned as far away from him as she could, but Flynn had taken that moment to move closer. She had nowhere to go. I almost felt sorry for her. "Why would you say such a thing?"

Rodriguez tapped the photo. "This man came here looking for your husband, and now he's dead. Murdered." He gave a little *tsk*. "Kind of an interesting coincidence, don't you think?"

"That's the guy who got killed?" Liza asked me. "The one you told me about?"

Flynn's voice dropped to a rumble. "Where were you Saturday?" he asked. "Between, say, noon and three o'clock?"

Liza's eyes widened. "You can't think I had anything to do with that. You even said you know I never saw this guy's face."

Flynn gave a chilly smile. "He was shot in the back."

"No, stop. No." Liza's panic was palpable. Her gaze darted around the room the way an animal's does before it escapes or bites. "I left California Saturday. I took the train to get here. I didn't get here until Tuesday. Ask Grace. I have proof. Tickets, receipts. Whatever you need."

Rodriguez asked questions about her route, jotting notes as she gave specifics regarding cities, timetables, and stops. She'd traveled from San Francisco to Chicago to D.C. before arriving in Emberstowne on Tuesday. How she'd survived that many hours on a train with her meager belongings and little money boggled my mind. There was no doubt, however, that she was telling the truth about her journey.

"We may have more questions for you," Rodriguez said as they wrapped up the kitchen table interrogation. "And, of course, if you remember anything that might help us, or you see your husband, you will let us know."

Liza pulled her cheeks in tight, but nodded.

Sliding his chair around to the end once again, Rodriguez addressed me. "What can you tell me about your visitor this evening?"

I gave him what little information I had.

"You ran him off, did you?" A corner of Flynn's mouth curled up. "I would have liked to see that."

Rodriguez grinned. "Our favorite curator is turning into a she-devil," he said as he hauled himself to his feet. "We'll have uniforms keep an eye on your house tonight, Grace. If he comes back, or you notice anything out of place, any time of the day or night, call us." He patted me on the shoulder with a beefy hand. "I know you will."

Flynn stood up. "Where's Bootsie?" he asked. "Haven't seen her at all tonight."

As though she'd expected the summons, she pranced into the kitchen from the dining room, little nose held high. Rodriguez began making his way to the front door. Flynn picked up the cat and followed. "How are you, sweetheart?" he asked as he scratched under her chin. "Hiding out, were you?"

I leaned close so as not to be overheard. "Bootsie takes cover when Liza's around."

Flynn shot a scathing look over his shoulder. "I know she's your sister, Grace, but that girl is trouble."

"Tell me about it," I said.

Chapter 19

THE NEXT MORNING, I STRODE INTO LIZA'S room to rouse her. I pushed open the door, wrinkling my nose at the stale laundry smell. The window shade hung all the way down, allowing no morning light. The limited clothing she'd brought with her, now freed from the confines of her overstuffed bag, had expanded into messy piles on the floor—the source of the unpleasant aroma. I picked my way around them to the single bed in the far corner. On her back, with one arm across her eyes and the other stretched overhead, she slept with her mouth open, gurgling throaty noises with every breath.

"Liza." I wiggled her elbow. "Wake up." She shifted her back to me. I pulled at her shoulder, then shook it with enough effort to get her attention. "Come on. Time to get up."

With a cry, Liza sprang awake. She pulled her legs in fast and twisted, drawing herself into the corner, blanket clutched tight in both hands. "What are you—?" As awareness settled over her, she smoothed her hair back. "What do you want?"

"You have a half hour to get yourself ready."

"Where am I going?"

"I've made arrangements for your safety while I'm at work."

"What kind of arrangements?"

I started for the door. "I've already showered, but still need to get dressed. Meet me downstairs when you're ready."

"Don't I get a choice here?"

"Sorry," I said. "You don't."

BRUCE WAS READING THE NEWSPAPER AND drinking a cup of coffee when I made it down to the kitchen. "You're up early," I said.

He wore sweatpants and a pale green shirt soaked with perspiration. Pinching the neckline, he peeled the fabric forward and fanned it while giving me a lopsided grin. "Went out for a run this morning."

"*You* went running?" I poured coffee and joined him at the table.

"Okay, fine. More like a jog." He held up a finger. "But I kept a good pace."

"When did this start?"

"You know how we're always talking about staying healthy? I thought it was about time I stopped talking and actually followed through." Pointing upward, he added, "I haven't been able to convince Scott yet."

"It's twenty degrees outside. Maybe you need to try when it's warmer."

He lifted the coffee mug to his lips. "Maybe." A moment later, he asked, "What's going on with Liza? Any update on how long she'll be here?"

The reunion between my roommates and my sister had been awkward at best. Ever since Liza's arrival, Bruce and Scott had begun coming home later and leaving earlier. I couldn't blame them.

"I'm so sorry to put you guys in the middle of this," I said.

"It's not your fault, Grace. Nobody saw this coming."

I told him about the second would-be FBI agent who had come to call yesterday as well as about Rodriguez and Flynn's visit. Bootsie leapt into my lap and I stroked her head as I shared the details of my plans for Liza today.

"She's fed, by the way," Bruce said when I'd finished. It took me a second to realize he meant Bootsie.

"So where's the worm?"

Bruce and I turned as Liza entered the room. Wet hair combed back from her scrubbed face, she was barefoot and wearing one of the oversized T-shirts I'd provided. She'd recaptured a measure of her usual insouciance, sauntering past my chair to pick up the coffeepot. Sniffing the brew, she wrinkled her nose. "Doesn't anyone know how to make decent coffee around here?"

Neither of us bothered to answer.

Pouring herself a cup of the brew she'd just maligned, she sat down. "The worm," she said. "Get it? We're early birds." Making a face at Bruce, she asked, "What happened to you?"

"There's my cue to head up for a shower," Bruce said. He rinsed his mug out in the sink then loaded it into the dishwasher. "See you tonight, Grace." He glanced at my sister. "Later, Liza."

She shouted to his back, "Can't wait," but lowered her voice again to me. "So, Sis, what are these big plans of yours?"

"You said you planned to be here for a week . . . ish."

"Tossing me out already?"

"Not quite. What I am doing, however, is keeping you out of harm's way until they find whoever murdered that man."

"The guy with all the aliases?"

"The same. He, and the one at the door yesterday, came here looking for Eric. You even admitted you suspect Eric might show up."

She didn't comment.

"Because I can't trust you to manage the alarm, or stay put when it's important, or tell the truth when I need you to, I've arranged for you to stay elsewhere while I'm at work."

"Elsewhere," she repeated, deadpan. "Like daycare?"

Leaning forward, I kept my voice low. It wasn't that I minded Bruce or Scott overhearing, it was that I wanted Liza to pay close attention to what I had to say next. "If Eric or more of his associates show up here, I don't want you in the house by yourself."

"Because you don't trust me to face Eric? You think I'll take him back?"

"No." I blinked and sat back in my chair. "Because it isn't safe."

I could tell my words startled her. She bit her lip.

"Whoever killed that man in the neighbor's yard is still out there," I said. "What's to stop him from killing you?"

She fiddled her thumbs against the side of her mug but said nothing.

"Do you have anything to read?" I asked.

"Like a book?" She laughed without humor. "Yeah, right. Isn't there a television at this daycare center?"

I got to my feet, ignoring her snarky attitude. I rinsed out my mug and loaded it into the dishwasher. "How soon can you be ready to leave?"

"Ten minutes. But because I'm all giddy with excitement make it five." She stood to join me, leaving her mug at the table.

I slid a glance at it. "We clean up after ourselves around here."

With a huff worthy of a cranky teenager, she grabbed the mug, whipped it into the sink, flushed it with water, and then added it to the dishwasher. The dramatics were over-wrought but as long as she played by house rules, I let her enjoy her tantrum. While she stomped and banged, I tapped out a text on my cell phone.

"Thank you," I said when she was done. "Hurry up and get dressed."

She disappeared upstairs and, true to her prediction, was ready in five minutes, wearing ripped jeans, another one of my shirts, and a pair of canvas flats.

"I guess you are giddy after all," I said. "Let's go."

I opened the basement door. Her abject look of horror gave me the biggest jolt of amusement I'd felt in a long time.

"You're not putting me down there, are you? You can't do that."

I couldn't stop myself from chuckling. "Yeah, I'm planning to chain you to the wall. Don't worry. There will be plenty of bread and water."

"This isn't funny, Grace."

"Relax," I said. "Follow me."

She did. She clearly trusted me enough to know that I wouldn't imprison her underground, but I could feel her trepidation as she made her way down the stairs.

"It's cleaner down here than it used to be," she said. Taking a sniff, she added, "Smells better, too."

"Amazing the good things that come with effort."

We headed toward the front of the house, past the furnace. I let the surprise speak for itself.

Liza pointed to the metal door in the wall. "What's that? That wasn't here when we lived in the house."

"It was hidden. Remember the old workbench?"

She blinked a few times. "Vaguely."

I lifted the countersunk metal ring and pulled. The heavy door swung open, silently, smoothly, revealing the underground tunnel beyond.

"What is this?" she asked.

When we'd first found this passageway, there had been a temporary wall set up a few feet inside, giving the casual viewer the impression of a small space. With the help of Hillary's construction crew, we'd taken it down and cleaned the tunnel out. "Come on, I'll show you," I said.

Ducking my head, I eased myself through the opening. We kept a few flashlights immediately inside the door. I picked up two and handed one to Liza. Wide-eyed and openmouthed, her expression was a mixture of wonder and apprehension. "You want me to come in there with you? Where does this go?"

"I'll explain on the way." I flicked my flashlight on and moved deeper into the tunnel, confident her curiosity would get the better of her. It did.

Five steps later, she'd caught up with me and as we made the underground trek to Tooney's house, I explained how we'd found the passage. I also shared a little bit of the structure's history we'd uncovered.

She reached out to skim her fingers along the cool brick wall. "How often do you use it?"

"Not very. I texted Ronny Tooney before we left," I said. "He and I have come up with a system. The plan is to use the tunnel only in case of emergencies. Hiding you from Eric and his associates qualifies. Tooney is waiting for us on the other side."

"Your neighbor has access to your house?" she asked, aghast. "Doesn't that make you nervous?"

"Quite the opposite."

By the time we made it to the far door, Tooney had swung it open, providing enough illumination to proceed without the flashlights. I clicked mine off. Tooney's homely, hangdog face hovered ahead of us looking at once hesitant yet eager. His cheeks flushed when he caught sight of us and he grinned. I was taken aback, not for the first time, by the transformation in his appearance. When Tooney smiled, he was positively good-looking.

"Good morning, Grace." His gaze shifted from me to my sister as he backed up, allowing us both to step out of the tunnel and into his basement. "You must be Ms. Liza."

"Yep, that's me," she said, looking around the wide, empty space. "This basement is like a mirror image of ours."

I bit back the correction: *Mine*. "Liza, I'd like you to meet a good friend, Ronny Tooney."

His face flushed again, but this time no smile. He held out a hand. "Pleased to meet you."

Liza tilted her head as she reached to shake. "Very nice to meet you, Mr. Tooney." Her voice was honey, her gaze soft, as she tugged her slender fingers closer, bringing his chubby ones along for the ride. Grasping his hand in both of hers, she leaned closer. "Grace has told me so many wonderful things about you. I can't wait to get to know you better."

"And I've heard a great deal about you as well." Red-cheeked, he extracted his hand. Wiping a trickle of perspiration from the side of his face, he stretched his chin and chanced a look at me. I caught a hardness in his eyes. Fleeting, it was gone in an instant.

"Grace hasn't been telling stories again, has she?" Liza asked. "I'll bet you're annoyed to be stuck babysitting me all day." Short hair or no, she tossed her head triumphantly as she tucked a hand into Tooney's arm. "We're going to be good friends, aren't we, Ronald?"

He peeled her fingers up and took a step out of her reach. The flinty hardness snapped back into his eyes as he faced her. "Don't pretend to be attracted to me," he said. "I'm twenty years older than you are, at least. Plus, I have a mirror."

Liza shifted. She tucked her hands into her pockets. "Wow, Grace has really done a number on you, hasn't she? Has she tainted everyone's opinion of me, or is there a law against being friendly around here?"

"Not at all." Tooney maintained the stare. "I just want to make sure we understand each other."

She raised both hands in surrender. "Have it your way."

"And for the record," he said with a sly glance at me, "my name isn't Ronald."

I gasped. "It isn't?"

His stern visage gave way to amusement. "The cops gave

me the nickname Ronny when I was trying to get on the force. It stuck." He gave a self-conscious shrug. "After you and I first met, when the cops told you who I was, they used the nickname. You were so mad at me back then I didn't have the guts to tell you they'd gotten it wrong."

"But since that time," I stammered, "you've had plenty of opportunity. Why haven't you ever said anything?"

Again, the shrug. Again, his cheeks blazed. "You always call me by my last name, anyway. I didn't see the need."

"Oh my gosh, Tooney." Catching myself, I slapped a hand over my mouth. "I'm so sorry. I had no idea."

"It's okay, Grace."

Ignoring Liza's eyeroll, I asked him, "What is it then? Your real name?"

A smile teased his lips. "Bronson."

"Bronson," I repeated. "Like Charles Bronson?"

Tooney brightened. "You know him? I figured he was before your time."

"Our parents were big into war movies," I said. "I loved him in *The Great Escape*."

"Oh my God," Liza said, dropping her head back to stare at the ceiling.

"My folks, too." Tooney grew more animated. "They were huge fans of his. When I was born, they considered naming me Charles, but I'm really glad they didn't."

"Charles is a lovely name," I said.

"Yeah, but Charlie Tooney?" he asked. "You ever see a Starkist commercial?"

"Ooh," I said. "Good point."

"For crying out loud, are we going to reminisce about boring old movies and TV shows all day?"

I ignored Liza's complaint. "Bronson is a wonderful name," I said. "I'll do my best to remember to use it. It may take me a while to break the habit."

"You can keep calling me Tooney, Grace. I don't mind."

Liza threw her hands up. "What is it with this town? Everybody here is madly in love with my sister." She shook her head and twisted her lips. "Gotta tell you, Bronson," she said, stressing his name, "I don't see the attraction."

He gave a matter-of-fact shrug. "Then it's your loss."

Chapter 20

THE BUSINESS DISTRICT OF EMBERSTOWNE FEA-tured a plethora of quaint stores, restaurants, coffee shops, and other small enterprises—like my roommates' Amethyst Cellars—much as one might expect in touristy areas. These establishments owed their livelihood to the masses who visited Marshfield annually and the Chamber of Commerce, which took great pains to preserve the town's considerable charm.

Thus, whenever residents needed to shop for various and sundry items unavailable in our local shops, they headed out of town to the nearest big-box store. Located off the express-way, twenty minutes from our business district, it was the best option for finding what I needed today.

At this early hour, the store's wide aisles were empty. The few shoppers present zipped in to pick up what they needed and zipped right back out. Exactly my plan.

There were three prepaid cell phones on display worth considering and a handful of others out of my price range. I had no idea how long Liza planned to stay but I wanted to be able to reach her if necessary. There was no way I'd go so far as to add her to my mobile account, but a prepaid cheapie could provide me peace of mind.

Only one cashier had her light on—lane eight. She couldn't be much older than nineteen, with pale hair pulled back into a messy bun, stayed-out-late red eyes, and earrings that were too heavy and dark to do her any favors. I got in line behind a couple unloading their handheld basket. Preoccupied with plans for the day, it took me an extra second to recognize them. "Mr. and Mrs. Tuen," I said.

They both turned at the sound of my voice. "Ah, Miss Wheaton," Jim said. "It is a pleasure to see you again."

"I must apologize for not being able to come down when you visited the other day."

Daisy patted my arm. "Think nothing of it," she said. "We know you're busy."

"Thank you. I was very disappointed to miss talking with you."

Jim finished adding their items to the conveyor. Basic vacation needs, it seemed: a six-pack of bottled water, shampoo, generic aspirin, several magazines, and a bag of salty snacks. "Yes, yes," he said. "But we trust we will see you Tuesday night?"

"Tuesday night?" I asked.

"Bennett's reception."

"The reception. Of course," I said, giving myself a little smack in the head. "It's too early for my brain, I guess."

They both laughed politely.

Jim excused himself to complete his transaction with the cashier. "It seems we are destined to have our conversations whenever my wife and I are making purchases."

My turn to offer a considerate chuckle.

As he signed the small payment screen, Jim leaned back into the conversation, speaking quietly. "Would you happen to know if Malcolm Krol will be attending as well?"

Malcolm Krol—the name zinged an immediate recollection of the blond gentleman with the Australian accent who had visited Bennett earlier this week. "I . . . uh . . . don't know," I said.

Daisy and Jim shared a meaningful glance. "But you know who he is," Jim said. Not a question, more like a confirmation.

"We met briefly." I hoped my helpless shrug would prompt them to tell me more about Bennett's mysterious visitor.

Daisy's crow's-feet wrinkles deepened around her eyes. "We only wish our encounter with him had been brief."

Jim placed a restraining hand on his wife's arm. "Let's not speak ill of those who are not here to defend themselves." They finished their purchase and moved forward as the cashier handed them their bags. Jim thanked the young woman, then nodded to me. "Until Tuesday," he said.

While we were saying good-bye, I became aware of another shopper joining the line behind me. I didn't pay any attention to him until after the cashier asked if I'd found everything I needed, and I responded that I had.

Before she could scan my item, the man behind me plucked it out of her grasp. "Now what would an upstanding resident of Emberstowne need with a prepaid cell phone?"

I spun. "Excuse me," I began, but the quasi-polite reproach I'd intended died on my lips. The man from my front door—the fake FBI agent, the second and still-alive one—had twisted the blister-pack holder and was skimming the words on the back.

"Look at these features," he said. "These burner phones are getting more sophisticated every day."

"Give that back to me."

He handed it to the cashier. Far from the flat, blank stare he'd worn when we first met, the playful wink he flashed was aimed to make her swoon. The cashier's breathless thanks left no doubt the ploy had worked. And from the man's self-assured grin, it was clear he was used to such reactions.

The cashier, eyeing the credit card I'd pulled out, tapped the pay station. "Swipe over there, please."

The fake FBI guy had placed deodorant, mouthwash, disposable shavers, and a mystery paperback on the conveyor. "Those phones are still traceable, you know."

As I completed payment I worked up a dismissive glare. "Thank you for that insight, Mr. McClowery, or whatever your real name is."

The cashier's bloodshot eyes glinted, taking in our conversation. She handed me my purchase without another word.

McClowery flicked his fingers against the bag in my hands. "No burner phone in the world can help Eric now."

I yanked the bag up. "This isn't for Eric. This is . . ." I'd been about to say that it was for my sister, but that was none of this guy's business. "I told you I haven't seen Eric and I don't expect to. Whoever you are, you can stay away from me."

"We don't want *you*," he said, speaking softly. "My 'thug brethren,' as you call them, merely want to have a talk with your former fiancé." As he pulled out his wallet to pay, he gave me that dead-eyed stare again. "Tell me where he is and you never have to see me again."

"Trust me," I said with as much swagger I could muster, "nothing would give me greater pleasure."

"Tell me where he is and your troubles are over."

"My troubles are already over," I said, wildly faking it. "The minute I leave here, I'm calling the police on you. Again."

I pivoted and made for the doors, which were about fifty feet away. Resisting the urge to run or glance back at him, I didn't even take time to zipper my coat. Once I made it into the parking lot, I hurried to my car, threw the bag on the passenger seat, and drove off. It bothered me that I was shaking, but it bothered me even more that this angry man still apparently believed I knew Eric's whereabouts.

Eschewing the radio, I spent the entire silent ride to Marshfield mulling my situation. I didn't call Rodriguez and

Flynn as I'd threatened to, but I planned to do so once I was safely in my office.

Frances looked up when I stormed in.

"Eric must be around here somewhere," I said. "Why else would all these brutes suddenly converge on Emberstowne?"

"What happened?"

I told her about my interaction with the second fake FBI agent. "I didn't sign on for this," I said. "When Eric left, I thought he was gone for good. All of a sudden, I'm in the middle of . . . whatever this is."

"Would you really tell that guy where Eric was if you knew?"

"Probably not." I blew out a breath of frustration. "I have nothing but contempt for the guy but that doesn't mean I want to see him killed."

"And you think they plan to do that?"

"I can't figure out what anyone's plan is."

She leaned forward on her desk, her fleshy forearms like loaves of dough set out to rise. "Don't put yourself in danger to protect him."

"Ha!" My laugh came out harsh and quick. "I have no intention of doing that."

"You may be doing it already."

"What do you mean?"

She worked her lips in and out, buying time. "By providing asylum for your sister, you're keeping yourself in the bad guys' crosshairs. If she goes, maybe Eric follows; maybe not. Like you said from the start—she's at the center of all this. Toss her out and I bet your troubles disappear, too."

I scratched the back of my neck. "I'd be lying if I didn't admit the same thought had crossed my mind."

She waited.

When I finally looked up, I caught Frances watching me with a gentle expression in her eyes. Pity, perhaps? She blinked it away so fast I could pretend I hadn't noticed. "I can't," I said. "I can't throw her to the wolves."

"She's plenty capable of fending for herself."

"But what kind of person does that to another human being?" I shook my head. "Sure, I could wash my hands of the whole business. McClowery would have his bait and I'd have my life back." Ever since Liza appeared, I'd operated on autopilot, protecting my sister even though I wished her gone. Here, now, putting it into words for Frances helped me understand my own motivations. "That's not who I am."

"You're right. It isn't," she said. "So what do we do about it?"

Before I could answer, the office phones rang. Frances looked at the display. "Emberstowne Police Department," she said, then handed me the receiver. "Tell them that man was harassing you."

"Grace Wheaton," I said into the phone.

"Hey, yeah." It was Flynn. "We have another update for you."

"About the man who was killed?"

I could almost hear him shake his head. "Nah." Flynn's tone was different this morning. Oddly amused. "You know that guy you chased off your porch last night?"

"I was going to call you about him," I said, sitting up. "Why? What did he do?"

"Ah . . ." Flynn drew out the sound. "Rodriguez and I dug into the guy's background. Came up empty on criminal records. We planned to try again this morning. I got in early to get started."

"What did you find?"

He made a noise that I could have sworn was a laugh. "Right in the middle of a follow-up phone call, guess who walks in asking for me and Rodriguez?" He didn't wait for a reply. "Yep. Sam McClowery is sitting here as we speak. Told me a little bit about your conversation in the checkout line this morning."

"Wait, what? Why did he come to you?"

"Turns out he's legit." Again, the low chuckle. "Sam

McClowery *is* an FBI agent. I verified everything myself, not two minutes ago."

"But . . . but . . ."

"I know. Kind of a shock, isn't it?"

I had no words.

"I explained how our victim came to visit you claiming to be FBI. Agent McClowery is beginning to understand why you were skeptical when he presented his bona fides."

"No way," I said. "He threatened me. Today, in the store. Would a real government agent do that?"

"They do what's necessary."

"What has Eric gotten himself into? Why are they looking for him?"

"There's a question I can't answer." He covered the mouthpiece and I couldn't hear more than low mumbles. When Flynn returned to the phone, he said, "Agent McClowery has a few leads he plans to follow today. He said he'll stop by your house tonight. I hope you'll give him a warmer welcome this time."

When we hung up, I stared at Frances for a long moment. "Well," I said when I found my voice. "I didn't see that coming."

Chapter 21

I BROUGHT LIZA BACK HOME THAT EVENING
via the underground passage. Tooney—that is, Bronson—
mopped sweat from his forehead as he thanked me for coming home earlier than usual. Liza watched Tooney with
predatory satisfaction as he explained that, although Hillary
and Frederick had popped in during the day, he'd been worried that my sister was bored.

She'd skimmed her fingers along his upper arm and didn't
react when he flinched. "Bored? Not me," she said.

"I'm sorry," I whispered to him before we left.

"It's okay, Grace. I'll be better prepared next time."

When we were finally back at my house I asked Liza,
"What did you do to that poor man?"

"Gave him a little thrill, that's all. What is with you
people? You're all so stuffy and straitlaced."

I ignored her.

"I'm probably the most exciting thing that's happened to
this town in a long time."

I smiled in spite of myself. Knives, guns, bombs, poisons.

Not to mention treachery and murder. We'd had more excitement in the past couple of years than most cities experienced in a decade. "Yeah, probably," I said.

"Cut me a little slack then," she said, dropping into a kitchen chair. "I'm adding spice to your life. Admit it."

I handed Liza the prepaid cell phone. While she fiddled with it to figure it out, I started getting Bootsie's dinner together.

"Why did you get this for me?" Liza asked. "I don't understand."

"I want to be able to reach you. And for you to be able to reach me. In case of emergency."

She stopped poking at the buttons long enough to look up. "You expect an emergency?"

"I've learned to be prepared for anything."

Bootsie padded around the corner, probably smelling the food I'd pulled out for her. I placed her filled bowl on the small area rug near the counter and waited for her to pounce.

Back arched, she edged along the room's perimeter.

"Who is that Frederick guy, anyway?" Liza asked.

Bootsie froze in place for a split-second before spinning around and racing out of sight.

"What have you done to my cat?" I asked, crossing the room in three strides to see where Bootsie had gone. She wasn't in the dining room.

"Nothing," Liza said with a little whine in her voice. "How could I? I've been in the other house all day."

"Don't touch her. Got it?"

I turned around in time to see Liza roll her eyes. "I don't. I avoid her like the plague."

Taking a seat across from her, I started in on the news of the day. "Guess what, Little Sister? It turns out that the man who showed up here last night really is an FBI agent."

She ran a hand through her hair. "No way."

"Way," I said. "He's coming by again tonight to talk with you."

"What does he want with me?"

"I suppose we'll find out. I'll go out on a limb here and guess that he believes you can help him find Eric."

"No, no, no." She dropped both elbows onto the tabletop and splayed her fingers across her forehead. "How would I know where he is? I'm trying to keep away from him."

"So you say."

Her mood shifted from rattled to irritated in the millisecond it took to make eye contact. "What do you think? That I'm pretending? That I'm meeting Eric on the sly and we have some elaborate conspiracy planned?"

The doorbell rang. I pushed away from the table. "I wouldn't put it past you."

She followed me through the dining room and parlor, complaining the entire way. "Fine. I'll talk with this FBI guy. You know I wouldn't lie to the law."

I threw a scathing look over my shoulder.

"No really," she said. "I wouldn't."

I made sure to peer out the window before I opened the door. "It's not the FBI guy." It was a woman. She stood sideways, her head turned toward the street as though she'd just heard a noise she couldn't place.

"Who is it?" Liza asked.

Instead of answering her, I pulled open the big door.

At the sound, the woman turned. It was the same one who had come to ask about renting a room. I went momentarily speechless. "Hello again," I said.

Before I could get another syllable out, she tapped her chest. "Oh good, you remember me." She had on a more winter-worthy jacket this time, but still wore cowboy boots and the fluffy red scarf. She carried the same brown leather tote, filled to bulging. "Can I come in?"

"I don't see the point. We still don't have room for boarders." I began closing the door.

"Wait, please. One question."

"What?" I asked, against my better judgment. "My room-mates gave you good suggestions for places to stay."

"Everything is booked solid." She bit her lower lip, and lifted her brows in one of the most pathetic puppy dog looks I'd ever encountered. "This convention lasts for only a couple more days. Couldn't you let me stay here until the hotels open up again?"

"This is ludicrous," I said. "I don't believe for a moment that you're here to rent a room."

"Your couch, then. I said I'd sleep on your couch."

"Whatever your real story is, I'm not buying it."

Liza had skittered away when I'd first opened the door. Curiosity, or perhaps relief that it wasn't the FBI man, had brought her out of the shadows. "Who is it?" she asked, coming up behind me.

I started to close the door, this time for good.

I don't know if it was the look on Nina's face or the gasp from my sister that stopped me. Either way, I twisted between the two women like I was watching a furious game of Ping-Pong. Score: Liza distressed, Nina exhilarated.

"Go away," I said to the woman on the porch. "Don't come back."

I slammed the door as firmly as I could, leaning against it as blistering red-hot fury simmered in my chest. "What was that all about?"

Liza pretended not to understand, but her eyes were wild. "What do you mean?"

I pointed. "Nina Buchman. Who is she?"

Liza tried to adopt a "you're crazy" glare, but failed. "How should I know?"

"You recognized her," I said, pushing off from the door to follow Liza into the parlor. "And she recognized you. What in the world is going on here?"

Liza shook her head, hands dancing. "You're imagining things."

Squaring off opposite her, I folded my arms. "Right here, right now," I said. "No lies. No omissions. Who is she and what's going on?"

Liza flopped into my favorite wing chair and leaned her head back against the upholstery. "She works with Eric."

I didn't budge. "Doing what?"

"Don't know exactly. I didn't even know her name until you said it just now. They've been working together for a while." With a halfhearted laugh she got up to pull the room's curtains closed. "Kind of shutting the barn door after the horse gets out. Isn't that what Mom used to say?"

She returned to the chair, giving a quick appraising glance around the room, as though double-checking that there were no other ways to see inside. Pulling her knees up, she wrapped her arms around her legs and stared up at me. "That's it. And now she knows I'm here. Which means Eric knows I'm here." She flung one hand upward. "Or will, momentarily."

"If he's with this other woman," I said, making the obvious assumption, "why is he coming after you?"

She leaned forward, her feet hitting the floor with vehemence as though to force the words out faster. "He isn't *with* her. Not like that. They're colleagues." Twisting her hand in the air again, she slumped back. "Or something."

I waited.

"He wants me back," Liza said in a small voice. "That's why he's after me. He'll do anything he can to win me back."

"Uh-huh," I said.

"Fine, don't believe me. See if I care."

"Why do you keep so many secrets?" I asked.

Maybe it was my frankness—pure curiosity, stripped of judgmental overtones—that persuaded her to answer in kind. "We all have secrets, don't we?"

I sank into the sofa opposite her. "I suppose."

"Mom had lots of them."

"What do you mean?"

Liza gave me a look that suggested she pitied my ignorance. "You know as well as I do that this house meant more to her than it should." She waved her index fingers to encompass our surroundings. "Anyone else would have given this place up if her husband needed the money as much as Dad did. Not Mom. Even though we couldn't afford the upkeep. Why do you think that is?"

My heartbeat quickened. Could Liza know that our mom's biological father—Bennett's father—purchased this house for our grandmother back when our mom was a baby?

"She loved Emberstowne," I said.

That pitying look again. Liza rested her elbows on her knees and clasped her hands together. "The only reason a person keeps a money pit like this house is because they're tied to it on an emotional level."

My breath was quick and shallow. I hoped my cheeks weren't blazing red. Did Liza know? Had our mother shared the family secrets with her? Why not with me?

"You still don't get it, do you?" Liza asked.

My mouth painfully dry, I could do no more than shrug.

"Look at you. Look at me." She sat up straight and lifted her hands. "We barely resemble each other. I think Mom had an affair."

Relief *whoosh*ed out of me so fast I got lightheaded. "Is that what you think?"

Mistaking my reaction for shock, Liza laughed. "Why do you insist on wearing rose-colored glasses, Grace? Or are they blinders?" She seemed far more delighted than she should have at the prospect of our mother having had an extramarital dalliance. The idea was preposterous; our parents' marriage had been as solid as they come. But people like Liza—willing to deceive those she loved—had to believe that everyone around her was capable of duplicity as well.

"I . . . wow." Pulling my mangled thoughts together, I took a deep breath. "That's quite a stretch," I finally said.

"It fits. You have to admit it. Mom had all sorts of papers she hid from us. Like the Treasure Map. I wonder what ever happened to that after I snitched that you found it. Did you ever come across it again?"

I had. Finding it had helped me make the connection between our family and the Marshfields.

The doorbell rang again. Liza jumped up. "I'm not here," she said, hurrying into the kitchen. "Tell her she was mistaken. Give her a fake name. Or tell her I left the minute you shut the door on her. Tell her I ran off to . . . to . . ."

The rest of her words were lost as I dragged open the door once again, ready to let Nina Buchman know that my next step was calling the police.

"Ms. Wheaton?"

Caught short again, I took a moment to recover. I ran my hand through my hair and unlocked the outer door. "Agent McClowery. Come on in."

Chapter 22

I LED HIM INTO THE PARLOR, RAISING MY voice to be heard in the kitchen. "It's all right, Liza."

McClowery remained standing until my sister emerged. The expression on her face was at once both relieved and freshly alarmed. Having Liza here provided a roller coaster of emotional thrills for us all.

"Liza, this is Agent McClowery. I told you he would be visiting tonight."

She sauntered into the room, in full sassy-Liza mode. "But you didn't tell me how handsome he was."

Agent McClowery's impassive expression didn't change with Liza's exaggerated attempt to disarm.

"Please have a seat," I said. "Can I get you a drink?"

His overcoat was unfastened, but he didn't remove it. "No, thank you." He pulled out a notebook and pen and remained standing.

"I want to apologize for kicking you off my front porch the other evening."

He offered a quick smile. "Your local law enforcement

explained. Given the circumstances, your reaction was understandable."

Liza had curled up in my favorite chair again, feet tucked beneath her bottom. She'd adopted the waifish, damsel-in-confusion air she relied on when confronted with real-life issues she didn't care to handle.

"That said," McClowery continued, "now that you know my intentions are aboveboard, perhaps you'd be more inclined to share information on Eric Soames's whereabouts."

"When I ran you off last time, I thought you were a killer. That's why I went on and on about how I'd been engaged to Eric—so you'd understand that I had no connection with him anymore."

"Are you telling me none of that is true?"

I rubbed my forehead. "No, you misunderstand. I was—unfortunately—engaged to the man. Though I don't have any idea where Eric is right now, you're welcome to question someone who might." I extended my arm to indicate Liza, but I doubt he missed her slack-jawed reaction.

Not knowing how much background Rodriguez and Flynn had chosen to provide, I went on to explain. "Remember me mentioning that Eric threw me over for someone else?" I didn't wait for him to respond. "Here she is. My sister. She's in a far better position to help you than I am."

I got the impression that there wasn't much that took McClowery by surprise. This did. One eyebrow jerked upward. He settled it back almost immediately.

Liza ignored him, fixing her considerable hostility on me as she unfolded her legs and sat up straight. "Grace is right." She blinked rapidly, as though fighting tears. "He is a monster. That's why I left him." Her hate-gaze at me morphed into a soft and vulnerable stare directed toward the FBI agent. "That's why I'm here. My big sister took me in, thank goodness. Otherwise I don't know where I would have gone."

McClowery waited for her to finish. "Where is Eric Soames now?"

In a move worthy of Scarlett O'Hara, she draped fingers at her throat and said, "Why, how would I know?"

"She believes he's nearby," I said. "Don't you, Liza? Or have you changed your story from fifteen minutes ago?"

"My sister exaggerates," Liza said.

Before she could continue, I beat her to it. "Moments before you arrived, Agent McClowery, a woman showed up at my front door. In fact, when you rang, I thought she'd returned. She gave me the name Nina Buchman."

McClowery didn't express interest in my words but he wrote down everything I said.

"Liza and this Buchman woman recognized each other. Liza said that Eric worked with her," I continued, giving him the highlights of our conversation, and adding details about Nina Buchman's initial visit to the house.

During my explanation, McClowery flicked occasional glances at Liza, who kept her arms folded and stared at the floor.

"Why would Eric Soames follow you all the way back to Emberstowne?"

At that she glanced up, bright challenge in her eyes. "I broke his heart. Is that so impossible to believe?"

McClowery didn't comment. "Did you take anything from him when you left? Could he be after you to retrieve something?"

"Absolutely not," she said. "I used the last of my money for my train ticket here. I didn't take a penny that didn't belong to me."

"What about valuables other than cash? Anything at all?"

"Valuables? Eric? Are you kidding?" Liza let loose with a full-on snort. "Grace will tell you: I arrived here with all my worldly possessions packed into a purse." She indicated its size with her hands. "I'm stuck borrowing what I can from her. And as you can see from the way the two of us are built, that ain't much."

Liza's face began to glow as she talked. Her teeth

clenched and she fisted both hands. I wondered what had gone on between her and Eric that had inspired this level of animosity.

Unmoved by my sister's outburst, McClowery kept writing. When he finished, he looked up. "Tell me about Eric Soames's business dealings."

"He's a master at running a business into the ground," she said. "He has no aptitude, nor enough savvy, to run anything besides his mouth. Oh, he's good at selling you on an idea, believe me. Career con artists could take lessons from the guy. But when it comes to real work, he's gone. Won't lift a finger. All he wants to do is talk."

McClowery rubbed his nose, waiting, watching. "Let me rephrase. Tell me about people that Eric Soames dealt with. Names of those he interacted with."

She sat back. "I don't know any of them."

"Them?" McClowery repeated. "More than one, then? Who were they?"

"I told you. I don't know."

"Names?"

"I just said, I don't know."

McClowery worked his jaw. "Descriptions, then. Tell me what they looked like."

"I never saw any of them."

McClowery's eyebrow twitched enough for me to recognize skepticism.

"Come on, Liza," I said. "You clearly recognized Nina Buchman. Who else is there?"

McClowery's steady observation of Liza broke long enough for him to turn to me, and for the second time tonight I got the impression I'd surprised him.

"Here's the truth," Liza said, appealing to both of us. "I did see that woman once or twice, but that's it. She's the only one. Eric told me he had a big deal coming his way, bigger than I could ever imagine."

McClowery remained silent. I watched, trying to determine if Liza was lying.

"He promised this big windfall," Liza went on. "He's been promising it for about a year."

McClowery wrote that down. "Since when, exactly? What month?"

"I don't remember," she said dismissively. "All I know is that he promised this time would be different. He promised to make us wealthy and told me it was a sure thing."

"Who else was in on it?" McClowery asked.

Liza ran the tip of her tongue along her bottom lip. "Eric worked with a lot of people. He told me it was better if I never met them." After a quick beat, she added, "I swear that's the truth."

"You never met any of Eric Soames's associates?" McClowery asked. "Not even socially?"

Liza shook her head. "Eric wasn't much for going out. He was always on his computer."

"I understand," McClowery said softly, then gave the smallest grin, showing dimples. "But you strike me as a woman who doesn't enjoy being left in the dark. Weren't you curious? Even a little?"

"Of course I was curious," Liza said, but without the snarl.

Pen poised, McClowery waited.

"Okay, I followed him. But only once."

Keeping his voice modulated, his gaze sympathetic, McClowery asked, "What did you see?"

"Eric and that woman. They met a man at a coffee shop."

"What did they talk about?"

Liza shrugged. "I could never get close enough to hear. When the three parted company, I followed Eric and Nina. I was afraid they were . . . that Eric was . . ." She pulled her cheeks in. "I never saw the other guy again."

"You know his name?"

"No."

McClowery nodded. "Description?"

"I don't know. He was sitting, so I don't know if he was tall or short. He was good-looking." With a contemptuous glance at me, she added, "Better-looking than Eric, that's for sure."

"Age?"

Another shrug. "Older than me. Forty, maybe?"

"Build?"

"Average."

The questions went on for a few moments longer until it became clear to me, and apparently to McClowery, that Liza's description wouldn't do much to narrow the field.

He turned to me. "Detectives Rodriguez and Flynn tell me that you work at Marshfield Manor."

He hadn't phrased it as a question, but I felt the need to answer. "That's correct."

"Is there anyone at Marshfield who can vouch for your character?"

"Vouch for my character?" I spit out the words. "Apparently whatever Detectives Rodriguez and Flynn told you is casting me in a bad light."

"Not at all," he said. "But I prefer to be thorough."

"Why are you investigating me?" I asked.

He offered the faintest smile. "Again, I'm thorough."

"What *are* you investigating, anyway?" I asked.

"Sorry," he said, not looking sorry at all, "I'm not at liberty to discuss it. And who did you say I could speak with at Marshfield regarding your service there?"

I had half a mind to sic Frances on him, but thought better of it. "Bennett Marshfield," I said, spelling the first name as the agent wrote it down.

"He's a member of the family that owns the estate?" McClowery asked.

How an agent from the FBI could be involved in an investigation in Emberstowne and not know who Bennett was boggled my brain. "Yes. He's the last surviving descendent."

I almost tripped on my words, thinking about the DNA test and how its results might change the official family tree. "He lives on the property. I report directly to him."

"Thank you." He nodded to me and then to my sister. "Good night."

"You'll have to make an appointment to talk with Bennett," I said.

McClowery had the blankest eyes I'd ever encountered. "No, I won't."

Chapter 23

I HAD A SLEW OF ERRANDS TO RUN SATURDAY and the thought of dragging Liza along as I puttered from the cleaners to the library to the grocery store, with a stop at Amethyst Cellars to visit with Bruce and Scott, made me weary. Not to mention that taking her out in public with a killer on the loose made me worry.

There had been far too many people looking for Eric, far too many odd occurrences, and one too many murders recently for me to leave Liza home by herself, so I texted Tooney and asked if she could hang at his house for a few hours. He replied that it would be fine.

"Sending me off to daycare again, are you?" Liza said as she entered the underground passage. "This must be what it's like to have a baby, right? Can't go anywhere without making sure it will be safe." Patting her purse, she added, "At least I have my trusty cell phone, in case my sitter tries to take improper liberties."

"He won't."

"Bet you can't wait until I'm out of here."

I sensed Liza's visit was far from over. "The important thing is for you to stay safe."

"That's my big sis. Always taking care of me," she said, but with muted sarcasm. She ducked into the tunnel, then turned. "This time, Grace, I swear, I'm going to make everything right."

"I'm sure you will. Telling that agent about the guy you saw was a good first step. If you remember anything else—"

"That's not what I mean," she said. "I'm going to pay you back for all this. And then I won't ever owe you anything. We'll be even."

"I'm not keeping score, Liza."

Her mouth turned downward so sharply I thought she might cry. "That's because you're not the one who always comes up short."

With that, she spun and hurried away, swallowed seconds later by the darkness. I waited at the entrance until Tooney texted me that she'd arrived. I closed the iron door and headed back upstairs.

Bootsie greeted me at the landing, clambering at my legs until I lifted her up and cuddled her close. She purred deeply. I brought her to my face so we were nose to nose. "It's only temporary," I said. "I hope."

I GRABBED THE SHOULDER OF MY CAR'S PAS-senger seat, twisting to see behind as I prepared to back out of my driveway. My rear tires had barely made it to the sidewalk when movement in my peripheral vision made me stop.

A man on my porch peered into my front window. I threw my car into Park, pulled the keys out, and opened the door.

Hunched, with his hands cupped around his face, the man jumped back when Bootsie leapt onto the sill. In the space of the four seconds it took me to get out of the car I decided it couldn't be McClowery. The guy on my porch, now knocking on the window in a manner that suggested impatience, wasn't nearly as tall as the FBI agent. He wore a dark jacket, blue jeans, and a baseball cap.

When I slammed the car door, he spun.

Three thoughts bombarded me at once, freezing me in place: I should have anticipated this; I *had* anticipated this, but never imagined experiencing such a visceral reaction; and, in what world had I ever found him attractive?

"Eric?" I remained standing on the far side of my car, one hand propped on the roof. I hoped it read as casual. In truth, I needed a moment to steady my nerves. Not only was I experiencing a turbulent roil of surprise, the sight of him brought forth a rush of memories. Whatever good times we'd had together had been eclipsed by the pain he'd delivered when he left me for my sister. That I was overjoyed with the eventual outcome was beside the point. Seeing him again, after all that had transpired, was a shock to the system.

"Grace!" he said with more enthusiasm than he had a right to. "You're home. I thought I'd have to come back."

I strove to personify self-assurance. The woodpecker-speed pulse pounding in my ears and the sparkles of contempt clouding my vision had other ideas. *Keep calm*, I told myself. *Oh yeah, and remember to breathe.*

"What are you doing here?" I asked.

He loped down the front stairs, his head tilted to one side, his grin widening with every step. The baseball cap sported an impolite phrase emblazoned in orange. Sallow and thin, Eric was far less handsome than I remembered, his beard both new and spotty, bringing to mind a dog with the mange. "You look wonderful, Grace. It's great to see you again. Really."

Had I initially been drawn to him because, like Liza, he had the ability to turn on the charm at a moment's notice? I'd never met anyone so talented at faking sincerity. I'd grown up with Liza; maybe that relationship had imprinted itself on me so strongly that I'd subconsciously sought out a similar personality—and found Eric.

Mentally shaking off the psychological analysis, I repeated myself. "What are you doing here?"

When he made a move to come around the front of the car, I was struck with the horrifying notion he intended to give me a hug.

My hand shot up like a stop sign, halting him in his tracks. "Don't even think about it." He gave me a sheepish "can't blame a guy for trying" look, which I ignored. "You didn't answer my question."

"Come on, Grace. No hard feelings." He did his best to look abashed, hanging his head and even going so far as to kick a nonexistent pebble. "I thought by now you would have, you know, gotten over me."

The laugh that bubbled out of me satisfied my soul far more than any words could have. "Yeah, who'd a thunk?" I asked, deadpan.

He shifted his weight, watching with enough of a guarded expression that I knew my sarcasm had hit its mark.

"And now, for the third and final time: Why are you here? And where's my sister?"

My tagged-on inquiry seemed to throw him. But only for a second. "Ha ha, Grace." He pistol-pointed at me. "Good one."

An awkward silence filled the cold air between us. I let it stretch.

Stomping his feet, he pulled his bare hands up to his face and blew on them. "Now that you're home, maybe I can come in and we can talk?"

"I'm on my way out." I half hoped that admission would tempt him to try breaking in. My alarm would bring the cops running. Maybe McClowery, too.

He jerked his chin toward the house. "Is Liza home?"

"She's gone." It wasn't a lie. Not really.

"What do you mean?" He took a panicked step forward. "Where did she go?"

"Your friend Nina showed up and Liza got spooked." I shrugged to convey that my sister's departure was no big loss. "Why, exactly, did you follow her here? And why is she suddenly so afraid of you?"

Eric's Windbreaker offered feeble protection from the cold. His jeans were frayed and floppy. Incongruously, he wore black wing-tips, albeit scuffed ones. Warming his hands with his breath again, he shot a longing look at my house. "Can't we talk about this inside?"

When I pulled out my cell phone, he stepped backward. "Are you calling Liza?"

"I'm calling the police." I punched Rodriguez's number in and poised my finger above the lime-green telephone icon. "Answer my questions or I'll turn you in."

"For what?" His bluster was beginning to slip. "What would the police want with me?"

"Isn't that a fun question?" I asked. "Why don't you tell me?"

"Has anyone else been here?" he asked. "I mean, looking for me?"

"Maybe."

"Who?"

"How about you answer me, first. Why are you after Liza?"

"She left me," he said. "She didn't tell you?"

"Traveling across the country to get away from someone is a big deal. Having that person follow you across the country—with a sidekick of the opposite sex—makes me very curious. Now, let's try this again." Speaking very slowly, I repeated my question. "Why did you follow her here?"

"I screwed up." His regretful, abashed, rejected-suitor persona returned to the stage. "I messed things up and I hurt her. I can't live without her." His voice trembled. "I need her back."

"Okay. What else?"

"There isn't anything else."

I wiggled the phone. "Don't lie to me."

Comprehension dawned on him—a little late, but with sufficient force to get him to drop the beleaguered husband act. "You're different, Grace. What happened?"

I remained silent.

He hesitated, weighing his options, eyeing my phone as though it held the solution he sought. A stalemate on my driveway—not quite the efficient morning I had planned.

Rubbing his neck bristle, he finally broke the protracted silence. "Here it is, okay? Liza has information. Information that I don't want shared with anyone. And I mean anyone. I'm in a bind here—I'm in trouble."

"Go on."

"Liza is mad right now. I . . ." He waved a hand in the air. "I really hurt her. I didn't realize how much until after she'd left me."

"So you're here to apologize?" I couldn't help my skepticism.

He squared his shoulders spoiling for a fight. He hadn't expected me to push back, and it was almost painful to watch his brain switch gears and reassess strategy. How had I ever considered this guy anything beyond a conniving hustler?

"No, Grace," he said, dropping all pretense. "I'm not here to apologize. I'm here to convince Liza not to talk with anyone about anything."

"That's real specific."

"You don't want to know."

I'd suspected Liza of withholding information from the moment she'd shown up at Marshfield. While vindication bolstered my ego, it didn't resolve the problems at hand.

"Pretend I do want to know."

He pulled his mouth into a tight line. I couldn't tell if it was a calculated move to buy time or an effort to warm up his lips. "Liza hasn't spoken with your boss, Bennett Marshfield, has she?"

"What does Bennett have to do with any of this?"

"Has she?"

"I refuse to answer," I said, "unless you tell me what this has to do with Bennett."

His hands came up, shaking violently, as though throttling an invisible opponent. "Don't you get it? This could be life-and-death for me. Who has Liza talked to?"

Suave and in control when he'd first arrived, he'd now lost himself in a high frenzy I couldn't understand.

In crazed distress, he took another step forward. "Who has she talked to, Grace?"

I was tired of playing this game. "Good question," I said, hitting the Talk button. "Let's see if the police know."

His eyes flashed, wide and frightened. Slapping at my hand to dislodge the phone, he shouted, "No, no, no."

I held tight, racing around the back of my car as the call connected.

"Where are you staying, Eric?" I asked. "I'm sure they'll want to know."

The anger in his expression was murderous. Could Eric have killed the fake Fed? Fear and awareness kicked in with a high-powered jolt. Eric was capable, all right. At this moment, I had no doubt.

"Rodriguez?" I battled a tremor in my voice. "Eric Soames is here, on my driveway."

By the time I'd gotten the words out, Eric had turned and fled. "He took off west on Granville," I said above Rodriguez's exclamation. "He'll be gone by the time you get here."

"What is he wearing?"

I told him, then listened while Rodriguez directed activity on his end. I heard him issue a BOLO, or Be on the Lookout, for a man matching Eric's description. When he returned to me, he said, "We'll do our best to nab him before he disappears again."

I took in my surroundings. "I don't see any unfamiliar vehicles on the street. I'm guessing he didn't drive here. Too bad. We could have set up a stakeout around his car."

"Good thinking, but yeah, too bad. Did you talk with him?"

"At length," I said, then recapped our conversation.

"Sounds like Liza could put her husband behind bars if she has a mind to. Spouses aren't *required* to testify against each other, but that doesn't mean they can't. If your sister is ticked off enough, she could probably inflict real damage."

"And if he killed your victim, that Ochoa guy, what's to stop him from killing Liza to keep her quiet?"

"My thoughts exactly."

The wind kicked up, whipping my hair across my face. "You're at the station on a Saturday?" I asked. "Aren't you supposed to take it easy for a while?"

"Open homicide investigation. No rest until we close it. Back to your sister for a minute. Eric knows she's here, obviously."

"I told him she left," I said, and then remembered to explain about Nina Buchman's visit the night before. I was beginning to forget who I'd told what. "No idea if Eric believed me."

"We'll proceed as though we expect him to return. I'll have uniforms keep an eye on your house until we get answers."

As soon as we hung up, I dialed another number and stomped my feet to keep warm. I'd dressed for the weather, but cold began to seep in.

"Two phone calls in one day, Gracie?" Bennett asked when he picked up. "What's the occasion?"

I'd called him shortly before I left the house this morning to alert him to Agent McClowery's threat to drop by.

"Eric left here a moment ago."

Bennett's mood shifted. "Are you all right? What happened? Do you need me to come there?"

"I'm fine and thank you, but I've already talked with Rodriguez. They're after him. The reason I'm calling you is because Eric came here looking for Liza, but then cornered me to ask if Liza had spoken to you." I waited for that to sink in. "As far as I know, you and Liza have had only the one conversation in my office. Is that right?"

"That's correct."

"What's going on? Why would he bring up your name? Are you in danger? Is that why you opted to skip the FAAC this year?" A blip in my brain reminded me that the convention was in full swing. "Isn't that an odd coincidence?" I asked. "Eric shows up the day the convention opens, and this is the first time in years you're not attending?"

"Hold on a minute there, Gracie," he said in his most authoritative tone. "You're jumping subjects and imagining connections where none exist."

"Then what's going on? You've been very mysterious lately. Eric bringing up your name makes me nervous."

"There's no need for you to be nervous, I promise you."

"Bennett." My tremulous tone was the product of frustration and cold. "What is going on?"

"Nothing at all. Nothing to worry about."

It wasn't like Bennett to stonewall me. "Please," I said.

"Gracie," he said, "I don't know what to tell you."

"How about the truth?"

He went silent for far too long. As much as it made my insides scream with impatience, I waited. Finally, he said. "Do you have plans for tomorrow?"

The question took me aback. "Nothing important, why?"

"Come see me tomorrow afternoon. Say around two o'clock. Will you do that?"

"Of course, but what's going on?"

"Leave your sister under Mr. Tooney's care. If he's unavailable, let me know and I'll make other arrangements."

"Bennett?"

"Tomorrow, Gracie," he said, and hung up.

Chapter 24

"THIS IS BEGINNING TO GET OLD," LIZA SAID Sunday morning when I informed her that I planned to send her over to Tooney's house again. "Don't you lighten up on the weekend? What do you need to do that's so important that I can't come along?"

I wanted to answer: "Practically everything," but chose instead to deflect. "A meeting at Marshfield. Not everyone is available during the week, so we're required to hold off-hour conferences like this from time to time."

Playing with the cornflakes in her cereal bowl, she regarded me thoughtfully. "Convenient excuse," she said before taking a spoonful. "Don't know if I believe you."

"Doesn't matter what you believe." I stood at the pantry door, pretending to decide between oatmeal and raisin toast. Rather than silently debating breakfast food choices, however, I was arguing the merits and pitfalls of telling Liza about Eric's visit the day before.

I'd chosen not to say anything to her and had waited until after she'd gone to bed last night to whisper updates to Bruce and Scott. They'd agreed with me. Letting Liza know that Eric had stopped by would do none of us any good. She'd sworn that she'd left him and had no intention of ever going back, but if there was one thing I could count on from my sister, it's that she rarely told the truth. Sharing the fact that Eric had come looking for her could send her skittering right back into his arms.

I made a face. *That would get her out of my life again, wouldn't it?*

"Do you take this much time to pick your food every morning?" Liza asked, snapping me out of my reverie.

"Not usually." I snagged the raisin bread.

"Where are your roommates?"

"Bruce and Scott took off early today." I didn't mention that I keenly felt the loss of our trio's Sunday-morning newspaper ritual.

"Seems like they're out more than they're in," she said. "Is that normal, or is it because of me?"

Chalk one up to Liza's perceptiveness. "There's a lot of extra work to be done with so many people in town for the convention."

She finished her cereal as I began toasting my bread. "Look," she said, getting me to turn around. She'd gotten to her feet to carry her bowl to the sink, where she rinsed it and added it to the dishwasher. "I can be taught."

"Awesome." I went back to my toast.

"Maybe you'll see that it isn't so terrible having me around."

However faint, the suggestion of extending her stay made my stomach drop toward my feet. I was glad I had my back turned.

When I didn't respond, she stood next to me. My toast popped just then and I set to buttering it.

"Is it so bad?" she asked. "Having me here?"

"It's an adjustment," I said, veering away from the topic of prolonging her time in Emberstowne. "You and I have never gotten along the way sisters should. That makes it harder."

"I can change," she said.

Was that desperation I detected? Or another attempt to play me? "No one is asking you to change, Liza."

Her face dropped like I'd slapped her. "Excuse me; you've been trying to get me to be like you since we were little."

Pressing my two buttered toast sides together, I sliced them on a diagonal. "When we were kids, yeah. You're probably right. Whenever I perceived you were making a mistake, I corrected you."

"And you still do that today."

Facing her, I shook the butter knife from side to side. "No. I stopped a long time ago. Remember when Mom and Dad found out that you'd been stealing money from the people you babysat for? And drinking their liquor?"

"Only after the kids were in bed."

"Seriously? You still think that's a defense?"

"None of the kids ever got hurt."

"You got lucky." I put the knife down. "My point is that Mom and Dad came to me and asked me to have a talk with you. A heart-to-heart. They were crazy with worry and had tried reasoning, punishment, threats. Nothing worked. Your transgressions kept escalating."

"You did talk to me."

"Only after I told Mom and Dad that I'd been trying, all along. That I'd given up and couldn't do it anymore." Showdown time here. "Yeah, I talked with you, but if you recall, I didn't ask you to change. What I told you was that I wouldn't tolerate your bad behavior any longer. That until you made the decision to show consideration to the people in your life who cared about you, I was done."

She scratched the back of her head and looked away. She remembered, all right. "I thought that was just another way of telling me how to behave."

"Nope." I picked up my plate of toast and set it on the table while I poured coffee. "I was telling you that I can't control your behavior. I can only control mine. And my choice is to let you deal with your troubles yourself."

I sat. Liza sat across from me. "Then why am I here?" she asked. "You're letting me stay with you and you've even made arrangements for my safety. How is this making me deal with trouble myself?"

"Fair question." I chomped toast as I contemplated how to phrase what I wanted to say. Using my pinkie as a pointer, I continued, "I've provided you nothing more than a place to stay and a semblance of security. You may have noticed that, other than urging you to tell the truth, I haven't offered advice on what to do, where to go, how to live. Nor will I."

Her brows came together as though this was a fresh realization.

Talking around a mouthful of cinnamon and raisins, I went on. "That said, house rules are not to be trifled with. If you want to stay here, you won't step a toe over the line." I finished chewing and swallowed. "Do anything to hurt me, my roommates, Bennett, Bootsie, or anyone at Marshfield, and you're outta here. It's that simple."

BENNETT'S APARTMENT SAT ONE FLOOR ABOVE our offices. I made it there five minutes before two. Despite the fact that he'd encouraged me to let myself in whenever I liked, this part of the mansion was Bennett's home and I never felt right barging in unannounced.

When Bennett answered the door himself, I was taken aback. "Where's Theo?" I asked, referring to the butler who was most often on duty. "Does he have the day off?"

Bennett offered a perfunctory smile. "Indeed."

"What's wrong?" In the space of time it took him to allow me in, I couldn't help but notice that the lines bracketing his eyes and mouth seemed to have etched deeper since I'd seen him last.

"You'll know in a minute." He took both my shoulders in his hands and faced me straight on. "I'm sorry, Gracie."

Every ounce of energy in my body puddled to my feet

while every neuron in my brain fired with awareness that something terrible had happened. "Are you all right? You aren't ill, are you?"

With a sad smile, he released my shoulders, pulling me into a hug. "You are my rock, child." His voice rumbled in his chest. "You do me good."

I stepped back, confused. "Tell me what's going on." Another thought bounced up. "The DNA results?" I could hear the disbelief in my words. "They came back negative."

"My poor girl, I'm making this worse on you. No, the DNA results haven't come in yet." He pulled my hand into the crook of his arm. "There is much to explain. Fortunately, there is someone here who can do it far better than I. He's waiting in my office."

"But Theo isn't here," I said. Bennett allowing a person to remain unsupervised in his private rooms was unthinkable.

"I made an exception."

"Who is it?"

He didn't answer, but I didn't have long to wait. At the door to his office, he motioned for me to go first.

The man seated at Bennett's desk with his back to me, rose to his feet.

"Hello again, Ms. Wheaton," Agent McClowery said.

I stopped. My hand snapped up in a "wait a minute," move. I turned to Bennett. "Why all the secrecy? Why are you sorry?" I asked, referring to his bewildering apology from moments earlier. To McClowery, I said, "Is there more we need to discuss without my sister around?"

McClowery and Bennett exchanged a look I didn't understand. "Your questions are reasonable and I intend to answer them," the agent said. "I have a few questions for you, first, if you don't mind."

When I hesitated, Bennett touched my arm.

"Sure," I said.

McClowery's soft words held an ominous chill. "Please, have a seat."

We settled ourselves—Bennett behind his desk, McClowery and I across from him. Bennett's office, unlike his other private rooms and the rest of the mansion, offered little personality. A handsome space, decorated with law books and antique furniture and a handful of Bennett's art treasures, it provided no insight into the man's soul. Bennett liked it that way.

McClowery began. "Mr. Marshfield assured us, from the start, that you could be trusted with highly confidential information."

"From the start?" I repeated, directing the question to Bennett. "This isn't the first time you've met Agent McClowery?"

Bennett kept his hands folded on his desk, index fingers extended. He shook his head and used his pointing digits to direct my attention back to the FBI agent.

"Mr. Marshfield wanted us to include you in our discussions, but in situations like these—where secrecy is critical to an investigation—the Bureau prefers to release information on a need-to-know basis. When Mr. Marshfield informed us of your phone call warning him about Eric, we agreed it was time to bring you in."

He took his time, waiting for me to acknowledge his statement before continuing. "Mr. Marshfield's confidence in your trustworthiness, and my own impressions of your character from our interactions, have influenced my decision to bring you into our investigation at this time.

"I need your assurances that you will keep this conversation confidential and that you will share what we will disclose to you today with no one, especially your sister."

"I won't say a word. Of course not." The promise came out automatically, though my mental focus was elsewhere. Bennett had been working with the FBI? "How long has this been going on?" I asked.

"The investigation itself has been under way for a very long time," he said. "More than a decade. Mr. Marshfield's involvement, however, is relatively recent." He turned to

Bennett. "We've been working together for about how long? Three weeks?"

"Five," Bennett said.

I fought to keep my stricken reaction to myself. I failed. "How does this involve Eric?" I asked McClowery. "You came looking for him, right? That couldn't have been a ruse to assess me because . . . that other man, the one who was murdered, came looking for Eric, too." I could hear shock in my fast, furious questions. "Is my sister involved in this? She must be, it's too much of a coincidence." Taking a breath, I finally managed the central question: "What is this all about?"

McClowery reached into a satchel he'd propped against his chair. He dug out a letter-sized photograph and placed it in front of me on Bennett's desk.

"Have you ever seen this?" The agent's square-nailed thick fingers pushed the sheet closer to me. He said, "Take your time," but I could tell he was assessing my reaction.

"I've never seen anything like this before." The item in the picture, photographed next to a metric ruler for scale, appeared to be about the size of a box of facial tissues, standing on end.

McClowery kept silent.

"Is this gold? Are these"—I pointed—"precious stones?"

With two solid lengths of gold that twisted like the double-helix of DNA, the piece was structured like the hereditary material, but its resemblance ended there. The space between the edges was solid, littered with whorls of sparkling jewels. I couldn't imagine what purpose this thing served, or what it was meant to represent.

"Yes, and yes," McClowery said. "Can you guess the worth of a piece like that?"

I laughed, forgetting the tension in the room for a moment. "Are you kidding? Without more information, I'd be guessing."

"Fair to say, however, that it could be considered valuable?"

I nodded. "Very."

"You know the conflict surrounding the Temple of Sree Padmanabhaswamy, I assume."

"I do," I said. "When the temple's vaults were opened and vast treasures uncovered, the royal family of India, the government, and the public argued over ownership." I pointed. "Is this from that temple?"

"No." He gave me a sly smile. "Let me tell you another story, one you may not have heard."

I caught Bennett watching me. His sorrowful demeanor had broken and eager delight shone through. He leaned forward, eyes glittering with anticipation.

"Not far from the Indian temple, and by not far I mean on the same continent—"

I cough-laughed. "Asia covers a whole lot of area."

"For reasons of security, I am unable to be more specific at this time."

"Fair enough," I said.

"Let's call this location a sacred burial ground. Legend has it that the ruler of this region had a magnificent palace built into a mountainside. This was where he and his family would eventually be interred. He kept the exact location secret from all but his closest advisors."

Mountains? I began to review geography in my head to narrow down possibilities. A futile effort. Asia was simply too big. What I said was, "Kings, emperors, rulers of all kinds have been making elaborate plans for the afterlife since the beginning of time. Is this someone I've likely heard of? Can you tell me that much?"

"I'd prefer to keep specifics out of the discussion." With a conspiratorial glance to Bennett, he added, "I can tell you, however, that Mr. Marshfield was unaware of this particular dynasty."

Then most likely, I would be unaware as well. "I gather then, that these folks were super wealthy but obscure?"

"The region's culture might have been lost forever if not

for the efforts of a small, dedicated group of historians who made it their mission to rediscover the lost burial ground."

"I take it they were successful."

He nodded. "The treasures they uncovered far surpass those from the vaults of Sree Padmanabhaswamy. The historians were smart enough to keep news of their discovery from making headlines, but unfortunately, not savvy enough to prevent insidious forces from worming their way in."

"The government of—wherever this is—is claiming ownership?"

"Not quite. The inhabitants of the area surrounding the burial ground are a passive people, eager to trust. Unfortunately, it appears they are also easily deceived. Before the historians could summon professionals to assist the government in evaluating the cultural windfall, an item of extraordinary value was stolen." He tapped the photo. "This."

I studied the picture more closely, rotating it counterclockwise, trying to determine which way was up. "What is it, exactly?"

"A puzzle and a key," he said, returning the page to its original orientation. "Here." He indicated one of the odd-shaped item's long golden edges. "See that small mark? This piece is made up of eight intricately designed segments. Once assembled correctly—as it is in this photograph—it fits into a hollowed-out niche, unlocking the door to the treasure tomb of the burial ground."

"You're kidding me," I said. He wasn't, of course. "Sounds like something out of *Indiana Jones.*"

I'd expected him to show a hint of humor. Nope. The flat stare continued.

"The historians locked the tomb to protect it, but then this was stolen." He tapped the picture. "The ancient name is long and difficult to pronounce. We call it the jeweled key."

"Why are you looking for it? I wouldn't think the FBI would be called in. Don't you guys handle mostly domestic issues?"

"That is correct. The FBI would not ordinarily be involved in this matter."

"And yet, you're here in Emberstowne. Showing me this photo and looking for my sister's husband. What's the connection? Whoever stole this item from the burial ground had to be exceptionally clever. Eric isn't stupid, but this is way above his pay grade."

McClowery folded his hands in his lap. "That's where you and Mr. Marshfield come in."

AN HOUR LATER MY HEAD WAS SPINNING. McClowery, with Bennett's assistance, explained the whole intricate and confusing story.

The rogue who'd stolen the jeweled key from the tomb had done so at the behest of an unnamed broker—McClowery referred to him as "Mr. X"—who dealt primarily in black-market art and priceless antiquities. Mr. X used a go-between to offer the jeweled key for sale to a high-stakes bidder. Eric had been that go-between. What Eric hadn't realized is that the high-stakes bidder he'd been courting—on Mr. X's behalf—was McClowery, working undercover. The Bureau wasn't interested in Eric; they wanted to use him to snag Mr. X.

"We intended to recover the jeweled key in the process as well," McClowery said.

"I take it something went wrong?"

"I asked Eric for proof of the jeweled key's existence. That's standard procedure in such matters," he said. "According to Eric, the broker refused to allow him to take possession of such a valuable item. I suggested Mr. X show himself, to complete the transaction in person. That would have been ideal. Mr. X, however, countered by offering to allow Eric to bring me three of the eight pieces in a show of faith."

"Only three?" I asked.

During McClowery's explanation, Bennett had gotten up

to bring glasses and a pitcher of water. McClowery took a deep draught before continuing.

"Without all eight segments assembled together, the key is useless and considerably less valuable."

"What happened?"

"Eric never showed up. We feared Mr. X had gotten wind of the FBI's involvement, but no. Once Eric took possession of the three pieces"—McClowery opened his fingers like a fast-blooming tulip— "poof, he was gone."

"Can't you track him via his cell phone? Or credit cards? Isn't that how it works?"

"The cell phone in his name hasn't been used since he disappeared. Same for his credit cards."

"Maybe he's using Nina Buchman's phone and credit cards," I said. "Can't you track her?"

"We ran the name after I talked with you and your sister. It's an alias."

"Wow," I said, stunned by Eric's wily maneuvers. "You wouldn't think it would be so easy to drop out of sight. Not these days."

McClowery didn't comment. "Our initial fear was that Eric intended to melt the segments down and sell the gold and precious stones individually."

"He wouldn't, would he? Doesn't he realize what a tragedy that would be?" I was hit with a thought so terrible, it felt like a brick had dropped in my gut. "Could my sister have the pieces? Is that why Eric is after her?"

McClowery shook his head. "Your sister was never aware of the jeweled key's existence. I never met Liza until the other night because Eric told me—during our many meetings—that he preferred to keep her in the dark. She clearly didn't recognize me when I came to your house, and I believe her when she says she took nothing from him."

"Then why would he care that she's gone? Or ask if she's been in contact with Bennett?"

My many questions may have been taxing the man's

patience, but his stone-faced expression provided no clue. "You must understand that whenever we're undercover, we establish a bond with our subject. It's necessary to earn the subject's trust. Eric told me a great deal about his relationship with Liza. She not only possesses knowledge about him and his business dealings that could land him in prison, she is a conduit to Mr. Marshfield via her relationship to you."

"Wait, what?" I asked. "What possible reason could Eric have for wanting to connect with Bennett?"

McClowery hesitated. "We have reason to believe that Eric has initiated talks with another buyer interested in the jeweled key."

"Oh?"

Bennett cleared his throat. "Remember that gentleman you met downstairs last week?" he asked. "Malcolm Krol?"

"Yes, I do," I said. "You wouldn't tell me much about him."

"While our initial fear was that Eric would melt down the pieces for some easy cash, we discovered, through other sources, that Eric connected with Krol. In the world of priceless antiquities, the jeweled key is of enormous importance. Those who deal in the black market are salivating at the chance to possess even a single piece."

"But without the key, the burial ground people can't open the tomb," I said.

"Not without damaging the mechanism and ruining historical artifacts surrounding the lock," he agreed. "Everyone involved in preserving the burial ground would prefer to avoid destructive measures. The return of the key is of paramount importance to them." He gave a one shoulder shrug. "There are, however, many collectors with deep pockets and shallow scruples."

"Krol believes I am one such collector," Bennett said.

I couldn't contain my indignation. "How can he? You're the most honorable individual I've ever met."

"Krol believes that because we made him believe it," McClowery said. "We're working on two fronts here. Our primary goal is to apprehend Eric and use him to unmask Mr. X, thereby closing down his operations once and for all. Our secondary objective is to assist in the recovery of the jeweled key. All eight pieces, if possible."

Bennett leaned forward. "I know you were confused, and maybe even hurt that I wasn't being more forthcoming with my reasons for skipping the FAAC this year, but we couldn't risk Mr. X, or Krol, or Eric, approaching me in a public setting. The reception planned for Tuesday night is designed to flush out the person who possesses the jeweled key."

"Tuesday's reception, then," I began, "is a stakeout?"

Bennett nodded. "I wanted you in on it from the beginning." He threw a displeased look at McClowery. "They refused."

"The situation changed," McClowery said.

"Why did you come to my door and identify yourself as an FBI agent?"

"My cover was blown, which is why—we believe—Eric took off. He needed to find a new buyer. At this point, I can accomplish more with my credentials than I can working undercover." For the first time since I'd walked in, McClowery smiled. "Well, except for at our first meeting."

"And I chased you off." I saw no need to apologize again. "What about the fake FBI agent? Who was he?"

"Eric's disappearance upset Mr. X. He sent Emilio Ochoa here to find Eric. Or, more accurately, find him, kill him, and bring back the missing pieces of the jeweled key."

"Then who killed Ochoa?"

McClowery shook his head. "We still don't have the answer to that."

Chapter 25

"YOU WERE GONE A LONG TIME," LIZA SAID when I retrieved her from Tooney's care. "That had to be some meeting."

"It was."

As we headed up the stairs from the basement, she fingered her hair. "I don't like stumbling through that passageway. It's dark. And dirty."

I didn't bother answering. My mind was still on my conversation with Bennett and Agent McClowery. I wanted desperately to sit Liza down and grill her with questions until I was satisfied that she had no knowledge of the jeweled key, but there was no way to do so without breaking confidence.

"That Frederick," she began again when we were back in the kitchen, "what does he do for a living?"

"I don't know, exactly," I said. "He helped Hillary establish her business and seems to have had a good influence on her. I'm not entirely certain whether he's a small-time venture capitalist or a life coach."

"Hmm."

Her tone snapped me out of my musings. "Why do you ask?"

"Just curious. Nothing wrong with that."

"You asked me about him before."

"Did I?" Giving an indifferent shrug, she pointed upward. "I'm heading up for a shower. That walk underground makes me feel gritty."

LIZA SPENT THE REST OF THE DAY FOLLOWING me around, making small talk. It wasn't in my sister's nature to prattle on without purpose, but I didn't detect any ulterior motive to her chatter. She helped prepare dinner and didn't disappear when it was time to clean up. For the first time since her arrival, I didn't loathe every moment of our time together.

Dinner was over, the kitchen cleaned, and—at least for me—it was time to relax until Bruce and Scott got home. I pulled out the book I hadn't finished and got a roaring fire started in the parlor. Liza, surprisingly, picked up a book instead of watching television.

When I got up from my favorite wing chair to add a log to the blaze, she asked, "So why haven't you kicked me out?"

I was crouched on the floor. She was seated in the wing chair that matched mine, watching me with a patently curious look on her face.

"I thought we covered this." I poked at the new log, wedging it into the thick of the flames.

"Then pretend I'm dense. What's really going on? I don't for a minute believe that your sudden meeting today didn't have something to do with my being here. You've been way too cagey since you got back home."

I pushed myself up and returned to my seat.

Liza didn't wait for me to answer. "Are you working behind the scenes on a plan to kick me out? You're not talking with Aunt Belinda, are you? She hounds me relentlessly. I couldn't bear to live with that woman."

Bootsie crept into the room and after a few seconds' hesitation, bounded into my lap.

"Have you called her?" I pointed to the prepaid cell phone that poked out from Liza's purse on the floor next to her chair. "Aunt Belinda?"

"Are you kidding? If she knew I was here, she'd have a conniption fit that you didn't tell her. I'm protecting you, you understand."

"You're such a giver that way."

"What's really going on?" she asked again. "You know I can tell when you're lying so don't even try."

"No lies," I said. *But no reason to share the whole truth.* "You're here, you're afraid of Eric." I held up two fingers. "You have nowhere to go and, whether we like it or not, we're sisters." Four fingers straight up, I extended my thumb. "Last and most important, the fact that the murder victim came here looking for Eric right before you showed up convinces me that you're in deeper trouble than you realize. You may annoy the heck out of me, but I'm not about to throw you into the arms of a killer."

"You think Eric did it, don't you?"

"It's crossed my mind." I waited a beat. "What do you think?"

Her eyes reddened as she stared into the fire. "Eric wouldn't hurt me."

With no sound but the urgent crackle of the flames and Bootsie's gentle breathing, I took a chance. "Then what does he want from you, Liza?"

She met my eyes. "I don't know," she said. "I knew he was hiding things from me, but I didn't pay attention. I was . . ." She stared away again. "My mind was on what I *thought* was important."

"Liza?" I asked, keeping it quiet, "What aren't you telling me?"

She shook herself and coughed up a smile. "Nothing. Nothing important, at least. It's done."

* * *

THE NEXT MORNING, FRANCES MET ME WHEN I walked in. She stood a few feet inside the door to her office, tadpole brows arched over her half-glasses and thick arms folded across her chest. "Well, well, well," she said, alerting me to her level of pique, "thought you'd pull one over on me, did you?"

I shrugged out of my coat and took my time hanging it on our office rack. "I don't have a clue what you're talking about."

Her sensibly shod foot beat a breakneck rhythm against the floor. "When were you going to tell me that the Mister invited you to attend his soiree tomorrow night?" At the word *soiree*, her chubby fingers untucked themselves from their tight elbow nests, flying high to pantomime air quotes. "Last I heard, you and I were to stay away from this one. Let the Mister have his 'secrets.'"

"Oh, that," I said. How did this woman always get the scoop so accurately and so quickly? I had to believe she was still in the dark about the FBI's involvement, but we were talking Frances here. I couldn't be too sure.

"Yes, that." The shoe kept up its frenetic pace. "Thought you'd sneak that past without me noticing, did you?"

"Not at all," I said. "You didn't give me a chance. I just walked in, remember? I would have told you."

She narrowed her eyes. "I talked with the Mister this morning when I first came in."

"Oh, so he told you?" That surprised me. "You see? No big secret."

"He did not." Frances's dark brows jumped with each word.

"Then I don't understand. How did you find out?"

She led me around her desk and pointed to her computer monitor. "Look at that."

An open e-mail took up the screen. I skimmed. It was a

message from Bennett to Terrence, Marshfield's head of security, confirming that I had been added to tomorrow evening's list of expected guests.

"But . . ." I said, pointing, "you're not on this e-mail string. How did you get it?"

She waggled her head. "It was sent to me."

I double-checked the header. "No, it wasn't. This was sent directly from Bennett to Terrence." Now I folded my arms. "Explain."

She pursed her lips. "Davey helped the Mister get comfortable with e-mail."

"I know that. It doesn't explain this."

Again the head waggle of discomfort. "I thought it would be good if I helped the Mister out when I could. The Mister had Davey set things up so that whenever he sent something, it would automatically send a duplicate copy to me."

"Are you telling me that you've read every single one of Bennett's e-mails? For the past—what?—two years?"

She lifted one shoulder in a "so what?" move.

"Why didn't you tell me about this?"

"Why should I?" Her back rigid with indignation, she clamped her fists into her hips.

"Because . . ." Having to explain the magnitude of this impropriety rendered me speechless. "Where to start?" I finally sputtered, "Your actions are unethical, dishonorable, immoral."

"Throw a few more of those fancy words at me, why don't you?" she said. "You know as well as I do that my job here is to protect the Mister. If keeping tabs on his e-mails helps me do that, so be it."

Making a mental note to talk with Davey to ensure Frances's access was curtailed, I shifted gears. How much did Frances know about Bennett's involvement with Agent McClowery? I couldn't very well come out and ask.

Adopting a brisk, businesslike attitude, I wiggled the fingers of one hand in a "give it to me" gesture. "What else?"

Her pupils were pinpoint sharp. "What do you mean? What else is there?"

"I'm asking you what else you know about Bennett's business that you shouldn't." I held up a finger, stopping myself. "Wait, let me rephrase that because I know you believe there is nothing you shouldn't be aware of. What else have you learned lately from reading Bennett's e-mail?"

Her cheek twitched. "After the way you attacked me just now, I should keep you guessing."

She was toying with me. Expecting me to explode. And I was close. With one arm across my body propping up the other arm's elbow, I kept one hand snug against my mouth in an effort to keep myself reined in. She took her sweet time deigning to answer me. I couldn't tell if it was because she knew about the FBI's interests or if there was some other bombshell about to drop.

"The stress of having your sister living with you is affecting your mood and that's why you're so confrontational with me."

The slow delivery was excruciating. Struggling to keep my impatience in check, I bit the tip of my thumb.

"You feel powerless to control your sister, so you're taking it out on me. That's it, isn't it?" she asked.

I strained for calm, reminding myself that Frances always cooperated better when she believed she held the upper hand. "My sister's presence *has* been affecting a lot of my decisions," I said. "Thank you for your concern. Back to Bennett's e-mails. I need to know everything you've uncovered, whether or not you think it's important."

She watched me closely. "Is there anything in particular?"

Teeth working my lower lip, I gave her a "whatever" look. "You never know what's important until you see it."

"As it happens," she said, "the Mister doesn't send a lot of e-mail messages. He's old-fashioned and prefers to pick up the phone. I think the only reason he sent this one instead of calling is because Terrence e-mailed him a couple of days ago, requesting an update."

"You get copies of every e-mail Bennett receives, too?"

"*Pheh*," she said. "Who would want to sift through someone else's junk mail? If there's something interesting I need to know, it'll be underneath when the Mister responds."

"You haven't answered my question. What else have you learned?"

She twisted her mouth to one side. "That's it. The only one. I told you that the Mister doesn't send very many. This was the first e-mail he'd sent in about a week. Nothing interesting in the prior ones." Frances seemed disappointed to be unable to offer a juicy scoop. "It's not that the Mister isn't savvy enough to navigate e-mail. He simply doesn't care to."

"Okay, good." My entire body relaxed and my fists unclenched.

She folded her arms again. "What's on your mind? You're about as tense as I've ever seen you." The foot started tapping again. "What aren't you telling me?"

"It all comes back to my sister." I managed a self-conscious laugh. "You remember how much she wanted to talk with Bennett and how we wouldn't allow that? I was afraid she'd attempt an end-run around me."

"You don't think I would have told you if the Mister had been e-mailing with her?"

I worked to sell the story I was fabricating on the fly. "Think about it, Frances. She doesn't have a computer. She would've had to hack into mine and use my account. Messages would've looked like they came from me."

Frances's pursed lips twisted to the other side of her face. I wasn't sure she was buying it completely, but she gave grudging acceptance. "She's a wily one."

"I've done my best to keep her out of trouble, but you never know."

Behind me, the door to Frances's office opened, and Bennett strode in. "Good morning," he said, his voice booming with such good cheer that I wondered if there had been a break in the jeweled key investigation. "Am I interrupting an important discussion?"

"An enlightening one, I'd say." Ignoring Frances's laser-eyed warning, I let Bennett know about my assistant's access to his sent e-mails.

He curled a finger in front of his lips and I watched as he ran through a silent, mental checklist. Nodding, he gave me a meaningful look. "No harm done," he said.

"Good. I'll talk with Davey and get that changed."

Frances grimaced. "I don't see why it's such a big deal."

Bennett recognized her hurt feelings. He took her hand and patted it. "You've seen nothing that I wouldn't have been willing to share in person." He spoke to Frances, but I knew his words were directed to me. My relief was complete.

Frances was not so easily mollified. "What about confirming Grace's invitation to your fancy reception here tomorrow night? It was bad enough when we were both left out. Now it seems I'm the only one who isn't worthy."

"That's not it at all," Bennett said. He didn't explain further. I was glad, because Frances could sniff out a lie in no time. I'd barely skated by with my lame excuse about Liza accessing my computer. "Let's switch to a far more critical subject."

Had Frances been a Martian from a '60s TV show, her antennae would have sprung to attention at Bennett's use of the word *critical*.

"What's going on?" she asked.

Bennett lifted his chin. "The DNA results are in. From both labs."

"And?" Frances shouted. Or maybe it was me.

Bennett's mood was upbeat, yet guarded. A little jittery. Not happy enough for me to believe that we'd gotten the outcome we'd hoped for. Not disappointed enough if our expectations had been crushed. He seemed nervous. I know I was.

"I've invited representatives from both labs to present their findings to us here. Tomorrow."

Frances went speechless, but only for a moment. "You didn't *ask*?"

He shook his head. "I wanted us to hear the news together. I want you to be there, Frances. And Hillary, and whoever else we deem *worthy*." Stressing the same word that Frances had used moments earlier, he winked. "Tomorrow's news could be life-changing. Let us give this momentous occasion the respect it deserves."

I folded my hands in front of my face, inexplicably glad to have one more day to not know the truth. I wanted to be related to Bennett by blood. I wanted to be his family. I'd allowed myself to believe it could be true. Tomorrow's news could destroy that possibility forever.

"Here, you say?" Frances asked. "What time?"

"Early. Before the doors open for tours. I'd like everyone here by seven. When planning began for tomorrow evening's reception, I didn't know the results would be in. Tomorrow, it seems, will be exceptionally busy. I'd like to know the truth before . . ." He faltered. "Before the day gets away from us."

My stomach clenched. Bennett wanted to know the truth—wanted everyone to know the truth—before the FBI confrontation tomorrow night. Fear clawed its way into my chest.

"Why before the reception, Bennett?" I asked. "Is there something you aren't telling me? Are you expecting problems tomorrow night?" What a stupid question, I thought, even as the words rushed out my mouth. Of course there would be danger. While the FBI would be present at the event, so might the killer.

"Problems?" he asked with a laugh and a penetrating look to remind me not to arouse Frances's curiosity more than we already had. "Don't be silly, Grace. I'm expecting tomorrow evening's event to be boring and bland."

Too late. Frances arched a brow. "Then why host?" she

asked. "Particularly if you've made it a point to avoid the FAAC."

"It is expected of me." The finality in his tone was impossible to ignore.

"What about that item you talked about?" she persisted. "Or rather, that you wouldn't talk about? The mysterious item you hoped to obtain? Any news on that?" Before he could answer, she lifted her chin. "Or is that the real reason for this reception? You hope to close the deal and you don't want me to know about it?"

Bennett raised his hands in supplication. "You found me out, Frances. I should have known not to try to hide the truth from you."

It was clear she couldn't tell if he was being sarcastic or truthful. "*Hmph*," she grunted. "That better mean you're planning a surprise for me."

Chapter 26

WHEN MY DESK PHONE JANGLED, I JUMPED, noticing, belatedly that Frances stood in the doorway.

"Who is it?" I asked.

"Your caller ID isn't working? How should I know?"

"It's Amethyst Cellars," I said, puzzled.

"Must be important."

Scott was on the other end. "We don't like to bother you at work, Grace, but we have a weird situation here."

Visions of Liza having slunk out from under Tooney's care made me grip the plastic handset tighter. "What happened?"

"Everything is okay," Scott said. "I didn't mean to alarm you."

The more he waited to tell me the reason for his call, the more alarm built in my twitching chest. "What's going on?"

"Do you remember that woman you met here the other night? Phyllis Forgue?"

"What's up with her?"

Scott told me he was in the back room, but still kept his voice extra quiet. "She's here again. She's been every day since she met you. We're thrilled because she buys wine every time, but it's obvious she's waiting for someone."

"Okay," I said, drawing the word out. "I'm not understanding."

Scott grew even quieter. "We think she's waiting for you."

"Why?"

"Call it a sixth sense, or whatever you want, but you've gotten me and Bruce to pay closer attention when something doesn't feel right," Scott said. "She spends time tasting and talking with the staff but always turns the topic to Marshfield and Bennett. And you. Especially you."

"It's not like she and I connected personally."

"Exactly. She seems disproportionately interested in your work with Bennett. Not to mention disappointed that she hasn't run into him at the FAAC convention yet."

"Nor is she likely to," I said. "But she'll see Bennett at the reception tomorrow night."

"Are you sure she was invited?"

I thought about how often Bennett had hedged on details recently. But ever since I'd been brought in on the FBI initiative, I'd assumed I was fully informed. "To the best of my knowledge, she was. I'll check on that."

"Thanks, Grace. I know this sounds like no big deal. But Bruce and I both think it's curious that this woman in town for the FAAC is spending so much time away from the convention to hang around us, talking about you."

"I'm glad you told me." I glanced out the windows. A soft snow was beginning to fall. "Is she still there?"

"She just pointed out three more wines she wants to sample. I assume she's sticking around for a while."

"I'll swing by now and have a chat with her. Maybe I can find out what's really going on."

"We don't mean to pull you away from work," he said.

"Your vague sense that something's wrong is good enough for me." Before he could answer, I continued, "Plus, I have news to share. I'll be there in about twenty."

When we hung up I called Bennett. "You mentioned Phyllis Forgue was invited to tomorrow night's reception."

"That's right," he said.

"Is there any reason why she'd keep that fact under wraps?" I explained Scott's phone call. "I'm going there now."

Bennett's voice was a growl. "I'm not certain that's a wise decision, Gracie," he said. "Is Frances within earshot?"

I knew the answer without looking up. "Most definitely."

"Then I won't expand. I will say this much: Remember that the item I'm seeking is also being sought by others. Others who may be willing to harm innocent people to obtain it."

"I know that."

Frances had moved closer to my desk, but not close enough to hear Bennett's end of the conversation.

"If Phyllis Forgue is part of this chase . . ."

"I'm sure she isn't."

"Gracie." His voice was a warning.

"It's the middle of the afternoon," I said, mindful of Frances's intense scrutiny. "And even though I've tried very hard to stay busy, I can't concentrate. I'm worried, worked up, and nervous about the DNA results. I'm taking the afternoon off, if that's all right with you."

Another growl from his side of the phone. "It seems you won't be talked out of this errand." Not a question. So I didn't answer.

What I did say was, "Just to be clear: You can't think of any reason why Ms. Forgue wouldn't brag about having an invitation to your event?"

"No."

"Would it be all right if I ask if she plans to attend?" I smiled innocently at Frances. "You know, to help confirm head count."

I could practically hear the aggravation I was causing him.

"Like I said," I continued, "it's the middle of the afternoon. I'll pop in and out. No problem. Unless there's a specific reason why I shouldn't bring it up. I mean, I know you confirmed her invitation the other day . . ."

Boy, it was tough to communicate with Frances hovering. What I wanted to ask was whether or not the FBI would have a problem with my interacting with Phyllis Forgue.

"Go ahead. But please be careful. Will you do that for me?"

"Of course."

When we hung up, Frances glared. "I don't know what's going on between you two, but I'll find out. Count on it."

PHYLLIS FORGUE'S PALE FACE LIT UP WHEN I stepped into Amethyst Cellars. I waved hello and unzipped my coat as she crossed the room to greet me.

"Grace! I was hoping to run into you again."

"Very nice to see you, Phyllis." I feigned surprise. "But why are you here? I would have expected you to be at the FAAC."

"Oh that," she said, flipping a dismissive hand. "The convention is so much less interesting without Bennett to chat with. How is he? Why haven't we seen him? The convention is nearly over and he hasn't made an appearance yet."

She didn't wait for me to answer. "His assistant called me to let me know that he wouldn't be able to meet with me, but didn't explain why. At that point I still believed I'd see the old devil at the FAAC, so I didn't press the issue. Now I wish I would have."

"Well," I said, trying to come up with a vague enough response, "we've been very busy at Marshfield lately."

Her fair brows came together. "His assistant wasn't forthcoming with information, let me tell you. A very brusque man. I don't understand why Bennett keeps an employee like that."

I'd put money on the "assistant" being Agent McClowery. For lack of anything better, I said, "Bennett is a patient man."

We made our way to the middle of the longer of the two bars in the wine shop, where she'd left her tasting notes. Amethyst Cellars was quiet at the moment. Two small groups—one at the far end of this bar, one group at the other—were participating in tastings. No one paid us any attention.

I had no reason to be there, really. I didn't suspect Phyllis Forgue of anything worse than narcissism. The only reason I'd made the effort to talk with her was because I trusted my roommates. I couldn't dismiss their worries.

"Phyllis," I began, doing my best to adopt a conspiratorial air, "you are planning on attending Bennett's reception tomorrow night, aren't you?"

In a heartbeat she shifted from eager to manic. "I certainly am," she whispered. "Everyone is talking about it, but I think the fewer people who know, the better." She winked.

"I understand," I said, as though I did. "Last time we met you mentioned a specific item you were interested in acquiring. Have you had any luck?"

She glanced about the room, taking in the busy wine tasters to ensure no one listened in. "There's a rumor floating around this year that Bennett has—shall we say—loosened up a little?"

She'd phrased it as a question, but I had no idea how to answer.

"Go on," I said.

"You don't deny it?"

Playing along until I had a better idea of her point, I fixed my expression and said, "I can neither confirm nor deny."

She pursed and released her lips in rapid succession so many times that her signature cinnamon tint began to smear. After another wary glance around the room, her green cat eyes bore down on me. "Bennett has always been Mr. Clean when it comes to provenance. He won't touch—won't even look—at a piece unless its ownership history is well-documented and pristine."

Phyllis wasn't telling me anything I didn't already know. "Recently, however . . ." She smeared her lips together again. "The high-rollers are talking about how Bennett has his eye on a certain piece. That this item is so important to him and he desires it so much that he doesn't care how he gets it."

Perspiration gathered at my neckline. "Phyllis," I said, "it seems we have a great deal to discuss." I removed my coat, buying myself time to play this moment correctly. Did Phyllis have the jeweled key? Was *she* the mysterious black market collector the FBI had been after all these years?

I detected a faint sheen above her sparse brows. She dragged her fingernails against her cheek, clearly impatient for me to continue. I think she was holding her breath.

"You do know that Bennett and I work together extremely closely," I said.

She nodded.

"Good. Then am I to understand you are in possession of this elusive item?"

"Hypothetically," she began, "if I were able to produce it, would Bennett be willing to meet with me? Alone, I mean?"

The last thing the FBI would approve—the last thing I would want—would be for Bennett to meet with anyone alone. I raised an eyebrow, serving up the best look of skepticism I could muster. "Maybe we need to confirm that we're talking about the same item, first."

The light in her eyes dimmed ever so slightly. She ran long fingers through her red waves. "Word is, the reason why Bennett hasn't made an appearance at the FAAC this year is because he's waiting for the item to come to him."

I made a so-so motion with my head, encouraging her to keep talking.

"That's why he's hosting this reception, isn't it? So that he can complete the transaction on his home turf?"

Choosing my words carefully, I said, "You have to admit it would be safer that way. For all parties."

She stared out the condensation-fogged windows for a moment as though considering her next move.

"The item?" I prompted. "Do you have it?"

Her green eyes snapped back into focus, lasering on me. "Lovely seeing you again, Grace." She spun her heavy coat around her shoulders, hitched her purse into the crook of her elbow, and started for the door. Over her shoulder she called, "Please tell Bennett that I look forward to meeting with him tomorrow night."

"What was that all about?" Bruce asked when she was gone.

I shook my head, unsure of what had happened. Phyllis had never confirmed that she was in possession of the jeweled key. And yet, would she have? Given the item's history and value, it wouldn't make sense to make such a risky admission in the middle of a wine shop to someone she'd met only once.

An assistant took over tasting duties for Scott, freeing him to sidle up in time to hear me answer. "I'm glad you called me down here. I can't say I know much more than I did, but Phyllis Forgue is definitely worth watching."

Scott grinned. "Glad to hear it. We felt a little embarrassed making the call. We don't want to be paranoid, but something wasn't right."

Quick to change the subject before they pressed for details I couldn't provide, I said, "I have another, entirely selfish, reason for skipping out of work to come see you. Bennett stopped by my office this morning." I drew a deep breath. "The test results are in."

The two of them chorused in unison, "And?" exactly the way Frances and I had.

"Bennett didn't ask. He wants to have the great unveiling tomorrow morning at Marshfield. With friends, family, and lawyers in attendance, of course."

Bruce wore a lopsided grin. "He seems pretty certain of the results. Are you sure he hasn't gotten a sneak peek?"

"Bennett wouldn't fib. Not about this."

"Does he seem nervous at all?" Scott asked.

"A little."

"Will you call us as soon as you find out?"

"Are you kidding?" I asked. "I want you both to be there. Bennett set the meeting up for seven in the morning. I thought that was early enough for you to still make it here before the shop opens."

The two of them whooped so loudly everyone in the place turned to stare. "Sorry," Scott said to the small crowd.

"I need to head home and make a few other arrangements before tomorrow," I said.

Bruce ran a hand across his chin. "Liza?"

"Yeah," I said. "Liza."

Chapter 27

ONCE HOME, I TEXTED TOONEY TO LET HIM know I'd be visiting via the underground passage. He and Liza met me in his basement. When I'd first come down here, while Todd Pedota still owned the house, there had been stale water puddles on the concrete floor and an overwhelming aroma of mildew. The first thing Hillary had done when she began her remodeling was clean the house from top to bottom, starting with this basement. Today, with updated light fixtures, scrubbed clean floors, and a fresh coat of white paint on the walls, the place smelled brand-new.

Tooney's relief was impossible to miss. "You're home early."

"Couple of glitches at work today," I said.

Liza's eyes sparked with mischief. "Do I have to go home already, Mommy? But I'm having so much fun here playing with Ronny." She tilted her head, resting it against Tooney's arm. He stepped away.

"Bronson," I corrected her. "Remember?"

"Oh, I like calling him Ronny. It's such a cute name for

such a cute playmate." She wiggled her nose at Tooney, the gleam in her eyes turning hard when she faced me. "I can't think of anything I'd rather do all day than sit in this dump and wait for you to come home."

"Poor baby," I said. "Listen, Tooney—er—Bronson . . ."

"Grace, please." A corner of his mouth curled up, but I could tell he was weary and the effort taxed him. "Call me Tooney. You always have and I've kinda gotten used to it."

I smiled. "Thanks. What I was about to ask is if you have a couple of minutes to talk?"

With an uneasy glance at Liza, he pointed a thick finger into his chest. "Me? By myself?"

Answering his unasked question about how to conduct a private conversation while maintaining watch over my sister, I said, "Let's go back to my house. Liza, you can find something to do upstairs for a few minutes, can't you?"

"Another meeting I'm not privy to?" She worked her jaw from side to side. "A girl could develop a persecution complex around here."

"Grace, is that you?"

The pointy heels of Hillary's boots clunked the bare wood as she made her way down the steps. Frederick, a smiling, spectacled lump of a man, followed her, raising his hand in greeting.

"Hillary," I said. "I'm glad you're here. Do you have a few minutes?" I gestured vaguely in the direction of my house.

Liza perched a hand on her hip. "Are you inviting them to your secret meeting, too?"

Bennett's stepdaughter either wasn't paying attention to Liza's complaints or had another matter on her mind. "Yes, I do have a few minutes," she said with emphasis. "You and I need to talk."

It suddenly seemed foolish to have five people traipse through the passageway only to ensure Liza's seclusion, but I couldn't trust her upstairs in Tooney's house alone. Who knew what sort of mischief my sister might get herself into?

"Hey." I remembered that I'd reset my burglar alarm when I'd first gotten home. Liza didn't know about the secondary alarm—the one that sounded here at Tooney's if anyone entered or left my house without disarming the system. "I have an idea, Liza. You keep complaining that I don't trust you. Here's your chance to prove yourself. Go on back to my house. When I'm finished here, I'll join you."

"What's the catch?"

"No catch," I lied, counting on the fact that my sister wouldn't think to check the burglar alarm's status. "In fact, we'll go upstairs now to talk. If you'd prefer to wait down here for me, that's fine, too."

Liza studied me for a moment. "Fine. I could use a shower," she said. A moment later, she'd ducked into the passageway and was gone.

"Let's go upstairs," I said.

Tooney frowned at the iron door. "You sure this is a wise move?"

Hillary's cheeks were bright pink. She looked ready to explode before we made it up the stairs.

"I set the alarm," I told Tooney.

"Ah," he said. "Then yes, let's go up in case we need to chase after her."

Clearly fuming, Hillary managed to hold her tongue until we were gathered in the kitchen. "That sister of yours." Spittle formed at the corners of her mouth. She wiped it away. "How dare she? How dare she?"

"What happened?" I asked, taken aback by her sudden vehemence.

"Who does that girl think she is?"

Frederick, standing close to Hillary, tucked her hand into his arm and patted it while whispering words only she could hear. Hillary's sputtering diminished but her eyes continued to blaze.

"Uh . . ." Tooney stretched his chin. "Your, uh, sister . . ."

Frederick shot me an apologetic look. "She doesn't mean any harm. Not really."

I wasn't sure if he referred to Liza or Hillary. "Who are you talking about?"

Hillary stifled an exasperated scream, but only barely. "He means your sister, but he's wrong." Turning to Frederick, she said, "I'm sorry but this time I know I'm right. I've been that girl—and let me assure you she knows precisely what she's doing."

"It doesn't matter though, does it?" Frederick asked Hillary, very quietly.

"What doesn't matter?" I was beginning to guess.

Tooney tried again. "Your sister seems to . . . uh . . . be, um . . . attracted to . . ."

Hillary faced Frederick. "Are you certain you aren't tempted? Are you sure? She's so young. With a killer bod. She's at least ten years younger than I am."

Closer to fifteen, but I decided to keep my mouth shut.

Frederick took both of Hillary's hands in his. I watched the woman's stricken, anguished face soften as her eyes searched his. "I'm not tempted," he said softly. He stared up at Hillary with sweet adoration. "How could I be when I have you?"

Clearing my throat, I took a quick look around. Again, a mirror image of mine, the kitchen's walls had been restored with vintage tiles. Mine were pink, these were white with blue accents throughout. With shiny new appliances and floral décor, it didn't scream bachelor, but was a warm and welcoming room. "This kitchen looks fabulous, Hillary. You've done a marvelous job."

Her body had returned to a more restful pose. "Thank you."

Tooney walked over to the wall where his end of the burglar alarm had been installed. "Your house is still hot," he said. "So far she hasn't disarmed the system."

"Good. I don't want to tempt fate by taking too long here, but I wanted to share some news with all of you."

I opened the basement door to assure myself that Liza hadn't returned to listen in from the stairway before continuing. "Frederick, I know you're aware that Bennett and I submitted DNA for tests to determine kinship."

He nodded. Hillary said, "Papa Bennett called me earlier to tell me that the results are in. He wants us all to gather tomorrow to hear the news together."

"That's right," I said. "Bennett wants us there early, before Marshfield opens for the day." I provided necessary details. "But until we know for sure, one way or another, and until I can sort things out with my sister, I'd prefer it if we still kept this from Liza."

"I expect you'll want to bring her over here extra early tomorrow morning," Tooney said.

Much like Frederick had done with Hillary, I turned to Tooney. Instead of taking his hands, however, I held both his solid forearms. "I made other arrangements for Liza tomorrow because I want you to be there for the results, too," I said.

"You want me there? For the big announcement? Why would you want me?"

"How can you ask that, Tooney? You've been here from the very beginning. You're one of my best friends."

He swallowed and looked away, his eyes reddening. I let my hands drop as he stepped back to tug a wrinkled white handkerchief from his pocket. He wiped his eyes and face and mumbled about there being too much dust.

"You'll be there, won't you?" I asked. "Whether it's good news or a big disappointment, I want all my favorite people around me when we hear it."

At that Tooney lost it. He hiccupped, excused himself, and bounded out of the room.

"Somebody's in love," Hillary said with a sly smile.

"Nothing like that," I said, touched by Tooney's reaction and more than a little weak in the throat myself.

"I know it isn't," Hillary said. "I know you feel for him

the same way you do for my stepfather. But the man clearly adores you." She twisted her mouth sideways. "They both do. I'm starting to worry that you've won over that nasty Frances, too. You have a bewitching way about you, kid."

That was one of the nicest things Hillary had ever said to me. "Thank you."

"The jury is still out with the two of us," she said, nudging Frederick.

He winked at me. "Very true."

I FOUND LIZA AT THE KITCHEN TABLE, CELL phone in hand. "Texting?" I asked.

"Who would I text?"

"Eric?"

"I couldn't if I wanted to." She put the phone down. "I had his number stored in the one I left behind. Never bothered to memorize it."

I picked it up. "Mind if I have a look?"

She started to complain about privacy when I noticed the last number she'd dialed. "You called Bennett?" I asked.

"How did you know?"

"I recognize the number."

"Nerd," she said.

"Why did you call Bennett?" I asked, pulling my own phone up and preparing to dial him myself.

"You can stop freaking out. I didn't get through. A guy answered the phone. He sounded old. Told me that he was in a meeting. Asked if I wanted to leave a message. I told him it was personal and I'd try back another time."

It must have been Theo who'd intercepted Liza's call. "Why did you want to talk with Bennett?"

"I need a job." She lifted one shoulder. "Duh."

I went momentarily speechless. "You're joking."

"You think I like living here with all your rules? I need

income so I can find a place of my own." She gave the back window a furtive glance. "That is, once it's safe for me to walk around like a normal person again."

"Don't ever call Bennett." I didn't believe her excuse but wasn't in the mood right now to challenge her. "If you want to work at Marshfield you'll have to apply like anyone else would." The idea of Liza working at Marshfield sent zinging aggravation up my spine. No, no, no. "Exactly what are you qualified to do?"

Another half-shrug. "I figured being your sister, I have an in. There's got to be some easy and fun job to do there."

I bit back a snippy retort. "Don't call Bennett again," I said for the second time in thirty seconds. "Are we clear on that?"

She stood, slamming her hands on the tabletop. "Yes, ma'am."

I stopped her before she stormed out of the room. "One more thing."

She pivoted. "Now what?"

"We—you and I—are going to Marshfield tomorrow morning."

Her mouth dropped open, but only for a moment. Her eyes narrowed. "If it's about me trying to get a job there, I don't really think you should—"

"It's not that."

She tossed her head toward Tooney's house. "How come your knight in shining armor gets a day off?"

"He needs to be there, as well."

"What, you don't trust me with those other two?" she asked. "I'm sure Frederick wouldn't mind keeping an eye on me while you're gone."

"Be ready tomorrow. Early. We leave by six thirty."

Chapter 28

I DROVE TO MARSHFIELD THE NEXT MORNING, aware of Liza's intense scrutiny. "What is with you today?" she asked.

I couldn't put it into words, nor would I attempt to. Despite the fact that I made the trek to Marshfield every weekday following this same route, I couldn't shake off the weirdness I felt. Though the weather, the hour, and the purpose were different, today reminded me very much of my first visit to Marshfield Manor when I applied for a job. Back then I didn't know what lay ahead of me. I'd been anxious, hopeful, and jittery.

Yep, that's exactly how I was feeling today.

My fingers trembled—this despite my rigid grip on the steering wheel.

When I didn't answer, Liza tried again. "The guys were up and out extra early today, too. What aren't you telling me?"

I mumbled about how I wasn't answerable for Bruce's and Scott's schedules.

She continued to study me, clearly unconvinced. "Are you nervous about something? You don't look right."

"I don't look right? What a nice thing to say," I said with exaggerated resentment.

"You know what I mean. You're jumpy and weird this morning."

I feigned nonchalance. "Bringing you to Marshfield has that effect on me."

"And what's the deal with making me leave the new cell phone at home? Who are you afraid I'll call?"

I didn't answer.

She faced forward. "Fine. Don't tell me."

I swung into Marshfield's underground employee parking lot and said hello to the guard at the gate before signing Liza in as my guest.

"It's like the Bat Cave," she said as I navigated to my parking spot. "Nobody would ever notice the entrance from the outside."

"Marshfield guests enjoy the illusion of being transported to an easier, simpler time. That's why vehicle traffic around the house is kept to a minimum and we run shuttles between the parking lots and the mansion."

Liza dawdled, taking in our surroundings as she followed me through the employee entrance up the back stairs to my office.

"Back door for a clean getaway?" she asked when we reached the third-floor landing.

"Don't get any ideas." I swiped my ID card through the final checkpoint and punched in the code, again taking care not to allow Liza to see. "Input the wrong number combination more than twice and you'll never get out of the place."

Sullenness swept over her. "I wasn't getting any ideas. I was making a joke."

I decided not to reply.

"Why is it you always think the worst of me?" she asked.

At the door to our office, I turned. "Start giving me reason to believe otherwise."

"I've done nothing wrong the whole time I've been here," she said. "I've followed your rules and surrendered myself to a babysitter. Not one step out of line in an entire week. How much more do I have to prove?"

Clearly, her idea of what was out of line was at war with mine, but I wasn't in the mood to debate. "We'll talk later," I said and opened the door.

Frances had gotten in before me. Wearing her customary frown and four different purple hues, she waved us in. "It's about time you showed up."

Liza made an impertinent noise. "After the way I was treated last time, I expected to be bound and shackled if I ever stepped foot here again."

My assistant's freshly penciled brows jumped high on her forehead. "My," she said, "you have a gift for hyperbole, don't you?"

If my stomach hadn't been rolling up and tumbling in on itself, I might have laughed. As it was, anxiety's tight grip kept me only faintly aware of the conversation around me. I hung up my coat and started for my office.

"Grace told me *all* about today's meeting." Liza spoke very softly to Frances as she hung her coat up next to mine. "But I suppose that's obvious, otherwise I wouldn't be here."

"Oh, right," Frances's voice boomed. "Trying to get me to tell stories out of school, are you? Think you can fool the old woman into spilling secrets, do you?" She took a step closer to my sister, her considerable bulk encroaching into Liza's personal space, backing her into a corner.

"I . . . I don't know what you're talking about."

"Then why were you whispering?"

Liza forced a smile. "Politeness. I didn't want to disturb Grace."

"Sure you didn't," Frances said, fairly roaring the words. "You whisper that you know everything and you expect me to believe you're not trying to pull an end run around your sister?"

Fascinated again by Frances's mama-bear behavior, I watched.

Liza gurgled a laugh. "I didn't say, 'everything.' How would I ever know if it really was everything? There's no way to know that." Babbling now, Liza backpedaled fast. "What I mean is, Grace told me what I needed to know. I wanted to set your mind at ease."

Frances folded her arms across her chest as she tapped her foot, regarding my sister coldly. "How kind of you."

Liza flashed me a "Help me out here?" look. I ignored it. With another strangled laugh, she shrugged. "Yeah, I thought that you might feel awkward with me here. Just trying to be helpful."

"Oh?" The lilt at the end of Frances's word held more contempt than inquisitiveness. "Why don't you tell me what you know, then?" She took a step back, holding a fleshy arm out toward me. "Better yet, tell both of us about today's meeting. Go ahead. Don't be shy."

Liza lowered her chin. To anyone else she might appear appropriately chastised. But when she raised her head again, I caught the burn in her eyes.

I took a protective step toward Frances, but she sensed me coming and cut me off. "Thought I was an easy mark, did you?" She closed in on my sister again. "You won't make that mistake again, will you?"

Liza sucked in her cheeks and worked her jaw.

"Will you?"

"What is it with you people? You're all such . . ." She grabbed at the air with wild fingers searching for the right word. "Rule followers. Don't you ever break out of your boring little cages and take a look around? There's a big world out there, where things happen and rules get broken. Where if you can't shift gears when trouble starts, people get hurt. You cling so tightly to your right and wrong and live your dull lives here without *any* excitement *ever*. You don't know what you're missing."

Frances and I exchanged a glance. Frances shook her head. "Yeah, we don't know about none of that stuff," she said, affecting a dimwitted tone. "Nothing *ever* happens around here."

"Rule followers," I repeated. Clapping a fist to my chest, I rolled my eyes. "You really know how to wound, don't you?" Turning to Frances, I asked, "Have you talked with Terrence? I thought he'd be here by now."

As if on cue, our head of security walked into the office that moment. "Good morning, Grace, Frances," he said with a cheerful nod.

Terrence Carr was perhaps the most chiseled man I'd ever met. Dark skinned and tall, he carried himself with an air of confidence and control that made him extremely effective in his position. When he'd first started at Marshfield—about the same time I had—he'd faced an uphill battle. With inadequate security measures and outdated equipment, he'd had to essentially establish new protocols and build a new system from the ground up. We'd suffered a few tragic losses in the interim and Bennett had, more than once, threatened to fire the man.

Terrence had eventually turned the tide, however, and while Marshfield couldn't boast of cutting-edge technology, we were far more secure than we had ever been.

Smiling at my sister, Terrence said, "You must be Liza. Nice to meet you. My name is Terrence Carr and I'm delighted to be spending time with you this morning."

My sister's confusion evident, she shook his proffered hand. Her accusatory glance to me asked, "What? Another babysitter?" but she exuded warmth as she greeted Terrence. Her lively gaze took in his sharp gray suit, shiny shoes, and conservative tie. From the moment she said hello I knew she'd tagged him as a well-off professional and fair game. I didn't have the heart to mention that he was a happily married father of three.

"We're running a little late this morning," Terrence said to me. "Sorry about that. My team is busy with the other guests." I knew he was referring to Hillary and Frederick, Tooney, Bruce, Scott, representatives from both laboratories, and the plethora of attorneys expected to attend.

"Your team?" Liza asked, all smiles.

"My apologies." Terrence splayed his hand across his chest. "Chief of security here at Marshfield."

Impressed, Liza exclaimed, "Oh!" Her voice lowered as she repeated herself, "Oh," this second utterance edged with disappointment and accompanied by a glare at me. Flinging her arms tight across her chest with such force that it twisted the straps of her purse around her waist and back again, she launched into a high-pitched snit. "Head of security? What's going on?" She took a step back, though where she expected to go, I couldn't imagine. "Why am I really here?"

I hadn't anticipated the reaction. Her claim that I didn't trust her rang a familiar bell in my brain. "This has nothing to do with you, Liza," I began quietly. "It's not safe to leave you home by yourself and I couldn't think of anyone else to keep you company."

She pointed a quivering finger at Terrence. "But why the head of security? Why him?" Twisting to indicate Frances, she asked, "What's wrong with that one keeping an eye on me? What's so important? Am I here for an interrogation?"

"An interrogation?" I repeated. "Of course not." I stopped, studying her. "Why? What are you afraid of?"

Her gaze hopped from Terrence to Frances before it settled back on me. "You," she said, but the bite in her tone had weakened. "I never know what you have planned for me. It's no fun having to follow new rules every day. *You* try living like that."

"Let's start again, shall we?" I said. "Terrence will be keeping you company for however long this meeting lasts. And before you ask, I don't know how long that will be. I can't imagine more than an hour, though."

Mollified, or at least less freaked out than she'd been moments earlier, Liza nodded.

Terrence and I exchanged a glance. "If you'll follow me, Liza, one of my staff is waiting for us," he said. "We are set up in a comfortable parlor on the second floor." He frowned at his watch, then said to me, "You're due downstairs now, aren't you?"

I nodded. A *whoosh* of terrified excitement blossomed in my gut, making me tingle from head to toe. The drama with Liza had momentarily taken my mind off the reason for today's precautions. This was it. There was no turning back. Bennett and I would know the truth today. Adrenaline zoomed up my back like a rocket, exploding into a million zigzagging pieces, sparkling in my brain.

"Why are you blushing?" Liza asked. Her eyes narrowed. "You're not getting married or something, are you?"

Despite my high-wire tension, I laughed.

The office door opened and Agent McClowery stepped in. He opened his mouth to speak, but was startled into silence when he spotted Liza.

"Agent McClowery?" Liza asked, punctuating the awkwardness of the situation. "What are you doing here?"

Frances fixed her glare on me. "Agent?"

Terrence closed his eyes for a brief, regretful moment. Had he and Liza left two minutes sooner, this unfortunate encounter could have been avoided.

McClowery's jaw tightened. His eyes flashed. "Ms. Wheaton. That is, Ms. *Grace* Wheaton, a moment of your time?" He pointed to my office.

I turned to Terrence. "Please take my sister down to the parlor, as arranged." He nodded, touched Liza's elbow, and gestured. "Let's go."

Like a cat might, Frances had puffed herself up. In mere seconds it seemed she'd doubled in size, wrath rippling like steam from her face. The moment the other two were gone, she said, "Apparently there's a great deal more I'm unaware of."

"One minute, Frances." I held up a finger. "One minute."

"They're waiting for you downstairs." Cheeks pinked with vexation, she tilted her head condescendingly. "Or did this 'agent' of yours make you forget about the most important day in the Mister's life?"

"I haven't forgotten. Please, I need you to go down there and let Bennett know I'm on my way. Take him to the side and tell him—very quietly, making certain no one overhears—that Agent McClowery is here. Please also inform him that my sister encountered the agent here in my office. Can you do that for me?"

She raked a gaze over McClowery, bunched her lips, and glowered. "I'm not feeble, of course I *can* do it." Raising her chin to indicate the agent, she asked, "The Mister knows this fellow?"

"Yes, yes," I said, trying to hurry her along. "Please, Frances. Trust me on this."

She growled a *harrumph*, but nodded, then stomped out the door.

The moment she was gone, I spun. "What are you doing here?"

McClowery responded in kind. "We have a major operation in place for tonight. You don't think that takes some advance planning?" He sucked in a deep breath. "Why is your sister here?"

This was bad. Very bad. Liza wasn't stupid. It wouldn't take long for her to realize that McClowery's presence here meant that the FBI expected Eric to show.

"I have a meeting this morning."

"The DNA results meeting." He didn't phrase it as a question.

"You know about that?"

"Of course," he said impatiently. "That doesn't answer my question. Why is your sister here?"

"There was no one to keep an eye on her at home."

"This is great, just great." Hostility tinged each enunciated word. "I was led to believe that no one—except you and the security staff, of course—would be in at this time. Bennett mentioned you'd be in early. I intended to talk with you about arrangements for tonight. How was I to know you'd have a crowd gathered here?"

"What did you need from me?"

McClowery rubbed the back of his neck. "What about the older woman? Your assistant. What's her story?"

"Frances is the biggest gossip I've ever met in my life."

"This is getting better and better." He began to pace the room. "Ten years tracking Mr. X and it all falls apart at the last minute."

"Now that Frances knows something is up, she's going to be relentless trying to figure out what it is. Bring her in on the plan, and I promise I'll be able to manage her."

He stopped to glare at me. "You're suggesting I risk the success of a major FBI operation by sharing details with the biggest gossip you've ever met? Are you out of your mind?"

"What other option do you have?" I asked, my voice rising to match his. "Come up with a better suggestion."

He shook his head and resumed pacing. "That doesn't solve the problem of your sister. She's the one I'm worried about. She's our loose cannon. If Eric—or anyone—gets wind of what's going on here, we're sunk. Our best bet right now may be to cut our losses and pull out before we're exposed."

"And when Eric shows up with the jeweled key tonight, where will you be?" I knew where I should be right now: downstairs in the banquet hall instead of arguing with an angry FBI agent in Frances's office. But I felt responsible. I massaged my forehead. "We can keep Liza here at Marshfield all day. Through tonight." Even though I believed my sister feared Eric, I couldn't swear that, given the chance, she wouldn't attempt to contact him. "We'll ensure she has no contact with anyone outside of me, Frances, and our security team."

McClowery smirked with such derision I wanted to slap

him. "You're talking at least fourteen hours. Maybe longer."

"After the meeting is over, she can stick with me." It was a halfhearted offer, but a necessary one. Not how I'd envisioned my day.

Coming back around to face me, he asked, "What about during tonight's reception?"

I held up my hands in a helpless motion. "What about it?"

"That's why I came to see you. I want you behind the scenes, in the control booth, where we'll have camera feeds rolling and be able to listen in on some of the conversations. What do we do with Liza then?"

"You wouldn't happen to have a spare agent willing to sit with her?"

"No. I don't. Every single agent on my team has an important job this evening."

"Why do you want me in the control booth?"

"You and I are the only individuals involved who have met Eric face-to-face. We can use your eyes."

I tapped my lips. "We can make this work. Frances can sit with Liza during the reception. When Frances believes she's involved, she's a real team player." That was a bit of a stretch if you considered my assistant's snarly attitude, but I knew we held a far better chance of keeping this operation under wraps with Frances's cooperation that we would by excluding her.

Seconds ticked by as McClowery considered this. He continued to rub the back of his neck, focusing his attention near the ceiling. When he finally turned to me, his sour mood hadn't improved. "As you said, what other options are there?"

"Do you want to bring Frances up to speed, or shall I?"

"When your meeting concludes, send her to Bennett's apartment. I've established our home base up there in several rooms he generously offered for our purposes. I'll assess

Frances's reliability and decide how much to share at that time."

"I have to go now," I said, "I'm late."

His mouth jerked sideways, as though annoyed. "I must caution you not to share any further details with your sister about my presence here."

Like I wouldn't have been able to figure that out for myself. "What should I tell her? It's probably a good idea if you and I come up with a cover story in case she runs into you again."

"I intend to avoid that situation." He took a deep breath. "But if she asks, tell her that we believe Eric left Emberstowne this morning. Tell her I'm leaving to follow him. I came to see you this morning to provide my contact information in case Eric doubles back."

"That's good," I said. "I think she'll buy it."

He pushed a quick smile, but I could tell his mind was elsewhere. "I will contact you before the reception to go over procedures."

Finally free, I headed down to the banquet hall to face my future.

Chapter 29

I SHOULDN'T HAVE BEEN SURPRISED WHEN every single person in the banquet hall turned to stare at me when I stepped into the magnificent room. Nearly two-thirds the size of a football field, this majestic space featured a stunning mosaic ceiling that soared nearly thirty feet above the floor, and a stone walkway—a gallery off-limits to tourists—that lined the room's perimeter, one story up from where I stood now.

Everything about this space was enormous. Hulking, matching fireplaces—so big I could stand inside them—bookended the room's far ends. Tapestries lined the oak-paneled walls and natural light filtered in from above: gothic windows—oversized, of course—were evenly spaced along the high, narrow walkway.

Although tourists were allowed to enter the banquet hall, they were prevented from stepping very far in. The long dining room table—with seating for thirty—sat twenty feet in from the velvet ropes, and attentive docents kept sightseers at bay. Today the ropes were gone and the giant, echoey chamber buzzed with conversation. All discussion ceased the moment I arrived.

"Sorry I'm late," I said.

The room was filled with people, including lawyers I knew and others I'd met at the lab. Hillary and Frederick were at the table, the only ones in the room to have taken seats. Hillary had one of her perfectly manicured hands near her mouth. I think she was biting a nail.

In the far corner, Scott, Bruce, and Tooney stood together. All three smiled when I waved to them, but I could read nervous expectation on their faces. The rest of the room was a sea of business suits and apprehension.

In the two seconds it had taken to make my way in, I noticed that the lab representatives, Doctors Lucatorto, Rabbat, and Lyon, were huddled together, away from everyone else. None of the three met my eyes. Security guards had been posted at all doors, as well as along the catwalk.

Stepping forward to take my arm, Bennett smiled. It occurred to me that he was as nervous about this outcome as I was. He leaned sideways to whisper, "We wouldn't dream of starting without you."

Lifting his chin, he addressed the rest of the room. "Good morning, everyone. Grace and I are delighted to have all of you here to share in what I sincerely hope is a celebration."

He signaled the nearest security guard. The young man nodded, spoke briefly into his microphone, and within seconds all the guards stepped out of the room, snapping doors shut behind them to provide privacy. That is, if one can consider divulging secrets in front of two dozen people private.

Bennett patted my hand before continuing, "As you all know, there is significant evidence to suggest that my father and Grace's grandmother had a child together and that that child was Grace's mother."

I knew the lawyers were here to bear witness and keep things official. Hillary was here because, as Bennett's stepdaughter, she had a personal interest in the results. Frederick was here for Hillary's moral support.

Though Frances continued to wear a disgruntled expression, it was right to have her here as well. My heart swelled most, however, to know that, whatever the result, my best friends in the world—Bruce, Scott, and Tooney—were here to support me.

My mouth was dry, my grip on Bennett's arm tight. He glanced down at my upturned face and patted my hand again. "We know the truth, Gracie, that's all that matters."

I could do no more than nod. What if? I thought. What if the scientists in the corner told us that it was all a lie—or, rather, a misunderstanding? Sure, my grandmother had had an affair with Bennett's father, but what if my mom was not Marshfield's child? My grandmother had been married at the time. What if this all had been spun out of control and my legal grandfather had always been my biological grandfather? What then?

Would Bennett still regard me as warmly, still welcome me as family if we knew beyond a doubt that we didn't share blood? From almost the very moment we'd discovered this connection, Bennett had been eager to bring me into the fold. At times I feared him too eager. Would disappointment crush so deeply that he'd turn away from me?

"Doctors," Bennett continued, "are you prepared to present your findings?"

They were.

"Gracie?" Bennett asked, loud enough for all to hear. "Are you ready?"

I knew Bennett better than to believe he'd ever spurn me. Of course he wouldn't. But when the reality that I was merely a devoted employee set in, his warm feelings for me could dissolve, too.

Looking away, I fought the heat behind my eyes and the pain in my throat that made it so hard to swallow right now.

Bennett had become more important to me than I could put into words. As long as we pretended—believed—we were related, I knew I wouldn't lose the bond we'd created. But now, today, all pretending ceased.

I tugged tighter at his strong arm, pulling him close for the last moments of bliss—the final few seconds where the world was perfect and I had an uncle I dearly loved. I blew out a breath, knowing I had to stay strong.

"Yes," I said, "I'm ready."

The room fell into a heavy silence. Dr. Lucatorto cleared his throat. "As you all know, DNA tests were performed on two subjects, Mr. Bennett Marshfield and Ms. Grace Wheaton, to determine kinship. We extracted blood and collected swabs from both subjects and samples were analyzed by two separate laboratories: Lucatorto Labs and Sarear Labs."

He pulled out a piece of paper and donned reading glasses. Again, he cleared his throat. "Because both labs have delivered the same result, I see no need to announce the labs' conclusions separately."

A quick, nearly imperceptible inhalation. As if the entire room had suddenly chosen to hold its collective breath. Or maybe it was just me.

"You will recall," Dr. Lucatorto continued, "that a positive result will indicate that the subjects are related. A negative result indicates that no blood connection exists."

Dr. Lucatorto knuckled the edge of his glasses, pushing them up his nose. After a swift visual survey, ensuring that he had our attention, he cleared his throat again. I got the impression he'd never enjoyed this level of attention and wanted to milk the moment.

I closed my eyes, concentrating.

Wishing.

Hoping.

Fearful.

After clearing his throat yet again, Lucatorto continued.

"After comparing DNA samples from both aforementioned subjects, our experts have concluded, with a high degree of certitude . . ."

He paused long enough to take a breath. What felt like three lifetimes passed before he exhaled again.

". . . that Mr. Marshfield and Ms. Wheaton are, indeed, members of the same family."

Air *whoosh*ed out of me too quickly. Throbbing sparkles narrowed my vision, threatening me with loss of consciousness. My knees went weak. Faltering on my feet, I gripped Bennett's arm harder, but he'd begun pulling me in, wrapping strong arms around my back and whispering into my hair, "Never a moment's doubt, Gracie. Never a moment's doubt."

The news had been met with a roar of approval from the gathered group. Even before Bennett had fully released me, they swarmed us with happy congratulations.

Acting on what must have been some prearranged signal, a half-dozen servers entered the room, bearing silver trays and Champagne flutes. Over the din of excited conversation I heard the unmistakable *pop* of bottles and within moments, a glass of bubbly was thrust into my hand.

The room fell into immediate silence as Bennett raised his glass for a toast. He turned to me, his expression suffused with joy. "To family," he said.

My throat was thick, my eyes hot. "To family," I replied.

As we clinked our glasses and sipped, the room erupted once again.

Every one of the lawyers jockeyed for position, eager to shake my hand and personally promise allegiance. Overwhelmed by the news and the staggering onslaught of good wishes, I shifted to autopilot—relying on my innate politeness to smile and nod appropriately—all the while scanning past the glad hands and glinting eyes, searching for the faces of those most important to me.

Bruce and Scott pushed through the congratulatory

crowd, cheering as they enveloped me in a group hug. "We know how much this means to you," Scott said.

Choked up, Bruce managed to say, "So happy for you, sweetie."

Hillary made her way over. "What does this make us?" she asked. "Sisters?"

The word sliced through my happiness. With effort, I forced all thoughts of Liza out of my mind. For now, I chose to enjoy the celebration and to revel in the truth that I had family—real family—once again. "More like cousins, I think." My voice betrayed the giddy happiness bubbling in my heart and before I could stop myself, I threw my arms around Hillary and hugged her with gusto, spilling a little of both our Champagne.

"*Oof*," she said as her body got smooshed into mine. Her free hand came up long enough to pat me gently. When she stepped back again, she said, "Yes, well, a new beginning, I suppose." She straightened her skirt and ran a finger down the side of her cheek to flip an errant hair from her face. She glanced at Frederick, still at the table, who gave her an encouraging nod. "Welcome to the family, cuz," she said.

Through it all, Bennett had remained next to me, the two of us an island bombarded by a tidal wave of good wishes. Now he reached for Hillary, grasping her small hand in his. "This changes nothing between you and I," he said. "You know that, don't you?"

"I know you believe that." She reached up on tiptoe and touched her lips to his cheek.

The lawyers continued to swirl around us, forming little eddies of chatter, whispering among themselves. Alight with glee, they bumped and wound around one another, their spirits high with what I could only deduce was delight at the prospect of how this change might generate more business for them. I wanted nothing to change—nothing financial, that is. The attorneys' happy buzz warned that I held the minority opinion.

Frances had waited for the initial uproar to die down before making her way over. She pushed through, positioning herself between me and Bennett, twisting her thick neck back and forth until convinced we were both paying sufficient attention. "Well?" she asked. "Have either of you given any thought as to how this affects me?"

"I can't say we've had time to consider that question," he said, playing along. "I gather you have?"

With a gleam of satisfaction, she wrapped her arms across her middle. If Bennett hadn't been Marshfield's owner, if Frances hadn't been in the habit of deferring to his wishes as she'd been required to for forty years, she might have sassed him back. Instead, she nodded, with vigor. "Of course I have." At this she turned to me with what looked like a conspiratorial smirk. "Grace won't have time to keep up with all the day-to-day, mundane, boring duties that keep Marshfield running smoothly."

"No, no," I began, "I love what I do, I wouldn't want to give it—"

"What *you* want is the important consideration here," she continued, louder, directing every ounce of energy toward Bennett. "You'll want Grace to learn more of the family history and all that other business stuff you like so much. She's going to be stretched too thin."

"And that's where you come in, I take it?" Bennett didn't even try to muffle his laughter. "With a selfless offer to help?"

She lifted her chin. "I'm willing to take on the role as chief curator and estate manager, yes."

Bennett clapped Frances on the shoulder. "I will take it under advisement," he said, then winked at me. "Or perhaps I should say *we* will take that under advisement."

The lawyers chuckled. Not to be put off, Frances piped up again, "I get it. We'll talk about this later, in private." Shooting me a triumphant sideways grin, Frances waggled her eyebrows and stepped away.

Only Tooney held back, shuffling off by himself to watch

from a distance. His soft, homely face had transformed—as it always did—when he smiled. When I caught his eye, he lifted his glass in a silent toast.

"I hope you know you may count on me for confidentiality and discretion." An older lawyer, one whose name I couldn't remember, grasped my free hand in his spotted one. "I've served the Marshfield family for years and hope to continue to do so—"

"Thank you, yes. Please excuse me." I tugged my hand free, making my way over to Tooney.

"Congratulations, Grace," he said, tapping his glass against mine. "I couldn't be happier for you."

After we both took a sip, I said, "Nothing's going to change. Not really."

"*You* won't change, but don't for a moment believe everyone around you won't." He smiled to take the melancholy out of his words and said, "I may never get another chance." Bringing his stubbly cheek next to mine, he brushed the side of my face with a quick kiss. When he stepped back again, he winked. "Couldn't resist."

"Thank you, Bronson," I said.

"I really am happy for you."

The celebration continued until one of the security team reminded us that the mansion was scheduled to open soon. Bennett sidled over. "We have a lot to talk about Gracie," he said.

I leaned closer to him. "What do I do about Liza?"

He transferred his glass to his left hand and placed his right arm around my shoulders. "As I suggested earlier, the better question is: What do *we* do about Liza?"

Chapter 30

I CORNERED FRANCES TO LET HER KNOW THAT Agent McClowery wanted to speak with her, and relayed his instructions to meet him upstairs. Her tadpole eyebrows shot upward. "It's about time," she said, but when she trundled out the door, she did so with a cheerful thump in her step.

Before Bruce and Scott left, I pulled them over to enlist their help, explaining—as well as I could without divulging the truth about the FBI operation—that plans had changed and that Liza and I would be staying late tonight, attending Bennett's reception.

"This reception will probably be a chi-chi-pooh-pooh affair, won't it?" Bruce asked.

"I suppose."

Giving me a discreet once-over, he asked, "Don't you need us to bring you anything? A change of clothes, perhaps?"

I stammered. I couldn't very well tell him that the FBI planned to keep Liza holed up out of sight and station me in their observation room, so I said, "That would be great.

I don't know what of mine might suit Liza though, so don't go to any real trouble."

"Oh no?" Bruce asked with a pointed glance toward Bennett, who was clapping Dr. Lucatorto on the back as he escorted the man out. "If you think Bennett Marshfield isn't going to use this opportunity to share you with the rest of the world . . ."

He wouldn't. Tonight wasn't about celebration. Tonight was all about catching Eric and recovering the jeweled key.

I couldn't share that, so what I said was, "I guess you're right. I ought to be prepared."

Scott nodded. "We'll bring a few outfits and accessories for you and Liza. And necessities from your bathroom."

"Sounds great."

"I don't understand why Liza is invited to this shindig though," Bruce said, latching onto the part of my story that made the least sense. He waved a hand, encompassing the group. "With this many people in the know, and the news being so big, how can you possibly hope to keep the truth from her?"

"Bennett and I intend to talk about that," I said.

Scott and Bruce exchanged a look of concern. "Good luck."

I RETURNED TO FIND TERRENCE AND LIZA IN opposite corners of the second-floor parlor. A female member of the security team stood immediately inside the door. Liza had her back to me, facing the wide window.

"Grace," Terrence said with enthusiasm when I walked in. His eyes were full of questions as he released the other officer. The moment she was gone he asked, "How did it go?"

Liza hadn't bothered to turn.

"It went well," I said, hoping to communicate with my eyes. "Very well."

Terrence's face lit up. "Glad to hear it."

Liza twisted her head. "I won't bother asking. I know you won't tell me. But hey, I can be supportive. Whatever good news you're hiding—yay, hurray. Congratulations. Whatever."

She spun, closing the distance between us. "Can I go now? I'm missing my favorite TV shows." To Terrence, she added, "You know that my sister keeps me locked up day and night."

"Thanks for sharing." To me, he asked, "Is there anything else you need?"

"As a matter of fact, there is. My sister won't be leaving Marshfield today."

"What?" Liza asked.

"It can't be helped," I said to her, before returning my attention to Terrence. "I'll explain more later."

Arms folded across her chest, Liza thrust a hip out. "Later meaning when I won't overhear?"

"That's right." To Terrence again, I said, "If things go well, Frances and I will keep my sister in our office for the rest of the day, and I'll ask Frances to help out during the reception tonight."

"Frances?" Terrence repeated. "She's invited to the reception?"

He knew that Agent McClowery had chosen to keep Frances out of this operation. Having her play a role was a change. A big one.

"Lots of last-minute updates," I said vaguely. "If there are complications I may need to borrow one of your more . . . um . . . taciturn officers to help us out."

"Whatever you need, Grace," Terrence said.

Liza and I made our way back. "I'm not an idiot," she said as we crossed through Frances's empty office into mine. "Whatever is going on is a clearly a big deal. Everyone I've encountered today, from that FBI agent, to Terrence, to you, is acting weird."

"Maybe there's a full moon tonight." I took a seat behind my desk. "Isn't that where the term *lunatic* comes from?"

"Nice try." She plopped onto the sofa along the wall. "I'll find out what it is. You know I will."

Not if I can help it. "Be my guest."

She leaned forward, elbows on her knees, hands crossed between them. "Nothing I come up with makes sense."

Fighting to keep my happiness under control, I pulled a spreadsheet file up on my computer. Our accounting department had reported a spike in admissions last month. Year over year, we were up 10 percent. We expected a bump from the FAAC convention, but wouldn't see those numbers until next month. Increased attendance during the colder months was always good news. Better still, we'd been trending upward for a while now.

I clicked away, analyzing and crunching numbers while adding notes to the margin. One of my goals was to grow Bennett's enterprise and to implement modernizations that would not only bring the magnificent structure into the twenty-first century, but would captivate a new generation of tourists as well. I smiled. Business was looking up. Literally.

Liza broke the silence. "You *didn't* get married this morning, did you?"

I glanced over to her. "You really do have an active imagination."

When she sprawled backward, one hand to her forehead, one leg stretched across the cushions, I realized she'd spoken aloud only to get my attention. In a pose every bit as melodramatic as that of an ingénue in a silent film, she worked up a woeful gaze. "Do I have to stay here all day? I'm bored."

"I can get you a book."

"Really? Is that the best you can do?" She lifted her head a couple of inches, enough for her to peer at the clock across the room. "It's not even ten in the morning yet." She let her head drop onto the armrest, fixing her gaze at the ceiling.

"Can't you at least let me wander around a little? Let me be a tourist. Ask one of your minions to tag along if you're afraid I'll try to escape."

She slid a sideways glance to ensure I was listening.

"What part of 'staying in my office all day' didn't you understand?"

She rose up, feet to the ground. "This is torture," she said.

"It's been ten minutes."

"Exactly. I have a whole day of nothingness ahead of me."

"I'm sorry about that." And I was. "The offer for a book stands."

She made an unpleasant noise. I got back to work.

A moment later she'd bounded from the sofa to settle herself in one of the chairs across from me. "If you don't trust me wandering, then how about you invite someone here for me to talk to?"

"Frances should be back soon."

Liza made a "You gotta be kidding" face. "How about somebody with personality?"

"How about I call upstairs for a book?"

"What about that Agent McClowery? He's good-looking."

She was fishing for information now. "I don't think so."

"What was he doing here, anyway? I was surprised to see him here this morning but you sure weren't."

"He's been here a couple times."

"That's right," she said with a knowing lilt. "You've always been a sucker for dimples on a man, haven't you? Don't think I didn't notice."

Before I could get another word out, she asked, "He had something to do with the meeting today, didn't he? You're interested in him, aren't you?"

Keeping my head down, I held tight to the storm of contradictions that fought to pour out of my mouth. Tempting as it was to correct her, every bit of information she got out of me—however slight—threatened to bring her closer to deducing the truth. I had two big secrets to hide from her:

the DNA results and the reason for Agent McClowery's presence here. I wasn't willing to jeopardize either one.

"Agent McClowery came to let me know that he's leaving Emberstowne today, that's all." The lie came easily enough.

"When is he coming back?"

"I don't know," I said, hoping to convey disappointment over the agent's fictitious departure.

"He's not your type," she said.

"Doesn't matter anyway, does it?"

"Where's he going?"

I looked up. "He's an FBI agent. Do you really think he'd tell me?"

"Does this have something to do with Eric?"

I opened my mouth then closed it again, as though catching myself just in time. "Can't say."

"But you know." She didn't phrase it as a question.

Hooked. Now to reel her in. I shrugged. "Sam—that is, Agent McClowery—couldn't tell me where he was going or how long he'd be gone."

"Sam," she repeated. "On a first-name basis now, are we?"

When I didn't answer, she thrummed her fingers against the top of my desk. "What about Bennett?"

"What about him?"

"You trust *him*, I know you do. While you putter on your computer, maybe he could give me a tour. He'd do it if you asked him to."

The door to Frances's office opened and closed. At the welcome sound of her heavy footfalls, I called out, "I'm in here with Liza," before my assistant had a chance to blurt something she shouldn't.

"So I gathered," she said, clomping into the room. She planted herself in front of my desk. "What's this about me having to work overtime tonight?" She thrust her chin toward Liza. "I better be earning more than time-and-a-half if you expect me to contend with her."

Agent McClowery had obviously brought my assistant

up to date. Before she could utter another word, however, I jumped to my feet. "A moment of your time?"

We left Liza sitting by my desk and had barely gotten into Frances's office when she whispered, "What do you take me for? An idiot?" She leaned back to peer around the doorway to reassure herself that Liza hadn't followed us to listen in. "I know not to mention any names." Holding a finger to her lips, she shook her head. "That girl won't get squat out of me."

"I wasn't worried about that," I said. "I wanted you to know that Liza is convinced I'm smitten with McClowery and trying to hide it."

She blinked in surprise.

"I'm playing along," I said quickly. "Let her think she's onto me."

Frances nodded, peeked around the doorway again, then reverted to the angry expression she'd worn when she'd first walked in. "I knew you and the Mister were up to something. What took you so long to bring me in on it?"

"Not now." My desk phone rang, sparing me further explanation. "Excuse me."

Liza had gotten to her feet in order to read my caller ID. Before I could beat her to it, she'd answered the phone. "Good morning, Mr. Marshfield, how are you?"

I grabbed for the receiver but she ducked out of my reach. "She's here, yes. We were just talking about you. Grace was hoping you'd have time to give me a tour today. Yes, completely. Her idea."

Wrenching the handset away from her, I glared at Liza. "Sorry about that, Bennett. I was in the other office with Frances."

"She's a wily one, that sister of yours."

Using my free hand, I shooed her away so that she wouldn't be able to overhear Bennett's side of the conversation. "I did *not* suggest you giving her a private tour."

"So I assumed, Gracie," he said. "I have a number of

things on my mind I would like to discuss with you, though. Would you be able to get away for a little while?"

"Absolutely. What time?"

I could hear the smile in his voice. "As soon as you can cajole Frances into sitting with your sister."

My assistant had followed me in and when I hung up, she and Liza looked at me expectantly. "Bennett and I have a few details to go over before the event this evening," I said. "He'd like me to come upstairs to discuss them. Frances, would you mind keeping Liza company for a little while?"

"As long as you share those details with me," she said.

I didn't see how that would be possible with Liza around all day, but this was not the moment to argue the point. "You know I always do my best."

The offices' outer door opened and a moment later, we heard a cheery, "Good morning. Anybody around?"

Rodriguez. And probably Flynn. "In here," I called.

The two detectives ambled into my office, Rodriguez all smiles. "Ladies." He tipped an imaginary hat.

Flynn lifted his chin. "We have good news about your lover boy, Eric." I couldn't determine if he'd targeted the announcement to me, to Liza, or to us both.

I kept my expression impassive, but strove to shut the detective up by sheer force of will. Rodriguez and Flynn didn't know about the ruse McClowery and I had concocted. One misstep and Liza would know I'd been lying about why McClowery had been here this morning. Not that she could do anything about it, but still.

"Yeah, we already heard. He left town." Liza's affected nonchalance didn't fool me. She was digging. "I forgot where Grace said he was going, though . . ."

I could tell that the news of Eric's leaving surprised them both, but Flynn shrugged. "Doesn't matter where he is. At least not as far as we're concerned," he said. "He's no longer a person of interest in the murder of Emilio Ochoa, a.k.a. Alvin Clark, a.k.a. Tomas Pineda."

She shot me an "I told you so" look. "I knew Eric was no killer. I can leave now."

"Not so fast," I said.

"Why? You were all so worried about Evil Eric coming after me. He's not only skipped town, he's no longer a murder suspect. That means, dear sister, that I'm free to go. I can see and talk with whomever I like. You can't stop me."

"First of all," I began, "as long as you're living in my house, I still make the rules."

"You sound like a cranky parent yelling at a teenager," Flynn said.

"You're not helping." Addressing Liza again, I continued, "And unless you've been holding out on me, you don't have the resources to go anywhere else."

She opened her mouth. I cut her off. "Lastly, as I'm sure our esteemed detectives will tell you, just because Eric isn't the killer doesn't mean you're safe. Whoever killed that fake FBI guy is still at large." I turned to Rodriguez. "Am I right?"

"Sell it, amiga."

I stopped short of poking Liza in the chest. "And don't forget, before he was killed, the victim came to see *me*. Which means the killer is fully aware of Eric's connection to *you*. You think he'll believe you know nothing? Or do you think he'll do whatever it takes to squeeze information out of you?"

I waited a beat before holding my hand out toward the door. "Still want to leave?"

She huffed. "Fine. Forget it." She crossed the room to fling herself back on the couch, resuming her angst-ridden ingénue pose.

Flynn smirked. "She sure acts like a teenager."

I asked Rodriguez and Flynn to follow me out of the office. "Frances, do you mind?"

My assistant settled her hostile gaze on Liza's recumbent form. "We'll be fine here, don't you worry about a thing."

"Well?" Flynn asked the moment we were in the corridor. "Tell us."

We continued down the long hallway of third-floor offices, toward the stairs. Not knowing how much McClowery had shared with these two, I opted to play it safe. "The truth is I don't know whether Eric has left town or not, but—for a lot of very good reasons—we need Liza to believe that he has."

The two men stopped walking and exchanged a puzzled look. "That's real nice," Flynn said, "but it doesn't answer my question."

My turn to be confused. "What are you talking about?"

"The test," Rodriguez said, impatient as Flynn. "The DNA. Have you found out if you and Mr. Marshfield are related?"

I raised a hand to my forehead. "This morning seems so long ago." And then I remembered that Bennett was waiting for me upstairs.

"Well?" Flynn prompted, fidgety as ever.

I took a quick breath. "Yes, we're related."

They congratulated me and offered speculation about how my life would change. "That's not why I did it," I said. "Knowing Bennett is my uncle is enough. I don't need anything more."

Flynn lifted his chin toward my office. "I take it *she* doesn't know. Your sister, I mean."

I felt the familiar flutter of apprehension. "No," I said. "She doesn't."

Rodriguez placed a heavy hand on my shoulder. "Maybe the sooner she leaves Emberstowne, the better."

Chapter 31

THEO THREW OPEN THE DOOR TO BENNETT'S apartment with far less decorum than I'd come to expect from the staid butler. "Miss Grace," he said, "Mr. Bennett told me the good news." He grabbed my hand and shook it with vigor. "Best thing to happen here in a very long time."

"Thank you, Theo." Touched by his enthusiasm, I wrapped both my hands around his larger one. "I'm so happy to be part of a family again."

"Mr. Bennett has considered you family for some time."

"Gracie, is that you?" Bennett called from deep within the apartment.

"I'll be right there," I said.

"I don't mean to detain you, Miss Grace," Theo said.

"Good news is fun to share." I patted him on the forearm. "But I suppose I ought to get in there."

Theo's pale eyes widened with emphasis. "He's antsy today, no question about it. I think the quicker you talk with him the sooner he'll settle down."

"Thanks."

He winked. "Welcome home."

Bennett was pacing his study when I walked in. Much homier than his office, bookshelves lined three walls of this room. The center of the eastern wall featured a carved oak panel that had been set between shelves. A secret room lay behind that panel, and one of these days I hoped Bennett would make good on his promise to allow me to dig through the dusty treasures that had been secreted there.

"Something wrong?" I asked.

He stood behind the room's low-backed persimmon sofa and I got the impression I'd stopped him mid-pace. "I wanted quiet time today. I wanted to spend time with you, talking about the future. I have plans, Gracie. Lots of plans. I want your input before moving forward."

"We have plenty of time for that now."

Bennett didn't smile the way I'd expected him to. "Close the door, please."

I obliged. He pointed toward the paisley wing chair that sat perpendicular to the couch. I sat.

"I trust Theo completely, but it's best to keep tonight's details to ourselves." Bennett began marching back and forth across the room. "We don't have a lot of time." Holding up two fingers, he shook them as though chiding me with the peace symbol. "McClowery wants to go over everything again."

"I'm sorry I'm late."

"No, no, Gracie. It's not your fault. It's that I'd hoped to have my plans in place before this whatever-you-want-to-call-it tonight. Stakeout? Sting? Whatever it is, occurs."

I got to my feet and went over to him, preventing further pacing. "What do you mean 'plans in place before tonight'? This isn't the first time you've said such a thing. What aren't you telling me?"

Although he smiled down at me, I recognized anxiety behind his eyes. "I don't like to leave things unfinished. Not that I have any real safety concerns, mind you," he added, reacting to my expression. "But after all the harrowing experiences you and I have lived through these past few years, I no longer take safety for granted. I told my attorneys to have everything prepared ahead of time. Once we had the proof in hand I wanted it to be easy. Sign, witness, done."

"Bennett, there's no need for changes."

"I know you feel that way, but ownership of Marshfield has always remained with family. I'm not about to break tradition now."

"You're afraid of not making it through tonight, aren't you?" Before he could answer, I said, "Call it off, then. No artifact, not even this jeweled key, is worth it."

His eyes were sad. "I'll be fine, Gracie. Again, it's merely unfinished business that's troubling me. I'm unsettled until I know everything is under control. The attorneys should have had everything ready to go, but . . ."

"It's because of Liza, isn't it?"

"She will need to be told. Better we face the consequences together, on our terms, than to have her discover the truth on her own. My attorneys believe it's in my best interests to come up with specific provisions excluding Liza before changing my will to leave the bulk of my estate to you."

"No, Bennett, no."

He pressed a finger to my lips. "It's my fortune. I'm allowed to do with it as I please."

"I'm not comfortable—"

"I know that. Which is why I'm determined to make it through this evening without a scratch. I intend for you to learn everything so that you become comfortable by the time I am no longer here."

"Please don't talk like that."

He seemed about to reassure me yet again when there was a knock at the door. "Come," he called.

"Another wrinkle in tonight's plan." McClowery pushed his way in and stopped short, his surprise evident. "Glad to find you here, Grace. The matter I wanted to discuss involves you both."

"Have a seat," Bennett said.

McClowery lowered himself into the wing chair as Bennett and I sat on the sofa. "My team is set up. We've tapped into your closed-circuit system to maintain surveillance this evening."

Without waiting for our acknowledgment, he went on. "As you know, Bennett, you'll wear a hidden microphone so we can monitor all your conversations."

"I don't understand," I said. "Why is that necessary? Don't you intend to apprehend Eric the moment he shows up?"

McClowery leaned forward, hands clasped between his knees. "As this event is open to all FAAC attendees, it's very possible that Eric Soames will show up tonight intending to negotiate the sale of the jeweled key to Bennett, personally. That would be optimal."

But. I was waiting for the "but."

"But Soames isn't stupid. A more likely scenario would be for him to use an intermediary for this initial contact with Mr. Marshfield."

"Someone like Nina Buchman?" I asked.

McClowery nodded. "Or another associate we aren't aware of. If Nina Buchman shows up here tonight, you'd recognize her?"

"Definitely."

"Good."

"You used the words *initial contact*," I said.

"Eric Soames will probably send an emissary to connect with Mr. Marshfield and then negotiate a price as well as a time and place for the exchange," he said. "We're guessing, but are fairly confident, that Eric will want to complete the transaction fast. Perhaps even later tonight, after the event."

"Wait," I said. "Do you intend for Bennett to meet with criminals? Alone?"

"We hope to bring our investigation to a satisfactory conclusion before any such meeting takes place." McClowery's
cold delivery held no compassion. "Mr. Marshfield has been
advised of the risks. He has agreed to cooperate."

I wanted to slap the dead-eyed stare off the agent's flat
face. "Did you forget that someone out there already killed
a man to get this jeweled key? How can you put Bennett in
danger like this?"

"Again, Ms. Wheaton, we hope it won't come to that."

"You hope," I repeated.

"We will be right there. Mr. Soames won't get away."

Flynn's recent warning echoed in my brain. *What good
will that do if you're already dead?*

Reading my thoughts, perhaps, Bennett patted my knee.
"It will be okay, Gracie," he said. "Let's get back to the plan.
You mentioned a wrinkle, Agent McClowery?"

The FBI man gave a quick nod, clearly relieved by the
change of topic. "As you are both aware, our agency's goal
is not so much to apprehend Eric Soames as it is to use
Soames's testimony to bring down Mr. X."

"And to recover the jeweled key," Bennett reminded him.

"That is, of course, an important objective," McClowery
said, "but the FBI's focus is to uncover the outfit responsible
for its theft in the first place. This organization is, if you
will, the engine that powers thousands of such thefts and
subsequent black market sales every year."

"Thousands?" I asked.

"I had no idea, either," Bennett said, "until Agent McClowery first approached me about working with the FBI."

McClowery looked at his watch and began speaking
more quickly. "Not every theft is as notorious as this one.
Not every item so valuable. That's why tonight's setup is of
the utmost importance. Back to the change in our plan. It's
very possible that the ringleader Soames was working for
will make an appearance here tonight."

Despite the fact that I was still processing anger at the

FBI's willingness to put Bennett's life at risk, I asked, "Why would he do that?"

"Our intelligence suggests that the head of the black market organization is an avid collector in his or her own right. Mr. X would blend in perfectly at tonight's affair, whereas one of the boss's hired guns would not."

"You've mentioned that before," Bennett said. "I don't understand what's changed."

"What's different now is our wild card." To me, he said, "I'm talking about your sister, Liza."

"I don't understand."

"We want her present at the reception tonight," he said.

"What are you, nuts?" I asked.

"Liza will not be made aware that the FBI is in attendance. She will merely be told—by you—that because Eric has left town and because security is tight at Marshfield, there's no reason to keep her locked away all evening."

He sat up straight, as though that explained everything.

I shook my head. "What possible reason could you have to want Liza there?"

"By now, whoever hired Eric Soames knows who Liza is. Allowing your sister to mingle among potential targets tonight gives us the opportunity to observe who approaches her and how she interacts with them."

"You want to use my sister as bait."

"She will never be in any danger." He blinked those flat eyes. "But essentially, yes."

"You don't understand my sister," I said. "She swore she knew none of Eric's business partners, but then admitted to recognizing Nina Buchman. My sister is a liar."

The two men waited for me to continue.

"What if she really *does* know the person who hired Eric? Or what if she recognizes the person Eric sends? Then what?"

McClowery's dead eyes finally glinted with life. "Even better."

Chapter 32

"I DON'T UNDERSTAND WHAT CHANGED YOUR mind," Liza said for the fourth time since I'd delivered the news. From the moment she knew she was attending the reception, she turned her behavior around. Abandoning both her perch on the sofa and her woe-is-me attitude, she'd spent the last twenty minutes walking around my office, nattering about how excited she was to be allowed a little fun for a change.

"I told you. This was Bennett's idea."

I hadn't had a chance to tell Frances the reason for the new plan. Red-faced and fidgeting with pent-up curiosity, she marched in and slammed on my desk a report I'd requested.

"I know you weren't thrilled with the idea of sitting with Liza," I said to her. "Now that she's joining the party, I'll understand if you'd prefer to take a pass on tonight."

"*Pheh*," Frances said, fairly spitting the sound. "Not getting rid of me that easily." She stormed back out.

Liza faced me again. "What I don't understand is why Bennett changed his mind about me."

"He didn't change his mind about you. He's being nice. That's it. No hidden agenda." Part of me hated how easily the lies spilled out. Part of me felt perversely proud.

"He didn't seem to like me very much."

Time to put an end to this discussion. I folded my arms across my desk with a *thunk* of finality. "Liza, can you understand that this is not about you? I made the mistake of telling him how bored you've been since you came here. Bennett is a very kind soul. He's really just being nice." I exaggerated a shrug. "What more do you want from me?"

My deadpan description of how Liza came to be invited didn't do anything to dim her spirits. "I love parties. I can't wait for tonight."

"I can't wait until it's over."

BRIMMING WITH WEALTHY GUESTS, THE BAN-quet room buzzed with a very different sort of energy than it had this morning. Had it been only today that Bennett and I had learned the truth of our familial connection? That moment, and the happiness I'd felt, seemed so long ago.

Next to me, Liza sipped Champagne. "Can you *imagine* living like this?" she asked, her eyes wide as she took in the room's soaring ceiling, priceless tapestries, and fireplaces the size of small bedrooms.

Thanks to Bruce and Scott's efforts, my sister and I blended in well enough with the eclectic crowd. As promised, my thoughtful roommates had dropped off clothes. Some I didn't recognize. I imagined those—in Liza's size—had been acquired from the local consignment shop this morning.

I wore my favorite little black dress, pearl pendant, and matching earrings. Liza's bohemian ensemble—a flowing, patterned skirt to her ankles, shiny scarlet top, and oversized fringed purse—was the perfect choice for my wild-card sister. The bright red would make it extra easy for McClowery to keep tabs on her.

My sister lifted her flute in a mock toast, the gesture reminiscent of this morning's celebration in a way that made me very sad. "You've done well for yourself, Sis, landing a job that lets you rub noses with these kinds of people."

"Marshfield is more than a job for me," I said, in a rare, candid admission. "I love my life here."

"Yeah." She studied me for a moment, then took another long look around. "Staying put after Mom died was the right decision for you." She sipped more Champagne. "I'm still waiting for my decisions to work out right."

I had nothing to add so I moved through the groups of guests, greeting those I recognized.

Liza seemed unwilling to leave my side. "Where's our host for this gala gathering?" she asked. "I want to thank him personally for inviting me."

"Bennett will be along shortly. He prefers to join a party once it's under way." I was back to lying; Bennett was undergoing a last-minute mic check in a small room off the second-floor balcony.

"How many people did he invite to this thing?" she asked.

The banquet room could probably hold more than three thousand people standing shoulder to shoulder. At the moment we had far fewer than that, though enough to fill it comfortably. "Two hundred and fifty," I said, "ish."

"Wow."

Frances elbowed her way through a group of people, who frowned and spoke in quiet voices. I'd taken notice of them earlier. There were fewer than a dozen of them, but they made themselves conspicuous by their antisocial behavior. None of these individuals had accepted a drink from a wandering waiter; several had, in fact, shooed servers away.

"Aren't they the life of the party?" Liza asked. With a nod toward Frances, she whispered, "She fits right in."

I caught a glimpse of one of the men, in profile. "Hey," I exclaimed quietly, but before I could get a better look, the group had swallowed him back up.

Frances turned around, following my stare. "Who do you recognize?"

"Nobody," I lied. "My mistake."

Frances fixed me with a disagreeable frown. My poor assistant still didn't know why Liza had been allowed to attend.

"I may need to disappear from the festivities for a bit," I said. Yet another falsehood. "I always like to ensure that events like this are running smoothly behind the scenes."

Liza shrugged her indifference.

Frances barely moved her lips. "Need any assistance?"

"I'll be fine, thanks."

Liza tugged my arm. "Tell me a couple of important things about collecting antiques." Her face was alight with anticipation. "Or give me the names of expensive pieces so I can make small talk with these people."

"Liza, don't even try. You wouldn't last thirty seconds faking a conversation about antiquities. Not with these people. They'll eat you up and spit you out. If you're uncomfortable mingling, stay close to Frances. She'll help you out."

I pretended not to notice Frances's pinpoint pupils and gritted teeth. I couldn't help but catch the glow of excitement in Liza's wide eyes. I placed a hand on her shoulder. "Do you understand? These people are way out of your league. Don't make a fool of yourself by pretending to be someone you're not."

She slid out of my grip, downed the remainder of her Champagne, and dropped the glass onto a passing waiter's tray. "You've got nothing to worry about from me."

Liza's assurances did more to unnerve than settle me as I made my way out and up to the FBI's control center.

Even though Marshfield security personnel manned the door, I was not allowed to pass until a federal agent confirmed my identity.

The moment I stepped in, I gasped. This former bedroom-parlor combination, with its close proximity to the family's personal quarters on the second floor had originally been designated to accommodate favored guests. These people would have been delighted by the high ceilings, expansive living space, and modern (for the time) attached lavatory. They may have overlooked the fact that the room lacked windows. Which is probably why McClowery picked it.

Even though the room's overhead lights were off, the quarters felt close and confined, warm from the heat of too many bodies and too much humming machinery crammed into a location designed for a single guest. Maybe two. Furniture had been removed, replaced by a dozen oversized monitors, a collection of collapsible metal desks, and as many rolling chairs. Illumination from the screens provided enough light to see clearly: lots of quiet people wearing headsets, tapping keyboards, and staring at images of the banquet hall crowd below.

McClowery and Bennett stood inside the door. They both glanced up at my entrance, but McClowery, wearing a headset around the back of his neck, didn't stop talking. "Remember that we will be watching and listening every minute," he said to Bennett. "Our goal tonight is simple: allow the thieves to make contact and when they do, express your interest in acquiring the jeweled key. Try not to be overanxious. If they suggest meeting later for a private exchange, agree to it, but don't let them think you're nervous."

"You've made all this abundantly clear, Agent McClowery," Bennett said. "I understand my instructions. We can go over them again if you like, but we're wasting time."

McClowery fitted the headset over his dark hair and adjusted the microphone near his lips. "Don't forget that we have agents at the party, too."

"I know," Bennett said with a trace of exasperation. "I will know who to trust by use of our code word."

McClowery slid a glance toward me as though worried I might overhear.

All I cared about was Bennett's safety this evening. "Is

Malcolm Krol one of tonight's attendees?" I asked. "I think I spotted him down there."

McClowery didn't answer.

Bennett's smile was grim. "I think it's time I went downstairs and greeted my guests, don't you?"

I fully intended to accompany him, but McClowery stopped me. "We'd prefer you stay in the control room for a while."

Before Bennett left, I gripped his arm. "Be careful."

"Are you afraid I can't handle myself, Gracie?" he asked with a playful lilt, but I caught the seriousness in his question.

"Of course not," I said. "But we're both so much stronger together than we are alone."

His eyes glistened. He opened his arms and I stepped into a hug. He kissed the top of my head. "Don't worry, Gracie. We'll stand together another day."

When he released me, McClowery frowned. "Careful. Those microphones are delicate."

Chapter 33

UNSETTLED, I SHIFTED MY WEIGHT FOR THE third time in as many minutes. McClowery and I stood behind a seated FBI agent who paid us no attention whatsoever. She spoke quietly into her headset, saying things like "Segment delta-four, zoom," and, "Alpha-three, pull out," as she clicked through alternating views of the room.

Down the line, five other agents maintained surveillance over the banquet hall, studying images from five different vantage points. I craned my neck to see what the agents across the room were doing. They, too, studied their oversized monitors with sights on key spaces outside the big hall: exits, nearby washrooms, the mansion's front door, and the gate where visitors signed in before being allowed access.

"Wouldn't that be the perfect spot to apprehend Eric?" I asked, pointing. "As soon as he gives his name to the guard, you'd have him."

McClowery gave me a withering look. "Eric will know better than to provide his real name. And I wouldn't be surprised if he's changed his appearance in some way. That's another reason why we want you here. You and your sister probably know him better than anyone else in attendance. If he's incognito, you're our best bet to see through his disguise."

If. I thought the whole setup was flimsy. Eric showing up tonight was a real possibility. No argument there. But having me up here, instead of next to Bennett, where I could be of real assistance, felt wrong.

The crowd in the banquet hall formed itself into a loose receiving line, as guests queued up to greet Bennett. Most of them offered the sort of small talk one might expect from wealthy antique collectors. Among these were Daisy and Jim Tuen. As they introduced themselves, Jim said, "My wife and I are pleased to be able to join you here this evening. This is the highlight of our trip."

Daisy asked, "Is Ms. Wheaton here? We haven't seen her yet tonight."

"That's right," Bennett said. "I'd forgotten that you've met Gracie. She and I were very sorry to be unable to spend time with you when you visited earlier."

The Tuens were quick to *tut-tut* his apology. Daisy assured him that they understood completely.

Bennett gave the room a cursory scan. "I'm sure Gracie will return soon." He seemed to want to prolong the conversation, but the Tuens thanked him again for the invitation and stepped away.

Among those waiting to get a word with Bennett was another familiar face. The red hair and body-skimming clothes would have drawn my attention even if I'd never met her before. Near the end of the line that continued to grow, Phyllis Forgue seemed more interested in assessing those around her than in getting closer to Bennett. At the same time, her body language screamed impatience. Finally, she stepped away and snagged a drink from a waiter. I pointed. "Looks like Ms. Forgue wants to wait until Bennett is alone."

I took McClowery's grunt as affirmation.

When I opened my mouth to ask a question about the woman, McClowery sliced the air with his finger. He cocked an ear toward the display. One of the attendees, an older gentleman, had leaned in close to speak softly to Bennett. It took me a moment to realize that this was the same man we'd run into at the restaurant after the DNA testing— the Texan Bennett hadn't introduced me to. The man he'd claimed he wanted to avoid. I searched my memory for the man's name.

"If I didn't know better, Bennett, I'd think you've been dodging me." As the two men talked I was amazed at how well the hidden microphone picked up their conversation without being drowned out by crowd noises. "What is this rumor I hear?" the man asked.

The woman seated before us clicked her mouse. Immediately, four different angles of the interchange came into view. We could see this man's face in profile from both directions and a slightly obstructed view of him from up and behind Bennett's right shoulder.

Bennett feigned confusion. "There are always rumors, Neal," he said. "Which one are you talking about?"

Next to me, McClowery raised his voice. "Neal," he called to his subordinates. "What do we have on him?"

Seconds later the reply came. "Neal Coddington. Age sixty-seven. Married. Lives outside Houston. Former owner and CEO of a pharmaceutical company. No priors."

McClowery continued to stare at the screen. "Any travel to Asia in the past year?"

The same agent called back, "Working on it."

Onscreen, Coddington smiled enigmatically and lowered his voice further, speaking directly into Bennett's ear. "My sources tell me that you may be interested in acquiring a certain"—he glanced about quickly—"missing artifact? Is this true?"

Bennett spoke softly. "Why do you ask?"

Emboldened perhaps by Bennett's open-ended question,

Coddington straightened and said, "Very unlike you, my friend."

McClowery had one arm across his middle, the other hand up at his mouth, fingers tugging at his bottom lip. "Careful," he said. Addressing the group again, he raised his voice. "Where are we on the Asia travel?"

"Nothing's coming up."

"Check private transport. Look at next of kin."

"On it."

Bennett held the man's gaze. "You find it unusual for me to attempt to procure one-of-a-kind treasures?" He offered a nonchalant wave, encompassing the mansion. "What I have on display is a mere fraction of my private collection."

Coddington shook his head. "Don't play coy with me, Bennett. We've been around too long for games. If the rumors are true, you're opening up a dark door." He waited, but Bennett didn't say a word. "Mind you, I do understand how a particular piece can drive one to explore options one might never otherwise consider."

"Are you speaking from experience?" Bennett asked.

"I admit nothing," Coddington said with a sly smile. Again he leaned in close. "I suggest you proceed with caution. If you are after the missing jeweled key, as I have been led to believe, know that spies are everywhere. You were wise to limit your exposure by entertaining here. I wish you luck, my friend."

He shook Bennett's hand and was about to move off, but Bennett held on a moment longer. "If you happen on information, you will let me know?"

Coddington's smile was melancholy. "This one is out of my league."

When Coddington broke away, McClowery's shoulders relaxed and he let loose with an audible sigh of disappointment.

"No Asia travel in the past five years for Neal Coddington," one of the agents reported.

McClowery waved the air. "Never mind."

"Didn't you have a guest list ahead of time?" I asked. "Wouldn't you already have all that information?"

McClowery didn't try to hide his annoyance. "Of course we performed a preliminary investigation on all prospective attendees." His right hand shot out toward the active displays. "Do you have any idea how many of these people fit our profile? Nearly all of them. If it were a matter of simply tracing steps or examining business dealings, we would have arrested the guilty party years ago."

I didn't say anything.

"The entire reason for tonight's setup is to flush the black market organization out into the open. Mr. X has been savvy enough to keep his tracks covered. With few exceptions, every single person down there is a suspect. The only way we're going to find Mr. X is when he makes a move."

The FBI agents manning the displays paid no attention as McClowery and I strolled back and forth behind them. Each of the six silent agents studied his or her assigned section of the banquet hall. I meandered, doing my best to keep tabs on Liza while at the same time looking for either Eric or Nina Buchman.

More guests made their way to Bennett, most of them offering little more than vapid small talk and forced chuckles. In separate instances, however, two guests, one man, one woman, made mention of "recent rumors" about a "priceless treasure" that might become available. Their follow-up questions and veiled references were enough to prompt Bennett to use these guests' names in conversation, thereby triggering McClowery's shouted demands for information.

"Say that again," he said to the tech across the room. "What was that about her preferences for Asian influences?"

The agent read from his screen. I tuned him out.

Instead, I watched Liza circumnavigate the room. Even though I'd encountered Eric mere days ago, I counted on Liza being able to recognize him faster than I would. I also counted on the fact that she'd be unable to mask her reaction.

Frances had been dogging Liza's every step, ignoring my sister's repeated scathing glances, until a guest insinuated herself between them. From Frances's surprised, then relaxed, body language, I deduced she recognized the interloper.

McClowery picked up on my scrutiny. "The agent is telling your assistant to back off. No one will approach Liza if she's not alone."

Liza wound through the gathered guests, occasionally stopping to chat. She didn't appear to quibble when it came to age or gender. One of the people she spent more than a few minutes with was Neal Coddington, whose body language suggested his delight in having caught the attention of an attractive young female. After that, she moved on to engage an elderly woman, even going so far as to help her into a seat and fetch the woman a drink.

Through it all, I continued to catch snippets of conversations. The woman who'd captured McClowery's interest had moved on, and whoever Bennett was speaking with now didn't command the agent's full attention.

Liza had moved on as well. Her body language suggested that she was eager to talk with Bennett. The moment he was free, she made a beeline for him. In her haste to connect, she collided with Phyllis Forgue. From my vantage point it seemed that Forgue had anticipated Liza's move and intentionally blocked her. With no microphones covering either of them, I was left to determine my own soundtrack for their silent performance. Perfunctory apologies. Insincere smiles. Two wary felines, sizing each other up.

Phyllis's interception smugly complete, she steered Liza one way and took off the other—headed straight for Bennett.

Her goal was so apparent that when Bennett—oblivious to the drama—took that moment to stride across the room to talk with someone else, I almost laughed out loud.

After a prolonged period of quiet, I asked McClowery, "Is Malcolm Krol dangerous?"

I got the impression the agent had forgotten I was there. He took an extra beat to collect himself. "We are all dangerous, Ms. Wheaton."

"You know what I mean. Does he pose a threat to Bennett?"

The dark metal doors behind McClowery's eyes slid shut yet again. "There should be no reason for Malcolm Krol to cause Mr. Marshfield harm."

Should be. "Wouldn't it be better if I went down there?"

"You're to stay here, Ms. Wheaton. That is the plan."

"And if I refuse?"

McClowery glanced toward the door. As if obeying some silent signal, the agent stationed there stepped in front of it, blocking my exit. McClowery's placating smile chilled me. "We strongly urge you to stay." He gestured toward the monitors. "Please resume watching the crowd, Ms. Wheaton. And don't distract me again unless Eric Soames shows up."

Chastised, I bit my bottom lip. Wouldn't Eric have arrived by now? My gut told me he wasn't coming. A straightforward approach wasn't really his style. No, he preferred to lurk in the background, sneak in, take whatever he wanted, and skulk back out. He might send Nina Buchman, of course, but that was starting to feel like a long shot, too.

I didn't really care about catching Eric. All I cared about was keeping Bennett safe. And the only way to keep him safe, it seemed, was to remain vigilant as I studied the activity below.

Chapter 34

PHYLLIS FORGUE AGAIN MADE HER WAY toward Bennett, working too hard at nonchalance for me to miss. Across the room, Liza had refreshed her drink and, eyes narrowed, watched the other woman stop Bennett in his tracks.

"More talk over here," one of the agents said, drawing McClowery's attention. "I think that old guy, Neal Coddington, is trying to drum up intrigue. I'm hearing chatter about the missing key in several conversations."

"I thought only Bennett was wired," I said.

McClowery ignored me.

The agent I stood behind leaned sideways. Without taking her attention off the screen, she whispered, "Our people are wired as well." She tapped her headset. "We're able to catch a lot and communicate with them."

Another agent raised a hand. "Coddington dropped the rumor into conversation here as well. It's all they want to talk about now."

"Eyes on the prize, people," McClowery said. "Separate the wheat from the chaff."

"Phyllis Forgue." Bennett reached to shake hands. A preemptive move, as she'd clearly been intent on an embrace. "It's wonderful to see you."

"And you, Bennett. You're dashing, as always." The moment he released her hand, she tossed her hair back. "I've missed you this week. Where have you been hiding yourself?"

"Not hiding," he said. "Business concerns kept me tied up."

Peeling a stray hair from the side of her face, she stepped closer. "And what an impressive estate this is." She inched ever nearer as her voice dropped a notch. "Still, I have a business concern that might be worth leaving home for."

"I'm listening." Bennett's tone was appropriately inquisitive, but I caught faint puzzlement in his expression.

McClowery tensed. "What do we have on Phyllis Forgue?"

All smiles, Phyllis whispered, "I recently came into possession of an item I know you want."

"You have full my attention," Bennett said.

She eased sideways, blocking the camera. "Where are my other angles?" McClowery shouted.

"Limited zone," someone replied. "We have only the one view here."

McClowery spoke under his breath. "I went over this with Marshfield multiple times. He knew where not to stand."

"She stopped him there," I said in Bennett's defense. "What was he supposed to do, tell her to stop talking until he could reposition her?"

McClowery ignored me.

The view widened, capturing a bigger slice of the party. Unfortunately, the angle didn't change. Phyllis still had her back to the camera, blocking Bennett nearly head to toe.

"Better?" one of the agents asked.

"No," McClowery answered.

"Your full attention?" Phyllis asked provocatively. "What a delightful prospect."

"What item do you have, Phyllis?" Bennett asked.

With her back to us, we couldn't see her expression. Her voice, however, rang clear. "I'm feeling playful tonight. I'll give you a hint."

The control room fell silent.

"You'd like a hint, wouldn't you?"

"I'd prefer you tell me straight out." Bennett shifted. I could see a sliver of his face. Again, I caught confusion in his tone. "Please."

"Remember that conversation we once had?" Phyllis's words were smooth, coaxing. "About the lengths people go to acquire special treasures?"

"I remember."

McClowery spoke into the microphone on his headset. "I want all eyes on Phyllis Forgue."

Below us, subtle shifts in the crowd revealed our under-cover agents. Their coordinated movements probably went unnoticed by other partygoers, but this bird's-eye view of the room made their objectives clear.

In what appeared to be spontaneous bustle, three agents moved in closer to Phyllis and Bennett. She continued to tease him. "And isn't there a particular artifact that stirs your blood? Something you've had your eye on, something that you believe has escaped your reach?"

Bennett played it cool. "Are you telling me that you have this artifact?"

"You're going to be so jealous when I show it to you." She held up her purse and dangled it in front of him. "Maybe I should make you close your eyes."

"You brought it with you?" Bennett asked. "Here, tonight?"

"Let's see." She reached into her purse. "Did I?"

As the FBI agents casually surrounded the couple, Malcolm Krol wandered into view. A moment later, Liza swung into the picture, clearly targeting the handsome Australian, who seemed oblivious to her attention. Liza tossed her head, straightened her shoulders, and moved in.

Bennett took Phyllis by the elbow. "Let's talk over there where it's quieter."

The moment Bennett hit his mark, McClowery *whoosh*ed relief. "Good man," he said. "Now keep her there."

Four views of Bennett and Phyllis popped onto the screen. Now we were able to see their faces, watch their body language, and, most important, see what it was that Phyllis was about to unveil.

"Be prepared for searing jealousy, Bennett," Phyllis said. "This moment belongs to me." She pulled out a cloth-wrapped bundle and held it in out to him. "Go ahead. You know you want to."

Bennett's eyes closed for an extra half-beat. I watched comprehension wash over him. His face broke into a wide smile. "You've found the snail."

McClowery shouted his disbelief. "Snail? What snail?"

Bennett gingerly opened the cloth to reveal a ceramic snail the size of a grapefruit. He picked it out of her hands and turned it from side to side. With giant white pearlized eyes and a disenchanted look on its flat-cheeked face, the snail looked more like a toy than a piece of art. "Wherever did you find it?"

"That's privileged information, Bennett, though I might be persuaded to tell you over dinner some evening."

"Dinner?" Bennett repeated Phyllis's not-so-subtle hint. "Although I would enjoy that immensely, I really have been rather busy of late. I don't anticipate that changing anytime soon." He handed the snail back to her.

She wrapped her fingers around his as she accepted it. "You know what they say about all work and no play, Bennett. And a man has to eat. Can't you find a little bit of time to share a meal with me?"

"It's very kind of you," Bennett said, "but again—"

Having tucked the snail back into her purse, Phyllis adopted a patronizing tone. "Don't give me that line about important business that keeps you home. I won't take no for an answer."

Liza swooped into the scene, slipping her hand into the crook of Bennett's elbow. "I've been looking all over for you," she said to him.

I clapped a hand over my mouth. "Oh, no!"

Shooting an over-the-top smile at Phyllis, Liza said, "Is Bennett referring to me as a business concern again? I keep reminding him that this is the twenty-first century and there's nothing wrong with a mature gentleman's interest in a woman my age."

I sneaked a glance at McClowery. The stone-faced agent fumed at the screen.

Liza squeezed herself against Bennett's arm. "Isn't that right?"

It was the first time I'd ever seen Bennett at a loss for words.

"Oh," Phyllis squeaked. Her gaze raked over my interfering sister for a breathless couple of seconds. "I had no idea," she finally said. Addressing Bennett again, she forced a smile. "You never fail to surprise me." She tapped his arm with the tips of her fingers, "You'll let me know when the item *I'm* interested in comes back on the market, won't you?"

Phyllis not only strode away from the pair, she headed straight out the door. "Ouch," I said to no one.

Liza let go of Bennett's arm and took a sedate step back. "I'm sorry if that was intrusive, but pushy people like her drive me crazy. She was about to sink her teeth into you and I couldn't stand to watch."

Bennett had completely recollected himself. "I appreciate your concern, Liza, but I could have handled the situation myself." He flicked a regretful glance toward the exit. "Without embarrassing the poor woman."

"Then I apologize again. My mistake." Liza fidgeted with

the straps of her fringed purse, as though preparing to walk away, but her eyes fairly begged him to ask her to stay. "I guess I'll leave you to your guests then."

Bennett didn't stop her.

Liza bit her bottom lip. "The reason you don't want to talk with me is because Grace says I'm trouble, right?"

Bennett frowned. He didn't answer.

"She thinks I can't be reformed. But I can, really. All I need is a chance."

"This is not the time for this conversation, Liza," Bennett said.

McClowery waved a hand in the air and spoke into his microphone. "Get her away from Mr. Marshfield," he said. "Make it casual. Unobtrusive."

I wanted to be down there. "Don't you think Eric should have arrived by now?" I asked.

"I told you that he may send a proxy."

"Then I really don't need to be up here anymore, do I?"

"You will remain in this room until further notice."

I was about to argue when movement on the screen caught my attention. Bennett laid a hand on Liza's forearm, drawing her closer. "What did you say?"

"If you do this for me, I promise I'll become the sister Grace wants me to be."

Between McClowery's orders and my request for release, he and I had both missed part of the conversation. "What did she say?" McClowery asked the agent in front of us.

"No, no," Bennett answered her. "Before that."

The agent started to reply to McClowery, but stopped when it became obvious that onscreen, Liza was answering the question herself. "I asked if you'd help me sell something Eric gave to me. I thought it was junk but now I'm starting to believe it may be kind of valuable."

Bennett made eye contact with the camera. I felt as though he was communicating both disbelief and sorrow to me personally. He lowered his voice as he returned his undivided attention to my sister. "Tell me about this item."

We were able to watch their faces and the sudden alertness in my sister's eyes made my stomach clench. "No," I said. "Please no."

"It's actually three pieces. Gold and jewels in weird shapes," she said. "I wasn't sure they were real, but I think maybe they are." Enthusiasm caused her voice to rise. "Would you like to see?" She reached into her fringed purse.

"How did we miss this?" McClowery shouted.

Onscreen, Bennett placed a hand over Liza's. "Not now. You and I need to discuss this privately."

She stepped back. "Are you putting me off? Hoping I'll forget and go away? Because I really need help."

"You say Eric gave these to you?"

Liza nodded.

"Liar," I said to the screen. "You stole it."

"I'm not putting you off, Liza, but I need your sister's assistance." Bennett adopted his most authoritative tone. He made eye contact with the camera again. "I'll send someone to find her. Where's Frances?"

"I'm going down there," I said.

McClowery didn't stop me.

Chapter 35

I MADE IT DOWN TO THE BANQUET HALL before Frances made it to Bennett's side. "Liza," I said with feigned affection. "Let's find a quiet spot to talk."

"What's going on?" she asked. "Where did you come from?"

"This is important." I kept a party-appropriate smile on my face as I steered my sister toward the exit door. Frances hurried over, but I waved her back. "Ladies' room," I said, loud enough for anyone nearby to hear. "Be right back."

Liza moved with uncertain stiffness but didn't fight. "Where are we going?"

I knew I had to keep her soothed until we were safely out of sight. "There's an office upstairs specifically set aside for confidential business transactions. It seems as though you've been invited."

"Wait," she said. "How did you know? You've been listening?"

"Yes." No need to deny at this point.

"How does Bennett know what I have to sell? I didn't get a chance to show it to him."

"If it's what I think it is, he's been looking for it for some time."

"So it is valuable?" she asked. "Do you have any idea how much I might get for it?"

I wanted to answer, "Fifteen to twenty years," but I held my tongue. My sister clearly didn't know what she was holding. "No idea."

We stepped through a door separating the public areas from the private, where we traversed a short hallway that opened to a staircase. As I'd expected, just inside, McClowery and two agents waited for us. "Hand it over, Ms. Wheaton," McClowery said.

Liza paled. Her eyes were wild things. Her breath came shallow and fast as understanding dawned. She wrapped her arms around herself, pulling her purse close.

I stepped away as McClowery and two female agents took over. One of the women pried the purse out of Liza's hands and drew out an opaque plastic bag. Its contents clanked like heavy jewelry.

My sister sank to the ground to sit cross-legged, head in her hands.

The first agent upended the bag into McClowery's cupped palms. "These are even more beautiful than the photos." He allowed himself two seconds of appreciation before resuming his angry agent persona. "Handcuff her," he ordered the women. "Take her upstairs while I try to figure out if there's any way to salvage this mess."

"You lied to me." Sobs strangled Liza's words as she was tugged to her feet. Her eyes shimmered red; black rivers of mascara streaked her hot cheeks. "Why are you doing this to me?"

I didn't answer.

We were far enough from the festivities to be unconcerned about Liza's wails. I waited until the three women were up the stairs and out of sight to address McClowery, "What happens now?"

With both hands on his forehead and his eyes closed, the agent shook his head. "She had them the whole time." Opening his eyes, he flung one hand up in frustration. "She's no good to us."

"But at least you have three of the pieces."

"Without the other five, these are useless," he said. "The pieces were never as important as uncovering the organization behind the theft. Now we may never find Mr. X. We needed Eric to make contact tonight. We needed to get him to spill. And we would have. I know it."

"He may still show up," I said even though I didn't believe it. It was obvious McClowery didn't, either. "You never know."

"Or, we can start all over again. Take another decade to find and target another weasely con artist, get that person to infiltrate one of the toughest black market art crime organizations in the country, and hope that, this time, the whole thing doesn't blow up in our faces." He glared at me before starting up the stairs. "Sure. Why not?"

The party was scheduled to continue for another hour, but the mood in the control room had changed. Everything from the agents' postures to their surly attitudes told me that McClowery wasn't the only one feeling the heat from this debacle, but he was the only one to voice it. "We've lost this one, boys and girls. Let's pack it in."

"You'll be able to use the three pieces to flush out Mr. X, eventually though, right?" I asked. "There's nothing to say that you won't apprehend Eric at some point."

"Do you have any idea how much effort or how many personnel hours it takes to set up an operation this intricate? No, of course you don't." McClowery massaged his forehead. "You may go now," he said. "Your assistance is no longer required."

Days ago, I'd asked McClowery if Liza might have possession of the pieces, but he'd assured me that was impossible.

I felt like reminding him, but decided against it as I grabbed my purse from the corner of the control room and prepared to leave.

"Good luck," I said.

He didn't respond.

Liza was being detained in the hallway outside the control room. Perched in a hard chair with her hands cuffed behind her, she was flanked by the two agents who'd met us in the stairwell.

Liza glanced up, then returned to staring at the floor. "I'm your sister, you know," she said in a steely voice. "You're supposed to have my back, not stab me in it."

I started to reply that she'd done this to herself, but knew my words would be wasted. "I'm sorry you feel that way."

"I thought I could trust you. I thought I could trust Bennett."

"By offering him stolen goods?"

Her attention snapped up at that. "I didn't know they were stolen."

"You took them from Eric."

"You know what I mean—really stolen. I only did it to hurt him—before he dumped me for that horsey-looking Nina. How was I supposed to know that those three gold chunks were so important? I didn't. Not until everybody started showing up here looking for him." She sucked in her cheeks. Her stare was hard yet broken at the same time. "I thought that if I waited him out, he'd give up. All I wanted to do was teach him a lesson."

"You don't realize it now, Liza, but you got lucky."

She snorted.

"Eric isn't in hiding from just the FBI. He's in hiding from the dealer he double-crossed. That dealer killed at least one person already. You're lucky they didn't find you."

"If the FBI knows all this, why don't they do something about it?"

"That's what tonight's reception was all about. They were hoping to nab Eric and get him to roll over on his former boss."

"You mean all this was just to bait Eric?" she asked, using her chin to indicate the banquet hall below. "That seems like a lot of effort."

"Whoever he double-crossed might be here tonight as well."

"But the FBI has no idea who Eric was working for?"

I shook my head.

"It could be anybody?"

"Yeah," I said. "It could."

Her brows came together and her lips pursed. "A lot of people talked about that missing jeweled key tonight."

"You should tell McClowery."

"Should I tell him who seemed interested in the three missing pieces?"

"You didn't tell anyone you had them, did you?"

"Of course not," she said. "But I may have hinted that I knew where they were."

I squeezed my eyes shut and rubbed my forehead. "Who did you tell?"

"A few people." She shrugged. "Can't remember their names."

"Do yourself a favor and try to remember *exactly* who you spoke with and what they had to say. Then, when McClowery questions you, tell him everything. You got it?"

"You think I can use it as a bargaining chip? Maybe get off with a slap on the wrist?"

I doubted it. "It's worth a try."

Behind me, the control room door opened. "Ms. Wheaton?"

I turned to see one of McClowery's subordinates hurrying over, his hand extended. "Is this your phone? We noticed it on the floor after you left."

"Thanks," I said, accepting the device from him. "I appreciate it."

"No problem," he said. "And don't worry about McClowery. He gets like this when things go wrong. Fortunately for us, that isn't often."

I hadn't been worried, but thanked the young man for his assurances just the same. When he returned to the control room, I turned my phone's ringer back on. I'd switched it to silent shortly before the reception began. My phone's display lit up and I gave it an absentminded glance. Two missed calls. Five text messages.

"Have a nice life," Liza said. "Make sure you tell Aunt Belinda where to write me."

There was nothing to say that would make things better between us, so I opted to remain silent. Walking away, I tapped in my phone's security code and pulled up its phone log. Ronny Tooney had called twice and left two messages on voicemail in the past three minutes. Before calling him back, I checked my texts. All five from Tooney and all variations of the same theme: Call me ASAP.

I stopped to dial his number, relieved when he picked up immediately. "What's going on?"

"Did you listen to my messages?"

"No. What happened?"

He took a deep breath, then spoke very slowly. "Flynn and Rodriguez are at your house. There's been a break-in."

I gasped.

"It's okay, Grace. They got the intruders. It was your buddy Eric and his girlfriend. They're in custody. I wanted you to know right away. Plus I didn't want you to panic if you came home while all the police cars were still here."

Panic? I was thrilled. "This is great news, Tooney."

"It is?"

"Absolutely." I pivoted, heading back to the control room. "Tell Rodriguez and Flynn that, under no circumstances should they let Eric go free. Can you do that?"

"There's no chance, Grace. They caught the two of them ransacking your house. They got 'em solid."

"Still, promise me you'll give them the message."

"You got it," he said. "They're taking off in a minute. I'll catch them before they leave."

"Thanks, Tooney. You're a gem."

Liza had been listening in and now she sat up straighter. "What happened?" she asked. "Who found Eric? What's going on?"

I threw open the door to the control room. "McClowery." He was working closely with an agent in the far corner, but looked up at my shout. I held my phone aloft. "Eric has been arrested. He's in custody right now."

McClowery's annoyance morphed into exuberance by the time I crossed the room. "What happened?" he asked.

"Eric got caught breaking into my house," I said. "That's all I know."

McClowery tagged the young man who'd brought me my phone. "Take over here, Wilson. I'll be back."

Chapter 36

I ASKED ONE OF TERRENCE'S OFFICERS TO LET Bennett know that I'd been called away and not to worry. McClowery left Wilson in charge and took off for the Emberstowne Police Department, where Rodriguez and Flynn were booking their prisoners.

By the time I arrived at my house, the place was quiet. No police cars. No nosy neighbors. The only thing out of the ordinary was Tooney waiting for me, just inside my front door. He had Bootsie in his arms.

He held the outer door open and showed me where the lock had been broken. "Sorry about this, Grace," he said. "They jimmied the big door, too. You're going to have to get them fixed right away."

"I will," I said as he handed Bootsie to me. I nuzzled her neck.

"Except for the doors and the mess," he said, "I think everything is all right. They didn't destroy anything. At least, not that I could tell."

"What happened?"

Tooney gave me a quick rundown. Eric and Nina Buch-man had successfully disarmed my burglar alarm but were unaware of the second alarm, which had sounded at Tooney's house when they broke in.

"I didn't know who they were, of course," he said. "Not until Rodriguez and Flynn showed up. That's when it finally made sense."

Tooney knew that Liza and I were at Marshfield this evening for Bennett's reception, so when the second alarm sounded, he wasted no time investigating. He'd first alerted the police, then trekked via the underground passage to my house to see what was going on.

"I could hear them upstairs," he said. "They were search-ing through the bedrooms, making a racket opening and slamming drawers and doors."

"Weren't you afraid the police would burst in and shoot you by mistake?"

He shook his big head. "I called Rodriguez directly and told him I'd be here," he said. "I also told him the front door was open, and that I'd unlock the back if he wanted." Tooney gave a self-conscious shrug. "I mean, you just had the whole house all fixed up. I didn't want them to ruin another of your brand-new doors."

"You're amazing."

"Anyway," he continued, waving the air as though his thoughtfulness meant nothing, "I could hear the two of them shouting to each other from different rooms. I got the impression they were looking for something. Sounded like they were searching for pieces of a key, but I didn't under-stand what that meant."

"They didn't realize you were here?"

"I know how to keep quiet." Tooney pointed to Bootsie, who purred contentedly against my chest. "I picked her up straightaway so she'd stay safe. I think the little girl knew exactly what was going on. She didn't make a sound. I stayed on this floor, listening to everything they said. They were mad at each other, that's for sure. I got the impression they expected Liza to be here." He blinked, pointed to the closed front door, and asked, "Didn't she come back with you?"

"Long story," I said.

"I wish I could stay until your roommates get back," Tooney said, "but I told Rodriguez I'd meet them at the station as soon as you got home."

"I totally understand. Do Bruce and Scott know what happened?"

"Once the cops arrived and made the arrest, I called them at the shop. They both wanted to close up and rush back here, but I told them the situation was under control."

"Thank you, Tooney. You have no idea what a good thing you did tonight."

"The pieces Eric and Nina were looking for, you know what they are?"

"Another long story," I said.

"For another time." He grabbed the doorknob and started out. "Oh, one more thing. Eric and Nina did a number on your primary alarm system; it's all torn up. I tried to get the company to send a repair team tonight, but the order has to come from you. Give them a call as soon as I leave. Tell them it's an emergency."

"I'm sure I'm safe."

"You never know, Grace. Promise me you'll call them right away."

"I promise."

The minute the door shut behind Tooney, I raced upstairs. I had to see what damage had been done. Now that we were alone, and the house was quiet again, Bootsie struggled to escape my arms. I let her down as I reached the top landing—the spacious square area where we'd positioned a wing chair, end table, and small stained-glass lamp. Bruce and Scott's door was to the left and Liza's to the right. My room was farther down the hallway, also on the right. We had two smaller rooms up there that sat empty.

All the doors were wide open, even Bruce and Scott's, which they usually kept closed. I peeked in. The overhead light was on, but otherwise nothing appeared to have been disturbed. I couldn't tell for sure, of course, but the bed was made, the dresser tops were tidy, and the door to their washroom was shut. I could imagine Eric having thrown the door open, realizing his efforts were better focused elsewhere, and moving on.

Liza's room was trashed. My sister could never be accused of being a neat freak, but this mess was far beyond anything she'd created before. Dresser drawers had been yanked out and upended on the bed and the floor. Liza didn't own a lot of clothing of her own, so the items strewn about were mostly the extra sheets and guest items I kept stored there. Her bed was unmade and stripped bare, the mattress and box spring tipped off the bed frame.

What made me saddest were the gouges on the newly painted walls where they'd pulled things down and tossed them aside. I picked up one piece of artwork, a landscape my mother had painted when she was very young. The gold metal frame was ruined. At least the painting had survived.

With a heavy heart, I made my way past the two vacant rooms, steeling myself against the disaster I might find in mine. Before I made it halfway down the hallway, however, I remembered my promise to Tooney. I pulled up my cell phone to dial the alarm company.

The woman on the other end of the line was brisk, professional, and efficient. When I explained the evening's events she assured me that a repair person would be dispatched immediately and that I would be hearing from him or her soon. I thanked her and hung up.

Deep breath, Grace, I said to myself and then stepped into my room.

So devastating was the wreckage that it sucked my breath away. Maybe because I'd left it clean and uncluttered, this damage seemed far worse than what I'd found in Liza's room. "No," I said, closing my eyes and wishing that, like a bad dream, it would all go away in a blink.

It didn't.

Behind me, Bootsie yowled a protest, then wound herself between my ankles, offering whatever solace she could. I picked her up.

With my hand over my mouth, I took a tentative step forward, seeing every piece of clothing I owned scattered across the bed, my dressers, the floor, looking like rummage sale offerings. I didn't wear a lot of jewelry, but what I had had been dumped and strewn about as well. My bed hadn't been upended the way Liza's had. Perhaps the police arrived before they'd had the chance to toss it.

When my cell phone rang, I jumped. Swallowing my stinging anger in an attempt to sound calm, I answered. "Hello, Bennett," I said. "How are things going over there?"

"Mr. Tooney called me, Gracie. Are you all right?"

"I'm fine. The excitement was over by the time I got home." I struggled to keep things light. "Seems that Tooney saved the day again. The alarm you insisted on worked perfectly, and both Eric and his girlfriend have been arrested." I forced a chuckle. "McClowery must be ecstatic at this turn of events."

"Is Bootsie all right?" Bennett asked.

"She's fine. She's keeping me company while I clean up. There's a lot to put away, unfortunately. I may have to cut this conversation short."

"I'm leaving Marshfield right now. I should be there in less than a half hour."

"You don't have to come, Bennett. I'm fine. Really I am."

"This is not up for discussion. You've been victimized. You shouldn't be alone."

I wrinkled my nose as I took in the shambles that used to be my personal haven. "Maybe you're right," I said. "Thanks."

When we hung up, I returned to the hallway, left my

phone on the table out there, and lowered Bootsie into the wing chair. "I'm going to need two hands," I said to her.

One by one, I slid my drawers back where they belonged. I began replacing the contents of the first one when the doorbell rang. I hurried down the stairs to answer, thinking that if this was the alarm company, they weren't lying about being tops in customer service. More likely, however, it was a neighbor being nosy.

Remembering to check before opening the door, I peered out the side window as I flicked on the outside light. It didn't work. I flipped the switch up and down several times as though that would make a difference. Nothing. Eric and Nina had apparently broken that, too.

I couldn't make out much beyond the fact that two people stood outside my door. By their shapes and sizes I guessed them to be the brother-sister team who lived across the street and whose names I couldn't keep straight.

Prepared to politely turn them away, I swung open the door.

"This really isn't a good t—"

Jim Tuen pulled open my outer door. "Good evening, Grace."

Daisy brushed past to storm into my home. "Where's your sister?"

Chapter 37

BY THE TIME I REACTED, JIM TUEN HAD SHUT
the front door and positioned himself in front of it. He wore
a dark puffy parka, blue paper booties, and purple latex
gloves.

"You were right, Grace," Jim said to me. "Bennett Marshfield is a most genial man. I'm sorry I must cause him such
sorrow."

"Sorrow?" My mouth was so dry it was like swallowing
sandpaper. "What do you mean?"

"Bennett regards you highly," Jim said. "It's a shame to
rob him of someone he holds so dear. But then again, I may
be doing him a kindness. This way, he might never discover
your subterfuge."

Behind me, Daisy trooped through the empty rooms,
calling Liza's name.

"She's not here," I said. "She's—" I stopped myself.

Daisy returned to the front foyer. She, too, wore blue
booties and purple latex gloves. The part of my brain that
remained heedless of danger pointed out that these were just

like the ones our phlebotomists from Lucatorto Labs had worn. I swallowed. Bennett was on his way.

"She's where?" Daisy asked.

"Get out of my house." I took a threatening step toward her. "Get out now."

Neither of them reacted with anything that resembled fear. "We aren't leaving until your sister fulfills her promise."

Jim reached under his coat. He drew out a weapon I recognized as an ancient Maori Mere club. Bennett had two in his collection, but I'd never personally handled either one. Resembling an elongated, flattened bowling pin but made of jade, it had rounded edges and a thick center head. Mere clubs were highly effective bludgeons. One well-aimed blow could easily crush an opponent's skull.

I took a step back, pointing to the control panel next to my front door. "I haven't disengaged the alarm. The police will be here in minutes."

Jim's eyes tensed. He handed the club to his wife, who swung it with authority. "Do not test me," she said.

"Your alarm is not operational," Jim said. "Don't toy with us. Where is your sister?"

Daisy wielded the club with ease, slicing the air in a show of power. "More important, where are the pieces she and Soames stole from us?"

"Stole from *you*?" Realization clicked in. More than killer collectors, these two were the black market leaders responsible for stealing the treasure to begin with.

Daisy gave a dark laugh. "Your sister is a fool. She offered us our own property tonight. But then, like her boyfriend before her, she disappeared before completing the transaction. Had we known you were part of this charade . . ."

I didn't bother to correct her.

"No matter. Hand over the pieces. We know they're here."

All I could think of were McClowery's warnings. Of the ruthlessness of Mr. X. He would be surprised, I thought, to discover there was a Mrs. X involved, too. Daisy held the club, but the look in Jim's eyes made me fear him more.

"We are not without mercy," Jim said. "Give us the three pieces and I will deliver a quick death. One blow. You will not suffer."

"I don't have them here. Liza . . ." I tried to come up with a plausible enough lie to keep them talking until Bennett rang my front doorbell. That might be enough to distract them, enough for me to jump Daisy and wrestle the Mere club from her weathered hands. She was old, I was young. I could do it. I had to.

"Where are they?" Daisy was getting jumpy.

"Liza took them," I said. "When we got back, I mean. She said something about finding a safe place. I didn't even know she had them until then. I wanted to stop her but she threatened me."

"Who was she meeting?" Jim asked.

"No one. She wasn't meeting anyone." The last thing I needed was for them to believe the jeweled pieces were lost to a buyer. Then they'd have no reason to keep me alive. "She said she would be right back."

Daisy and Jim exchanged a look. "I saw her speaking with Malcolm Krol this evening," Daisy said to her husband. "I told you we should have insisted she leave with us. For all we know, she's with him now."

I heard a car door slam out front.

Daisy looked out the window. "It might be her sister returning home." She returned to my side and grabbed my arm. "Away from the front door. We don't want her running out if she sees us."

So much for the element of surprise I'd hoped for. "She won't." I worried now that if Bennett pushed through my unlocked door, he'd become a target. I needed to stay between them and him.

"Don't fight me," Daisy said. She clutched my upper arm

with her free hand. Though dulled by the purple latex covering them, her nails bit into my skin.

Jim pinched back of my neck, spinning me into the parlor. "Get in there."

Almost on cue, the doorbell rang.

Daisy waved the club. "Not a word," she said.

I held my breath, hoping it was the alarm company repair-
man. Hoping that, when no one answered the door, he would
report my non-response and alert the authorities.

Bootsie twisted around the doorway into the room. She
snaked sideways against the baseboard, her back arched,
her pupils wide, watching us as she tiptoed along the room's
perimeter.

The doorbell rang again. Moments later, pounding on
the window. Though muffled, I heard my name. "Gracie?"

"Who is that?" Jim asked.

"I don't know. A neighbor, probably."

Daisy's nails pinched tighter into the soft skin of my
upper arm. "Bennett calls you Gracie."

"Everybody calls me that."

"She's lying," Daisy said. "Bring him in here."

By the time Jim started for the door, Bennett had pushed
his way in. "Gracie." His voice was like thunder, echoing
in the foyer. "Where are you?"

Bootsie jumped and hissed, startling Daisy enough for
her to loosen her grasp of my arm.

I lunged for the Mere club, fingers writhing along the
smooth stone, fumbling for leverage. She took less than a
moment to react but just as she tried to wrench it away from
me, my hands clamped around the glossy club's narrow
neck. Bare skin triumphed over smooth latex. I heaved hard,
twisting it from her.

Daisy shouted for her husband. I heard Jim shout, too.

"Run, Bennett! Get out," I roared as I shoved Daisy to
the floor. I wobbled backward, off-balance from the skir-
mish. In the moment it took to regain my footing I registered

two things: Daisy, staring up at me with such hatred I could almost see waves of heat rising from her body, and sounds of a struggle coming from the foyer. I raced to the front door.

Furious, Bennett was on his hands and knees in the foyer. Jim had his back to the door, watching me with wary eyes.

I reached out a hand to help Bennett to his feet. "Are you okay?"

"Yes." He got up quickly and stood next to me. "What's going on?"

Daisy stepped into the foyer. The two faced us, eyes murderous. I hefted the Mere club and stared back. "Heavy," I said. "Now I understand why these are such effective weapons."

"You don't know how to use that," Jim said. He took a tentative step forward.

"I swing at your head, you go down. What more do I need to know?"

"That is a spiritual weapon," Daisy said. "You haven't yet learned its secrets."

"Give it to me." Hand out, Jim took another step forward. "I promise we will leave you in peace."

I swung the club back and forth the way I'd seen Daisy do earlier. "I might not have a spiritual connection with Maori weaponry," I said, "but I am a championship softball player. Oh, you didn't know?" I didn't give them a chance to respond. "Been playing since I was a kid." I pantomimed swinging for the fences, feeling the weight of the club nearly wrench my arms from their sockets. "You don't want to mess with me."

Jim spread his lips into a painful smile. "There are two of us. And only one club."

Daisy moved closer.

Bennett placed a hand on my shoulder. "Grace has taken down assailants far younger than either of you," he said. "If you want to go in peace, prove it. Leave now while you have the chance."

As though operating on some silent signal, they rushed me. I swung the heavy club, smashing Jim's shoulder with such force I nearly lost my footing. He toppled sideways, catching himself with one arm before scrambling back to his feet.

When I swung at Daisy, she spun, dodging the blow and using the momentum to launch herself at me again. As I had done earlier struggling to get the club from her, she grappled for control now, her fingers inching toward the narrow handle.

Bennett had taken advantage of Jim's imbalance to grab the man's parka and twist it up and around his head. Grunting, he shoved the disoriented man into my front door and pulled his right leg out from under him. The blue bootie slipped smoothly against the hardwood, sending Jim face-first to the floor.

I shot a foot into Daisy's leg, hitting her straight in the knee. She cried out, and crumpled to the floor.

For about five seconds all Bennett and I could do was breathe, our gasps coming hard and heavy. Daisy wrapped her hands around her knee and wailed.

Jim started to roll toward us, clawing his way out of the coat. I held the club like a baseball bat and whacked him in the side. He doubled over in pain. The heavy jacket had softened the blow, but it had been enough to keep him subdued. For now. I didn't want to crack his head with the weapon, but I couldn't allow the man to get up.

Shaking, I said, "Call the police, Bennett. Tell them to hurry."

Chapter 38

"DO YOU HAVE YOUR CELL PHONE?" I ASKED.

"Not with me."

I pointed to the back of the house. "Landline in the kitchen."

Bennett strode through the parlor and out of sight. Chances are he'd left his cell phone in the car with his driver. That man was probably outside right now, waiting patiently, completely oblivious to the commotion inside.

"You foolish twit." Daisy coughed out the words. She'd managed to sit up, leaning against a nearby wall for support. Her face contorted in pain. "Jim, stay down. Stay down."

His gyrations had caused him to roll closer. I stepped back, lest he kick out a leg or try to grab one of mine. Seconds later, his face, red with exertion, surfaced from within the folds of his coat. He pushed the fabric away and made a move to stand up.

"Your wife is giving you good advice." I waved the club. "Don't try it."

He maintained eye contact as he slowly worked his way to his knees, practically daring me to come at him.

"Stay down," I said, but another noise caught my attention. A creak from outside, the sound of my front door opening.

The doorknob turned slowly, as though whoever grasped it was being careful not to make noise. "Grant," I shouted, assuming he was Bennett's driver tonight. "Call the police. Don't come in. Call the police."

The door flew open. Malcolm Krol stepped in, gun in hand and determination in his eyes. "Where's Liza?" He took several seconds to assess the scene. "Tuen?" he asked when comprehension dawned. "What are you doing here?" His Australian accent was thick with anger.

"Same as you, fool. She tricked us all."

"Where is she?" He kicked the older man. "Tell me." I sensed it was confusion more than anger that drove Krol's mental state right now, but the effect on Tuen was visceral. He rolled onto his side, moaning.

Krol faced me. So did his gun. "Where's your sister?"

"Gone. Took the pieces with her."

I'd started a countdown in the back of my mind. If Bennett had gotten through to the police when I believed he had, we had a chance. As long as Krol didn't get crazy. As long as his trigger finger didn't twitch.

"She's selling them to me, you old moron," Krol said to Tuen with staggeringly misplaced confidence. "Eric and I had a deal. She's making good on it."

I inched sideways, out of a bullet's likely path. I still held the Mere club like a bat, but the weapon would be no help against Krol's gun. Even if I managed to get closer, he could blast my brains out before I completed my swing. Speaking loudly so that Bennett would hear and stay out of the room, I said, "Liza is gone, and the pieces are gone with her. The police are on their way. You better run before they get here."

"Don't try to bluff. I heard you sniveling when I came to the door. Nobody's coming."

"Take us with you," Jim Tuen said to Krol. "We will reward you. Forget the pieces. We can revisit that another day."

"Why would I do that?"

"Together we have more power. Get me and my wife out of here and I will pay you well."

Krol seemed to be having difficulty understanding.

"The police *are* on their way." Jim's words came faster by the moment. "Marshfield is here. In back. He called the authorities. Get us out of here, now, and I promise you great reward."

"Like you promised Soames?" Krol asked. "No thanks."

Jim's whole body seized up. He bellowed, "Get us out of here, you idiot. Daisy, come on."

Over the course of her husband's bizarre conversation, she'd managed to get to her feet. "I can't," she said. Jim started for her.

I'd called the police to my house too many times to not know how long it took them to get there. I hefted the club again. "Don't move," I warned the Tuens.

"Put that gun down," Bennett ordered. He stepped into the foyer behind me.

"Tell your girl here to put that club down," Krol said. He pointed the barrel at Bennett.

I heard sirens. We all heard them. Krol paled.

"They're here," I said. "You should have run when I told you. Hurry. Go now. Get out."

"I want the jeweled pieces." With his arm fully extended he took a step closer to Bennett, pointing the gun at his forehead. To me, he said, "Put down the club."

"The pieces aren't here. Your only chance is to run."

"Put down the club. Now."

I dropped it. Jim Tuen scurried across the bare floor, grabbed it, then wrapped an arm around his wife. "Out the back," he said to Daisy. "Let's go."

She cried out as he dragged her forward.

Krol swung his arm to point the gun at Daisy's head.

"I'm not taking the fall for this. No way. I figure as long as I keep one of you alive, I have a bargaining chip. You try to move again, and that chip is cashed. Got it?"

Jim's eyes blazed, but he nodded. Daisy whimpered. He murmured softly into her ear.

"Now you put down the club," Krol said.

It fell to Jim's feet with a formidable *thunk*.

The Australian raked an appraising glance over all of us. "You," he said to Bennett. "You're coming with me. You're my ticket out."

"Not Bennett," I said. "I'm a better choice."

"Gracie, no."

Using his free arm, Krol pushed me aside, taking Bennett by the shoulder. "We're getting out of here," he said, shoving him forward. "Let's go."

"I refuse," Bennett said.

"Don't make me shoot you."

Outside people yelled and—for the first time in my life—I was thrilled to distinguish Flynn's voice above the fray. "Police. Hands on your heads. Everyone. We're coming in."

"I'd think twice if I were you," Krol shouted back. He lifted the gun above his head, pointed it to the ceiling, and squeezed the trigger. The shot made me cry out and cover my ears. Everyone froze.

"You can't escape." Flynn's voice was muffled by the ringing in my ears. "Put down your weapon. Now."

"Don't try to come in here," Krol replied, "or the next one goes into someone's head." He pointed the gun at Bennett.

I screamed. "No!"

"Take it easy." Flynn's voice rose, but he spoke calmly. "We only want to talk to you."

Krol smirked. "I thought they might."

Although I could make out what Krol and Flynn were saying, the aftermath of the shot still dampened the sound; it was like listening to a conversation from underwater.

Daisy Tuen's knee had swollen up to nearly twice its size;

her anger, however, had grown exponentially. She shook her fist at Krol's chest. "You've ruined everything."

Krol answered, keeping his gun trained on Bennett. "For you, maybe. Not for me."

Daisy grimaced with fierce determination. She surprised me—and Krol—by launching herself at the man, fingers crooked like claws, raking his face. At the same moment, Jim Tuen, in a single, fluid motion, snagged the Mere club from the floor to swing it against Krol's skull. The moment the jade cracked bone, Krol's sympathetic muscle response kicked in. He squeezed off another round. And then he fell, senseless, to the floor.

Jim Tuen whipped off his booties, shoved them into his coat pockets, and shouted for his wife to do the same. He peeled off his purple gloves and grabbed my arm, spinning me to face him. "Tell the police that Krol held us all captive. Tell them nothing about our connection to the jeweled key. I will make it worth your effort. I will take care of you. You have my solemn oath."

His words barely registered. I wrangled free of his grasp and ran to Bennett, who lay bleeding on the floor. "No," I cried. "No, no."

Chapter 39

I PAID NO ATTENTION TO ANYTHING ELSE around me. All I cared about was getting medical assistance for Bennett. Flynn and Rodriguez had had the foresight to call for an ambulance when they'd first arrived; paramedics rushed in almost immediately.

"Bennett, stay with me, okay?" I knelt next to him, holding his right hand as the professionals moved in to stanch the blood. There was so much everywhere, I couldn't tell where he'd been hit. "It's going to be okay."

Bennett's eyes shone with pain and he pressed his lips together. "Tell them," he rasped. "Tell the lawyers that I want—"

"You're going to be fine." My words choked out, uneven and hot. "Do you understand?"

"If . . ." He grimaced, then shut his eyes.

My heart dropped to my stomach. "Bennett . . ."

He sucked in a shallow, ragged breath.

It wasn't until Rodriguez pulled me to my feet that I

realized the paramedics had been talking to me. "We need to transport the patient," one said.

"Keep thinking positive," the chubby detective whispered into my ear. "He's in good hands."

As they loaded Bennett onto the stretcher, I watched for signs of life—a blink, a breath, a reaction to pain. He was pale. Too pale.

"I need to go with him." I pulled away from Rodriguez. "I *am* going with him."

Rodriguez didn't argue. "We'll need a statement from you later."

I turned to survey the scene. Bennett couldn't die. Not here. Not in my house. And yet . . . A hard, hot ache rose up in my throat. This was the house his father had purchased for my grandmother. This was where our blood connection had first been established. This story had come full circle. I held a hand to my mouth, and fought the anguish building in my heart.

Another set of paramedics tended to Daisy Tuen. Jim rushed over, grabbed my limp hand, and held it tight. "We send our best wishes with you for Mr. Marshfield," he said before lowering his voice. "Please remember my promise." He raised our joined hands and made malevolent eye contact directly over them. "We will be a friend to you forever if you are a friend to us now."

I shook my hand free.

"I have your promise then?"

Without answering, I turned and walked out into the frigid night, realizing I hadn't thought to grab a jacket. Rodriguez lumbered after me, my down coat in his hands. As he placed it around my shoulders, he said, "You need anything Grace, you let me know."

"I do, Detective," I said. "Don't believe a word Jim and Daisy Tuen tell you. Let Agent McClowery know that they are Mr. and Mrs. X."

Rodriguez looked confused. "Mr. and Mrs. who?"

"Get McClowery here, pronto."

"He's interrogating Eric. Doesn't want to be interrupted."

"Tell him the Tuens are Mr. X. But before you do, surround my house and don't let the two of them out of your sight."

Bennett's stretcher was being lifted into the back of the ambulance. I hurried across my snowy front lawn so they wouldn't leave without me. Over my shoulder I shouted to Rodriguez, "Trust me."

I SAT ALONE IN THE SURGICAL WAITING ROOM, staring at the pastel painting on the wall across from me. Great horizontal swaths of pink and purple gave the illusion of a sunset over a sand colored foreground. In essence, the framed art was an image of nothing. Soothing blandness, I decided. A wholly appropriate choice for placement here.

The bullet had gone through soft tissue on Bennett's left side. He'd suffered extensive blood loss, but no major organs had been hit. His advanced age worked against him, but I hoped his fitness level and the paramedics' quick response would work in his favor.

I stood, stretching my back, as I'd done twenty times so far. There was no music piped in here, no one else waiting for updates on a loved one, and the dog-eared magazines piled in the corner didn't interest me. This place was quiet. Too quiet. Except for the occasional squeal of carts rolling by or murmurs from the nurses' station in the next room, the place was silent.

When I heard Rodriguez ask for me, I hurried out to meet him. Flynn was there, too. They both looked exhausted.

"How you doing, Miz Wheaton?" Rodriguez asked. "How's the boss?"

"I don't know." My words were weak and shaky.

Flynn scowled away. I didn't understand until he waved. "Over here," he said.

Frances hurried over, her brows halfway up her forehead. "You left me there, with no word. Nobody told me anything until I finally got through to these two." She thrust a hand out. "And now this." She glared at me. "What do you have to say for yourself?"

I shook my head.

"Where's Hillary?" Frances asked.

"I called her." Gesturing vaguely toward a courtesy phone the hospital had set up for those, like me, without a cell phone, I added, "I called Bruce and Scott, too. And Tooney."

She crossed her arms. "Hillary ought to be here."

"I'm sure she will be."

Rodriguez cleared his throat. "We have a few questions for you, Miz Wheaton. You up for it?"

I gestured into the quiet room and its army of empty chairs. "Have a seat."

AFTER I TOLD RODRIGUEZ AND FLYNN EVERY-thing I knew—Frances peppering us with questions throughout—I demanded a few answers of my own. "I assume this means you know who killed that fake FBI agent."

Flynn scratched the top of his head where pale fuzz was beginning to soften the shine. "McClowery will probably have a cow to hear us talking about this outside the station, but . . ." He gave an exaggerated look around the room. "Do you see anyone listening in?"

"Let him complain," Rodriguez said. "Go on."

Flynn continued. "When Eric disappeared, the Tuens sent Ochoa—our victim—to find him. Ochoa figured he could use Liza to get to Eric. He traced her here to Emberstowne. No one knew she'd stolen the missing jeweled pieces, though. Everybody thought Eric still had them."

"Ochoa got here well before Liza did," I said. "He had to know she wasn't here yet when he came to talk to me."

Rodriguez nodded. "Ochoa's dead, so we can't know for sure, but our best guess is that's why he posed as FBI. He wanted to enlist your help so that you'd lead him to Liza."

"If he'd have found her, you would have been spared all this trouble," Frances said to me. "And the Mister wouldn't be up in surgery right now."

"That's one way of looking at it," Flynn said. "Incidentally, Malcolm Krol is dead. But I'm assuming you knew that."

"I suspected. When Jim Tuen cracked him in the head with that club . . ." I shuddered.

"That dirty, rotten man, asking you to cover for him and his wife," Frances fumed. "I can't believe the nerve."

Rodriguez gave her a patient smile. "Since we can't question Krol, either, we're going to have to wait for forensics to tell us if he's Ochoa's killer. But I'd put money on it."

Flynn leaned in. "It's a free-for-all down at the station. McClowery and his FBI team have taken over the place. We've got Eric and his girlfriend singing on the Tuens, Liza negotiating for leniency by spilling on Eric, and the Tuens themselves holding tight to the story that they were merely innocent bystanders and it was Krol behind everything all along."

"McClowery is in his glory," Rodriguez said. "Never seen such a happy Fed."

The sound of heels hammering against the tile floor alerted us to Hillary's arrival seconds before she rounded the corner. Her pretty face was pink with exertion, her usually perfect hair mussed from sleep. "How is Papa Bennett?"

As though in answer, a doctor *whoosh*ed through the far glass doors. Her scrubs were stained, the surgical mask loose around her neck.

"You can all go home," she said as she peeled off her latex gloves.

I sucked in a terrified breath and gripped the chair's arm. "No," I cried.

"That's not what I mean," the doctor said quickly, holding her hand up. "I meant to say that he's fine. Mr. Marshfield is stable. He's heavily sedated, however, and will likely remain so through the night. Go home, get some rest, and you can be here when he wakes up."

I dropped my head into my hands. "Oh, thank God."

Chapter 40

I WAS STANDING NEXT TO BENNETT'S BED when his eyes fluttered open the next morning.

"So I'm still here, am I?" he asked.

I reached down to lay my hand atop his. "You're expected to make a full recovery."

"Guess it wasn't my time."

"If it were up to me, it will never be your time."

Though his hand was tethered to an IV, he twisted it, palm up, to wrap his fingers around mine. "Ah, Gracie." He tried to sit, but pain made him wince.

"Take it easy."

He shot me an impatient glare. "The harder I push myself, the quicker I get out of here."

"Take it easy," I repeated. "For today at least. Push tomorrow."

"Yes, ma'am." He settled back. "Everything all right?"

"Now it is, yes. We weren't sure for a while there."

"You're a tough cookie," Bennett said with admiration. "All that chaos and you stayed calm. You kept your head."

"I could say the same about you."

"I don't know." He pantomimed swinging a club even though it hurt him to do so. "I'm a championship softball player," he said, falsetto. "Watch out."

It felt good to laugh. The unexpected recap of my on-the-spot fib reminded me just how desperate I'd felt in that moment, how high the stakes, and how lucky we were to have survived. With Bennett lying here, safe, making jokes, I could finally relax again.

"That Mere club felt like a bat in my hands. It was the first thing I could think of."

"Did you really play softball in school?"

"Hardly." I tamped down a giggle. "I stunk at sports as a kid."

"I want to know more about that. I want to learn everything about your childhood, your family, your life before you came to Marshfield."

"You already know a lot of it."

"I want to be like a real uncle, who's known you from birth," he said. "And I want us to plan for the future."

"Not today."

"Fair enough. But soon." He reached for my hand again. "Tell me what else has happened."

"McClowery's keeping the Tuens' arrest out of the papers." I held a finger in front of my lips. "He plans to take control of their organization and use it to discover the extent of their reach. I predict more black-market bad-guy arrests in his future."

"Makes sense. And the jeweled key?"

"The Tuens had it in their hotel room safe, believe it or not." I shook my head. "And although the three pieces Liza tried to sell are a little scratched, they're still in good shape."

"Where is Liza?"

"Still in custody." I held back from spewing the contempt I felt for my sister right now. Always looking out for her own best interests, always oblivious to how her actions might impact others, her deviousness had put my life and Bennett's at risk.

Because of Liza, Krol was dead and the person dearest to me in this world, Bennett, had come close to joining him. "She's been assigned an attorney. They're hoping for leniency."

"She could be out soon?" Bennett asked.

"It's possible."

"Where will she go?"

I looked away. "I don't know." It had taken all my self-control to resist dumping my sister's meager possessions at the police department this morning. I would never forgive her for what she'd put us through.

Bennett waited for me to make eye contact. "She has to be told."

"Bennett, no. You've seen for yourself how toxic Liza is. I don't know how, but she'll ruin everything."

"Gracie, listen to me. For most of my adult life, I've faced adversaries. Most were far more cunning than your sister. The secret to winning is not hiding the truth, but shining a bright light on it, making it transparent to all. Angry, spiteful people like your sister are afraid of truth. They don't know how to behave when light hits them. In order to live our lives the way we want to, she will have to be told. Not now, but when the time is right." He squeezed my fingers again. "Are you with me on this?"

I swallowed my frustration. "I trust you, Bennett. I suppose that's all that really matters."

"Good. Now, next topic." He let go of my hand to wag a finger at me. "You and I need to work harder to stay out of trouble."

"Exactly my point," I said. "If my sister hadn't been part of it—"

"This one wasn't your fault. If I hadn't agreed to work with McClowery, neither of us would have encountered the Tuens nor Malcolm Krol."

I thought about that. "I don't know, Bennett. Something tells me we still would have gotten into the middle of this one."

A corner of his mouth curled up. "I suppose it was inevitable."

"Let's agree to keep things quiet from now on. What do you say? No more fighting bad guys. No more battles to the death."

Bennett chuckled. "I'm afraid quiet isn't our lot in life. You and I are not content to sit and wait, we are people of action." He cupped his mouth and whispered, "Speaking of which, how soon can you break me out of here?"